Hristina Bloomfield

Becky

Becky

London, 2022

hrisisart@gmail.com

Facebook: @Hristina Bloomfield Author

Instagram: @HristinaBloomfield

All characters in this book are fictional, and any resemblance to persons living or dead is purely coincidental.

To John

Hristina Bloomfield

1.

The sun hadn't set yet. Its rays reflected in the calm ocean and reflected softly in the waves. The sky was clear, with only a few wispy clouds drifting to the west. To any tourist this sight would have caused a cry of admiration, but to Becky these sunsets were part of her life, part of her daily routine, and she watched the rapidly changing landscape with no interest. She was tired, her legs hurt, and her stomach was rumbling. Becky's day had been long and, even though it was nearly nine in the evening, she still had things to do. She couldn't wait to get home and have dinner. She hadn't eaten since morning. Her day always started with a light breakfast, followed by a full day at school and then three hours of work at one of the warehouses near Penzance. It took her almost an hour to walk from Penzance to the farm where she lived with her parents and her little sister.

Becky looked outside again. The hedges along the shore were in bloom and the ground seemed to be covered with a yellow-green carpet. She noticed a few tourists walking along the coast. They looked happy and were smiling. This place gave them the peace they were looking for. Becky wished she could feel that sense of awe and peace too. A piece of paradise, that's how the tourists described the place where she was born and where she spent her life. However, for her, that was not the case. The farm where they lived and worked was by no means a piece of paradise, nor did it smell of the sea and flowers. The smell was of manure, and the cold, salty sea air came in through the gaps in the window frames and seeped into the walls. It was not bright and pleasant on the farm where Becky had lived since she was born. The rooms' small windows didn't let in much sunlight, and the stone walls didn't often get warm, especially on cold and wet days. However, today was warm and dry. At least she wouldn't come home wet, Becky thought. She looked again at where they were, and they were not far from the farm. The bus she was riding in was speeding through the narrow streets, passing through the small villages where it stopped and would soon be nearing where Becky lived. It was May, and there weren't many tourists standing in its way yet. A few more minutes and David, the bus driver, would be calling her to get off. Although there was no stop, he always stopped near her home. He was worried about her, especially in the winter when it was pitch dark here. Becky wasn't worried, she knew the way and was in no danger of getting lost. She could go home blindfolded because she had been walking this way for years. Almost no one else used this stony road, especially in the evening.

However, David was worried about her and did his best to close the distance for Becky a little. If it was up to him, he would have taken her to the farm himself, but the bus was too wide and would have gotten stuck in one of the hedges bordering the fields. It was still light, and the driver wasn't too worried about the young girl this evening. There was at least half an hour until dark, by which time she would be back at the farm, he thought.

As they approached the road that led to her home, he stopped the bus and called out to the young girl. Becky got her bag, got out and thanked the driver.

From here, she had to continue her journey on foot. She had to walk almost a mile. The road meandered, bordered by flowers and hedges that prevented people and animals from reaching the fields behind them. At its beginning, on either side, were several houses recently bought by a wealthy Londoner. Becky hadn't seen the owners yet, so she was surprised to see a car parked in front of one of the houses. Loud music was blaring from the car and clouds of smoke were coming out of the windows. Inside the car, she noticed young men, apparently very drunk, who were talking loudly and, noticing her, they looked her over from head to toe. A chill ran down Becky's spine. She was worried by their eyes following her every step. Her instinct told her to run, to get out of their sight as quickly as possible, and she hurried past the car with the drunken young men inside, even starting to run lightly, so as not to attract their attention with her escape. But the men did not lose their interest. On the contrary, two of them leaned out of the windows and stared at her. They jeered and whistled and laughed loudly at her worry. Becky ran faster, her heart was racing. She passed the car and continued to run towards the farm, which, however, was far away. She just thought she had gotten rid of them when she heard the sound of an engine behind her. The car raced in her direction and Becky sped up even more, scared of the people in it. The young men were shouting, three of them appeared from the windows and beckoned her to stop and talk. It wasn't long before the car caught up with her.

The road was very narrow, with thick hedges on both sides, and there was no place for Becky to stop or hide, so she continued to run as fast as she could. She let go of her bag and tried to get through a hole in the hedge but couldn't. Then she tried to jump over into the field beyond, but this attempt also failed, only slowing her down even more. The car was chasing her, and the men in it, who had reclined on the seats, were shouting something enthusiastically. Becky was so scared that she started calling for help, hoping that someone would be nearby and hear her. She ran as fast as she could, her legs starting to ache from the effort, her knees weak and her breath short. She turned to see if she had gained a lead but saw that the car was following her and almost at her feet. The driver was laughing in a throaty voice, pleased with his pursuit of his victim, and the others cheered him on with ecstatic shouts.

Finally, apparently, the driver got tired of the cat and mouse game. He stepped on the gas and hit her lightly enough to knock her to the ground. Becky fell, but got up quickly and started running again, stumbling down the country road. At a wider spot in the road, all the men got out of the car, caught up with her and pounced on her. They grabbed her and pulled her back. She screamed and struggled, but the nearest houses were so far away that the likelihood of anyone hearing her was minimal. Becky felt sick at the thought of what might happen to her. She started kicking and screaming even louder and tried her best to get away from them, but the men had grabbed her tightly and put her in the car. The driver obviously knew the area because he said he would drive to one of the beaches known only to the locals. As they travelled, several hands attacked and groped her. Some were busy groping her breasts, others were putting their hands under her skirt and struggling to get her panties off. Becky was trying to cry for help but couldn't. One of the men covered her mouth with one of her socks. She realized what was about to happen to her and even more furiously began to fight the men in the back seat, but they wouldn't let her go. On the contrary, one of them pulled down her panties and lifted up her skirt.

'Look what we have here,' he said, pointing to the girl's naked body. The men in the car stared at Becky's legs and body and a lustful smile appeared on each of their faces. She started kicking and struggling again, but the drunken men, seeing that they were far from populated areas, didn't pay much attention to her anymore. Three pairs of hands groped her and caused her pain. Only the driver had not yet directed his hands at her and was concentrating on driving. The car shook from the rough road and when Becky realized where they were, the fear in her heart turned to terror. The sun had almost set, but there was still a faint light around. The car's headlights illuminated part of the road, but the driver soon turned them off. He motioned for his friends to get Becky out, and, excited by what was to come, they roughly yanked her out of the back seat and dropped her onto the hard, stone-strewn ground. Two of them grabbed her legs and dragged her, letting her head hit the rocks like it was a piece of meat. The other two were taking something from the car and ran towards their friends. Becky screamed, hoping someone would hear her and come to help her. Her head ached from the blows she received as the two men dragged her. They had grabbed her by the ankles, each taking one leg in their hands. Her legs were spread, her skirt still up, and the men occasionally turned to enjoy the view. The other two illuminated her body with small flashlights. They dragged her for a few paces and finally put their victim on the ground. She tried to escape, grabbed a stone, and threw it at her attackers, but the stone didn't hit anyone.

'Now we're going to draw lots,' said the driver, pressing his foot on Becky's right wrist. The four of them looked away from her briefly and after quickly deciding who would be the first, they set about removing her skirt and shirt. Within seconds, Becky was down to her bra, which was quickly ripped off by the driver. The men's movements were rough and caused her pain. Becky shivered at the cold and damp air. She wanted to think that someone would come at the last moment and save her, but there was no one. The driver leaned over her, grabbed her chest roughly then took off his pants and moved his hands to her lower body. His friends watched him, in the eyes of two of them Becky saw envy. They envied him for doing this to her.

She closed her eyes, anticipating the inevitable pain, and began to cry softly. And the pain was intense, something tore inside her, and she screamed loudly. One of the men covered her mouth with his hand, squeezing her so hard that Becky felt small stones enter her scalp, and she screamed even louder. She blacked out from the pain she felt with every cell in her body. One of the men found her sock and stopped her screams with it. It was hard for her to breathe. She could feel the blood flowing from her and the sweat coming from her rapists. Everything hurt her, she tried to resist but with each resistance one of them hit her and caused her even more pain. Becky closed her eyes, her head throbbing. Her consciousness could not cope with what was happening to her, and, after a few minutes, she passed out.

'Wake her up,' said one of them. 'I want her to look me in the eye while I do it.'

Two of the men were trying to wake her up. They doused her with water and slapped her twice in the hope that this would revive her. After the third hard slap she regained consciousness, and her rapist gave her a satisfied smile.

'I want you to remember this,' he whispered in her ear.

Becky wanted to pass out again or die. That would be best. To die and not feel what these freaks were doing to her, but the men kept her awake. They didn't give her any rest. They raped her one after the other and then again until they got tired. She was crying, big heavy tears falling from her eyes, but they didn't notice it. They looked into her eyes as they played with her, and her tears seemed to turn them on even more.

'That's enough!' said the driver, finally. 'Let's dump the bitch here.'

'I have a better idea,' said one of the men, his dark eyes shining with excitement. 'Do people come here often?'

'No. In the off season almost no one comes,' said the driver confidently and grinned. 'What are you up to?'

The men were already out of control, drunk and stoned, intoxicated, and satisfied with the pleasure they had just been given. One of them went to the car, then returned with a small pocketknife.

'Let's scar her for life, huh? One scar from each of us. This is how she will remember this night forever,' he said and without warning he stabbed the young girl in the left shoulder. Becky winced in pain. The sock was still in her mouth. The driver smiled, took the knife, and plunged it with all his might into her left thigh. Before he could pull it out, he twirled knife into her flesh. Becky blacked out. She wanted to die. The pain was so intense that she finally passed out.

One of the men slapped her several times, doused her with water and hit her until she regained consciousness. He removed the sock from her mouth and said:

'If you tell someone who did this to you, you're dead. Although looking at yourself will make you want to die before that,' he spat at her. Then he raised the knife and plunged it into her right shoulder. She couldn't even gasp, only tried to curl up into a ball, but the last of the four forced her to lay onto her back and

11

plunged the knife into her right thigh. Then the four of them left her and went to the car. Becky felt the blood drain from her body and, when she felt that nobody was around, she screamed. Her first scream was loud, but after that her cries became feeble and weak. The chances of anyone hearing them were slim. Her blood flowed and fell between the small stones that were on the ground. Then it filled the space between them and soaked into the soil. Her tears were also falling slowly there. She was sobbing and begging to die. Five minutes later, Becky passed out. She sank into a white weightless field full of cotton-white clouds. Then the clouds began to take on a light pink colour and finally turned red. Becky decided she was dead and told herself with relief that it was for the best. She laid back on the red fluffy clouds and fell asleep.

2.

When Becky woke up, it was hard for her to breathe. She tried to open her eyes, but something was pressing them. She felt thirsty, her throat felt parched. She tried to lick her lips but failed. She felt fabric against her body. She squeezed it and realized from the material that it was a sheet. There was someone next to her, she could hear his breathing. Someone was moving, doing something above her head. Becky gripped the sheet again, hoping she would be able to find the strength to get up and see where she was and who was next to her, but she couldn't. Someone gently grabbed her arm and pulled her away.

'You need to rest,' said a female voice and someone gently caressed her hand. 'In a few days you will feel better.'

Becky relaxed and fell asleep. She dreamed of the men all hanging over her and cried out. The memory was so clear that she screamed at the top of her lungs. She woke up, opened her eyes and this time it didn't take much effort. Becky blinked from the bright light, raised herself slightly, just a few centimetres and looked around as best she could. She tried to get up, but something seemed to stop her. She tried again but quickly got tired and collapsed slightly on the bed. When she opened her eyes again, she saw two nurses standing by her bed.

'Everything is fine,' said one of them, seeing the terror in the girl's eyes. 'You're safe.'

Becky looked around again. She was in a hospital room. A policeman entered the room, worried by the commotion inside. The nurse motioned for him to come out and he did. He remained outside at his post. The young girl calmed down. She still couldn't move and realized her whole body was in bandages. She tried to move her arms, but a sharp pain stopped her, so she laid back on the bed.

'Now I will give you some medicine to calm you down,' said the nurse and left the room. The other nurse was checking her blood pressure and looked at her face.

'Are you okay?' she asked.

Becky closed her eyes and leaned back against the pillow. She wasn't dead. Becky didn't know whether to be happy about that or not. She looked down at her left arm and saw an IV injecting fluid into a vein in her arm. The nurse came back and put something into the IV.

'Now it will be less painful for you,' she said to Becky and stroked her hand again. There was sympathy in her eyes. Becky wondered if her mother and father were nearby and whether it was them that found her. Then she fell asleep again. When she woke up, she was alone in the room. It must have been night because the lights in the hallway were dimmed. She heard muffled voices from somewhere. Someone was whispering outside the door, and, when Becky listened, she realized that the whisper was coming from the policeman who was guarding her room. He was talking to his girlfriend and whispering something gentle to her. Becky's eyes watered. She wished she was dead. What was she going to do now? After what happened, no one would want her, everyone would point the finger at her. Her crying turned into sobbing. She closed her eyes and let her tears flow. After a few minutes, she calmed down and listened to the steady voice of the policeman, who continued to speak to his girlfriend. Becky drifted off and fell to sleep again.

A few hours later a doctor entered the room. An elderly man, with glasses and a good-natured face. He looked at the girl in the hospital bed and a nervous smile appeared on his lips. 'Good morning!'

Becky looked at him, the presence of a man in the room bothering her and unnerving her. She nodded and waited to hear what he had to say. The doctor seemed to sense her worry and stood away from the bed.

'My name is Doctor Vincent, and I am your attending physician at the clinic in Truro. First of all, I want to tell you that I am very sorry for what happened to you.'

Becky nodded.

'How do you feel?' he asked her.

She nodded again.

'Okay. I'm glad you're better. I have good news. Your test results are good, and your body is recovering quickly. Today we will be able to remove the oxygen tube and you will be able to speak. It will take you a few hours to get used to it, but I think it won't be a problem for you.'

He was silent for a moment as if he was hesitating about something. Finally, he said, 'I will come in a little while with a nurse. Before that, I want to make sure that my presence in the room will not disturb you.'

Becky looked at him nervously. She imagined his body above her, and her eyes widened in fear. This didn't go unnoticed by the doctor. He nodded.

'I will ask my colleague to help with this. I'll just watch from a distance. Is that, okay?'

Becky nodded and closed her eyes in thanks. Doctor Vincent also nodded and left the room. After a few minutes, he returned with his colleague, who helped Becky free herself from the oxygen tube.

'Drink water in small sips and try not to talk today, just focus on your recovery. The investigating officer who took over your case is coming tomorrow and wants to talk to you.'

Becky nodded, but just the thought of talking about what happened made her feel sick. The doctor saw her concern and asked the nurse to stay in the room while he spoke with the patient. 'Rebecca, you need to talk to the police inspectors so they can catch the perpetrator faster. Point them to clues so they can start searching. We will also assign a counsellor to help you overcome the stress you have experienced. A counsellor is a woman who talks to girls like you. As I can see that you are worried about my presence in the room, I will call my very good doctor friend to attend the interview tomorrow.'

Becky nodded again. Even if she could shave spoken, she preferred to remain silent now. The nightmares she was having were nothing compared to the mere thought of talking about it. The doctor looked at her sympathetically and left the room. The nurse stayed by her side for another two or three minutes to make sure she was okay and left the room as well. Becky got up, looked down the corridor hoping to see her parents, but the only one standing there was the policeman making sure no one entered her room. Where are they? Why didn't they come to see me, she asked herself. Then she looked away from the corridor and looked at her body for the first time after the rape. Most of her torso was still in bandages. They were squeezing her chest and it made difficult for her to breathe. Her upper arms and thighs were also bandaged. Apparently, they were dressing the knife wounds. The memory of the knife made her faint again. She rested her head on the pillow and stared at the ceiling of the room. She had survived, despite their desire to kill her she was still alive. Becky didn't know how she had ended up in the hospital, but she hoped to find out soon. She closed her eyes for a moment, but the faces of the men who almost killed her were before her again and she opened them. She stared at the people passing by in the corridor.

How much time had passed? How long had she been in the hospital? She must have been kicked out of school by now, she thought. Were her friends thinking about her? Becky was entangled in questions. She tried not to think about what had happened, but it was all about it. Exhausted by thoughts of the unknown, she finally fell asleep.

She didn't wake up until the next morning. The lights were still dim, as if it were night, but the sun had risen outside. It was probably five or six in the morning, which for early June was normal. The policeman outside the door was whispering something tender to his girlfriend again, and Becky listened to his monotonous, soothing voice. At first glance, he resembled her rapists, but his eyes had been warm when he looked at her yesterday. There was nothing aggressive about this man and even though Becky didn't know him, she felt a certain security with him. She was just starting to drift off again when the lights in the hallway went out and a young nurse came into her room. She asked Becky how she was, then quickly went out to check on the other patients. Doctor Vincent also visited her briefly, just to make sure she was well. At half past eight, several people appeared outside Becky's room. She didn't know any of them. After a brief conversation with the doctor and the policeman, the newcomers entered her room. A middle-aged man and woman watched her with lowered brows. Becky shifted uncomfortably under their stares. She wondered again where her mother and father were. Shouldn't they be here and present at these conversations? Becky swallowed loudly and stared at the people in front of her.

'I'm Inspector Becks, and this is Inspector Ramsey,' the man introduced them. Becky nodded but said nothing. 'We want to talk to you about what happened.'

'Where are my mum and dad?' Becky asked hoarsely. It was difficult for her to speak. Her throat was scraped.

'They didn't want to be present, but they allowed us to talk to you,' answered the woman. 'You are now sixteen-years-old, and you will have to testify without their presence.'

Becky looked at them sadly, leaned back against the pillow, and tears suddenly flowed from her eyes. They flowed and sank slowly into the pillow fabric. The two investigators stood by the door and didn't know what to say or how to react. Crimes of this magnitude were rare in Cornwall.

This girl's case had become even worse after her parents refused to cooperate and did not want to talk to their daughter, which, according to Inspector Ramsey was an even worse crime than what the rapist had committed. You must have a heart of stone to abandon your daughter at a time like this, she thought. Then she approached Becky, caressed her hand gently, and asked her to talk to them.

'Dr Vincent called his good friend who deals with cases like yours. She will attend the conversation instead of your parents. I hope you don't mind.'

Becky nodded, unable to speak again. Tears fell and blurred her vision. She tried to wipe them away, but she couldn't raise her hands. Inspector Ramsey reached out and wiped them with her hand, then nodded to the woman who was standing alone in the corridor. She approached, introduced herself, and asked Becky to quickly retell, without much detail, what had happened. Becky agreed, swallowed hard a few times, looked away from the people in the room and stared at the far-right corner. Then she began her story slowly. When she reached the part about the four young men, everyone in the room gasped in surprise. Not one, but four? Ramsey's face turned red, and her colleague simply turned his head and stared down the corridor. The ferocity of the men's behaviour astonished everyone in the room. Becky's tears continued to stream down her face. Unconscious tears, the woman conducting her therapy had called them. And healing, she had told her, washing away some of the emotional pain.

'I know it's hard for you, Becky, but can you remember what happened to the knife?' Ramsey asked her.

'No.' Becky cried this time, remembering the pain of the stabbings.

Doctor Vincent, who was watching the interrogation from the sideliners, asked everyone to leave and let Becky recover. But she couldn't rest. All day long, the tears streamed down her face. She didn't know which pain was stronger, the one caused by young, drugged, and drunk men or the pain of realizing she was abandoned by her parents. What would happen to her after she got out of the hospital, she wondered. Where would she go? She just turned sixteen.

Late in the evening, the doctor appeared at her door again. It was getting dark, almost no one was walking along the corridor, only the police officer was on duty.

This time it was a female police officer, as Inspector Ramsey had recommended after hearing Becky's testimony. Doctor Vincent turned on the light, looked at Becky, and shook his head dejectedly. He didn't dare to approach her bed, he didn't want to frighten her with unnecessary movements, so he remained on the threshold without entering the room.

'Your father has come to see you,' he told her. Becky smiled reassuringly. When her father entered, she quickly realized that there was no cause for joy. Her father looked sad. He had been drinking and smelled strongly of beer and whiskey.

'Becky,' he said, approaching her, looking at her and caressing her forehead with his palm. His eyes were glassy, tears were about to fall from them, but he held them back. 'Your mother sent me to say goodbye to you.'

'But why?' she asked.

'She doesn't want you at home. You know what she is like.'

'And you? Do you want me home?' Becky raised her head and looked into his eyes. She saw his tears and understood. He would do what her mother asked him to do.

'Why did you come?' she said coldly and turned her eyes away from him.

'We spoke to your cousin, Arnie. He'll find you a room to rent in London and will help you get a job.'

'London? You're sending me far away, aren't you?'

'Becky...' the man appeared to suppress his emotions. 'I have no choice. I brought you money. I hope it lasts you at least a few months.'

Becky turned her head. She didn't want to look at her father again. The tears kept flowing, but she no longer knew what exactly she was crying about.

Her father placed a paper envelope on her bedside table, leaned down and kissed her forehead. His breath reeked of alcohol. He had mustered up his courage in the pub for a long time, she thought. Then he slowly made his way to the door and turned to her once more. This time he met her gaze. He left before everyone could see his feelings. Becky pulled her covers up, buried her face in it, and cried her heart out.

The policewoman watched her from the window and thought that in all her conscious life she had never seen such anguish. She felt sorry for the girl and furious with the rapists and her family. Then she turned around and called her friend to buy flowers and candy for the poor girl. At least one human being had to show her compassion, and, at that moment Officer Simpson decided that, at least for a few days, it would be her.

3.

Becky stayed in the hospital for another three weeks. The police were looking for her rapists, but so far there was no trace of them. There was no sign of the car either, and the owner of the house Becky saw the car in front of, had an alibi and hadn't been in the area those days. The investigation continued, but with each passing day the likelihood of finding the men decreased. Becky was afraid of her rapists, but she spared no detail from Inspector Ramsey and her colleague, describing the men and the car as best she could. Though the memory pained her, she tried to recall anything that might help in their identification and capture. She had nothing left to lose. She had no relatives and no friends. No one came to visit her in the hospital, no one called her or tried to contact her. The policeman, the doctor, and one of the nurses took care of her, bringing her books, candy, and generally anything that could cheer her up. In the end, however, they had to separate. After several operations and severe psychological trauma, Becky had to get up, recover and take the train to London, where the unknown awaited her. Her legs and arms still hurt, her wounds had begun to heal, her body was still weak, but she had nowhere to go. She had to take her cousin Arnie's hand and accept his help.

There was £1,200 in the envelope her father left her. Becky had never seen so much money. She was sure that neither her mother nor her father had that much, and she wondered how he had gotten it. Becky had decided to return the money to her parents. The moment she got a job and felt better she would send them back every penny they gave her. She didn't want anything from them anymore. Dr Vincent and the inspectors tried to talk her out of it, get her to stay and move her to another clinic, bring in a few more sessions of therapy, but Becky decided to leave. People's sympathy was killing her, as well as the fear that one of her abusers would find her and finish her off.

Becky had worked up the courage to give as detailed a statement as possible, but the men she had described as her rapists were never found. The weeks she'd been in the ER had given them a head start and an opportunity to cover their tracks. Becky had no doubt that they knew she was alive. Her case had appeared in the local media and almost everyone was talking about it. Police were searching for the car and looking for witnesses. The two inspectors had given her their word to continue the investigation, but with no clues and no witnesses, they were making no progress. The only clue that was found at the crime scene was Becky's sock, which had been used to gag her mouth. Her bag and clothes were missing. The four men had left her naked with blood dripping from all her wounds. Everyone was horrified and Becky kind of understood why her parents wanted her away. She had to go to London, although she was not yet physically or mentally stable. She needed to hide and recover as quickly as possible. Away from everyone who knew about it and away from where it had happened. So, one morning she got up, said goodbye to everyone in the hospital and left. The policeman took her to the station, bought her a ticket and stayed until the train left.

The train Becky was traveling on was almost empty. Despite the warm weather, the children had not yet broken up for the school holidays. Out of tourist season only small number of people came to Cornwall during this time. Becky watched the scenery outside and wondered if she would ever want to return to this tourist paradise. If this was a corner of heaven, what awaited her in other places, she wondered. She had decided to forget everything, put it in a faraway part of her brain and lock it there. Becky was going to start a new life and she was going to do her best to make sure nothing like that happened to her again. She had survived thanks to her last cry for help. From Inspector Ramsey, she learned that a couple heard her cry, saw a car speeding away and found her there, covered in blood and tears. She would never let anyone hurt her like that again, Becky promised herself. Then she thought fondly of her little sister, Summer. Her twelve-year-old sister would be left there, in that horrible place, on that horrible farm with parents who didn't deserve her. They would keep her there until they could take advantage of the benefits for her, and then they would throw her out of their lives as an unnecessary item.

Tears welled up in Becky's eyes again. This time she stopped them, swallowed hard, wiped the moisture from her eyes with her hand, and stared out the window again. The train had picked up speed. They were expected to arrive at the station in London within two hours, where her cousin had promised to meet her.

Arnie was twenty-four years old now. Becky hadn't seen him in six years. He was also ostracized by their family. He hadn't done anything wrong. He just didn't fit in. Arnie was good-natured. He wanted to study, get an education and one day to work in a big financial firm. That was why he had gone to London. Six years ago, he said goodbye to Becky and his sister, Aya, and they hadn't seen him since. Arnie's sister had inherited her mother's character, never forgave her brother for leaving and spoke of him as a traitor. Instead of making money and bringing it to his family, she thought, he had run off to live his life in the big city and she didn't even want to know where he was or what he was doing now. But Becky often wondered what had happened to him. Now, traveling on the train, she began to worry that he would not recognize her or that she would not recognize him and the two would drift apart. Or that he wouldn't come to meet her at all. What would she do then, she wondered.

A woman standing next to Becky saw the girl's concern but said nothing. She turned her head to the window and looked out. Becky did the same, and though troubling thoughts and questions raced through her head, she managed to pull herself together and put on a calm face.

Becky had never left Cornwall before. She had dreamed of leaving the farm, but not like this. She wanted to leave the way Arnie had, with her chin up and faith in the future. At least there was money to begin with, she thought, and wondered again where the money had come from. Her mother and father couldn't keep five pounds in their pockets, where did they get twelve hundred? Becky leaned back and tried to calm down and not think about anything. After almost an eternity the train finally approached Paddington Station. When it stopped, all the passengers eagerly started to get off. Becky hesitated, afraid of the unknown, but finally she pulled the plastic bag that contained the few things that the people at the hospital had given her, and slowly got out of the train.

She walked in the direction of the crowd as Inspector Ramsey had advised her, passed the ticket barriers, and stared at the people standing in front of the platform. She looked for Arnie but didn't see him. Panic began to rise inside her, her heart pounding and her legs growing weak. She was wondering what to do, should she stay at the platform for a while or should she go somewhere else? A young man approached her, she got scared and started backing away.

'You have grown up,' he said and gave her a happy smile. Arnie's smile. Becky relaxed in relief and let him put his arms around her.

'Arnie,' she said. 'I didn't recognize you. You have a beard.'

'And you don't look like the little girl I left at the farm anymore,' he said and smiled at her again. 'Let's get your luggage and I'll take you out to eat. You must be hungry.'

Becky looked at him uncertainly while Arnie looked around for a suitcase or something that held her belongings. Finally, he realized that she had nothing, just a plastic bag filled with books, magazines, and get-well cards. Arnie tried to quickly recover from the shock, but Becky saw his concern.

'Don't worry,' he told her. 'I will buy you everything you need.'

'I have money,' she said.

'You will need that for accommodation. I will buy you clothes and food, I have some savings.' He smiled at her, took her by the hand, and led her to the nearest cafe. Becky was still struggling, her wounds aching, and Arnie had to help her up the steps. When they arrived at the cafe, she sat down with relief in the first chair she saw. She couldn't stand straight for long, and meeting strangers made her nervous and caused her lower lip to tremble slightly.

Arnie sat down next to her and stroked her hair. He knew what happened to her mostly from the media and from social networks. The frightened young girl he saw next to him now was a pale copy of Becky. His cousin had always impressed him with her strength and independence. Now she couldn't even look him in the eye. Her hands were nervously clutching the hem of the sweatshirt she was wearing, her gaze darting from person to person as if assessing potential danger. Arnie looked around the room, saw an empty table in the far corner, and helped Becky move there, away from most of the people in the cafe. That seemed to calm her down. She relaxed her hands and placed them on the coffee table in front of her. Her gaze was still nervous, but there was also curiosity in it.

'I'll be back soon,' Arnie told her and went to order tea and sandwiches.

Left alone, Becky looked away from the crowd and looked around the room. On one wall was a large photograph of an Italian scene, with steps leading to the sea and lots of flowers. Becky stared at the photograph for a while, and it calmed her down. Then she looked away and stared at Arnie. Her cousin hadn't married. His dark hair was pulled up in the style that most men his age currently wore. He was still thin, but his arms had already taken on a muscular appearance. Overall, the change in Arnie was good. As if sensing her gaze, he turned. His eyes looked at her worriedly. Her appearance had probably shocked him. Maybe he was already regretting agreeing to help her, Becky thought.

'I ordered you tea and sandwiches,' he told her, approaching the table with several utensils in his hands.

'Great,' answered Becky and looked again at the people in the cafe. Everyone was well dressed, with trendy hairdos and expensive smartphones. It reminded her that she needed to buy a phone. As they ate, Arnie helped her make a list of the things she needed first. She was dictating to him, but her gaze never stopped studying everyone who entered the cafe. Her fear was felt not only by her cousin but also by the visitors. Arnie watched her and decided they had better leave as quickly as possible. He picked up the remains of the sandwiches and helped Becky to her feet. He supported her the whole time as they walked down the street. Every few meters, Becky asked him to sit somewhere to rest. Finally, she reached into the bag and pulled out some pills.

'Painkillers. My doctor prescribed them for me. I forgot to take the pill in the morning,' she explained to him.

Arnie nodded, sat with her for a few minutes on a bench until Becky felt relieved and they continued on their way. She moved more quickly this time, the pills had worked and eased her pain. They stopped at a few stores, got what they needed and headed for the tube station. Even before they entered the tube station, Becky was nervous. It was full of people going in and out. She had plucked up the courage to get on the train, but the very idea of being meters underground with all these strangers and nowhere to run terrified her. She stopped, her breath quickened, and instinctively headed for a quiet corner of one of the nearby buildings. Arnie followed her. He saw her worry and wondered how to get her into the tube.

'Everything will be fine,' he whispered to her. 'I am with you, no one will hurt you.'

But Becky was fearful. The second time they tried to enter the station, she shook and almost screamed when a young man walked past her. Arnie pulled her up quickly and took her to a quieter and safer place for her.

'Okay,' he finally said thoughtfully. 'We have to find a way to get to Stratford. I would take a taxi, but they are very expensive, so that isn't an option. How about we try to take the bus home?'

Becky nodded. Her breathing calmed. Arnie waited a little longer for her to regain her composure and led her to the bus stop. It took them more than two hours to get to Stratford, and twice Becky cried out in terror as a man approached her. Arnie squeezed her hand reassuringly and told her that she was safe. When they finally entered the house, he was relieved. They were both very tired. They sat down on the sofa in the living room in silence for half an hour.

'I'm so sorry,' Becky told him. 'I panic only at the sight of an unknown man. I still can't control it, but the doctors told me it will go away in time.'

Arnie stared at her. Her skin was pale, her eyes still had that nervous look that scanned the entire house marking potential dangers. He took her hand and tried to calm her down.

'Everything will be fine. I will help you recover. But I don't think you're ready to live on your own. You will have to stay with me for a while.'

'You don't live alone, do you?' she asked him, noticing the many men's shoes in one corner. Some of them were a different size than the ones Arnie was wearing.

'I have two roommates. One is studying to become a doctor and the other works in a law firm. I have been living with them for four years and I completely trust them. You will have to trust them too.'

'Where are they now?' Becky asked, continuing to look around.

'They went to their families for the weekend. Paul is from Wales and Alexander from North Yorkshire. They'll be back on Sunday night or Monday morning, so you and I will have two days to sort out your emotions. You will settle in my room, and I will temporarily stay here and sleep on the sofa.'

'I don't want to bother you and your roommates. I don't know if I will be able to live with men,' she said frankly. 'We'd better find somewhere else for me to stay.'

'Becky, you won't make it. You are startled by every man who approaches you and every stranger makes you nervous, even women. Give yourself time, calm down. Stay here, I'm sure my roommates won't mind. And it will be useful for you to get used to having men around you.'

Becky nodded and rested her head on the back of the sofa. She was very tired and couldn't argue. All she wanted right now was to lie down and sleep.

Arnie let her sleep and went to prepare the room for her. Then he went out to buy her a phone and a prepaid sim card. While he was out, he called Paul and Alex to tell them about Becky. He didn't tell them what she had been through, only that she needed to stay with him for a few days. At this time, Becky woke up and started walking around the house. She looked around the kitchen, then went out into the well-tended garden. One of the men living with Arnie had gardening skills, she thought, as she saw the roses blooming in almost every corner of the garden. She sat down on one of the chairs and stared at the bees and butterflies attracted by the blooming flowers. It was nice and peaceful. This was exactly what she needed. When Arnie returned, he joined her. They stayed outside together until it got dark.

'Will you tell me what happened?' he asked her. Becky nodded, looked down at the cup of tea she held in her hands, and quickly recounted what had happened to her. She told it as if it was not about her, but about another person. Cold, emotionless, just facts. When she finished her story, Arnie hugged her.

'We'll make it, Becky. We will find the people who did this to you and bring them to justice. But before that, we will give you back your life and self-confidence,' Arnie said.

'But we won't be able to fix what they've done,' she told him sadly.

Becky was grateful for his support, but she didn't know how to handle her emotions. His presence calmed her, yet any other male presence made her unnerved. She took one of the books she had been given and was carried away into the imaginary life of the heroine. Nothing helped her forget what happened like reading about other people's lives. So, her life didn't seem to matter. She was transported to another reality, with other people and destinies. Towards midnight she finally put the book aside and got ready for bed. Arnie was asleep on the sofa, she wrapped a blanket over him, turned off all the lights and slowly, with great effort, climbed the stairs to the second floor where her room was. Five minutes later she was asleep and for the first time since the rape she didn't have any nightmares.

4.

When Becky woke up in the morning, the house was quiet. She got up, dressed as quickly as she could, and went down to the first floor to see what Arnie was doing. To her surprise he was gone. He had left her a note saying he had to go out for a bit and would be back as soon as possible. Becky decided to make herself some coffee and sit in the beautiful garden. It was a sunny day, and there was a nice fragrance from the roses there. She was just walking there with a cup of warm coffee when the kitchen door opened, and a man walked in. Becky panicked, jerking back, and dropping the glass in fright. The hot liquid spilled over her bare feet. She screamed in fear and pain. The man looked terrified and could not move. He came to her aid, but this made her panic even more and she screamed for help. Screaming, she ran to her room stumbling down the steps, closed the door and continued to shout out, 'Help! Help!' Becky opened the window and continued to scream. People gathered on the street, they were talking to her, but she couldn't hear them. She was so scared, and she didn't know what to do. She stayed at the window curled up in a ball until she heard Arnie's voice.

'Becky, open the door,' he said in a calm voice. 'Please, don't shout. Everything is fine.'

She slowly climbed down from the window frame, approached the door timidly but didn't unlock it.

'Becky, it's me. Open the door, please,' he begged again.

She stood for a moment, then unlocked the door and let him in.

'Everything is fine,' he told her and hold her.

'There was a man in the kitchen,' she said. Her body trembled, her eyes still staring at him in terror.

'That's right. This is Alex, my roommate. He came home early,' Arnie spoke soothingly to her. 'I'm sorry he scared you. Everything is fine. Just calm down.'

'Your roommate?' she asked and immediately realized what she had done.

There was a knock at the front door.

'Police,' said a male voice.

Becky started even more, but Arnie motioned for her to calm down and opened the door. Two police officers entered the house, looked around and questioned everyone. Becky's mother and Inspector Ramsey were then called to confirm her story. After realizing that everything was a misunderstanding, the police officers left the house. However, the neighbours continued to stare.

Becky stayed in her room for a while. What had happened totally shocked her. She was about to get Arnie's roommate arrested. She was so ashamed of what she had done that she gathered her courage for a while before going to the kitchen. When she got there, she found the two young men talking animatedly. At first, they didn't even notice her, then, feeling her gaze, they turned and stared at her.

'I'm really sorry,' she muttered.

Alexander got up, approached her slowly and gave her his hand. She stared at the hand, unable to touch it. He nodded at her and motioned for her to join them.

'Do you feel better?' Arnie asked her.

'Yes. I feel better. I'm so sorry for the yelling and screaming. And for the police. I don't know what happened to me, I just got scared.'

'A normal reaction after what you experienced,' Alex told her.

So, he already knew, thought Becky.

'I told him what happened, Becky,' Arnie explained. 'So, he knows what he's dealing with. Alex doesn't mind you staying with us for a while.'

Alex nodded and stared at her. She had calmed down, her blue eyes studying him, but he didn't look away. She also held his gaze. There was still a hint of vulnerability in her, especially when she bit her lip, but at the same time Alex sensed determination. He didn't know how to deal with a rape victim, although he had seen a few in court. But he would try to help her overcome her fear. Or at least he hoped she would let him help her.

The two looked at each other for a while longer, then Arnie broke the silence. 'Alex came back early to study for an exam,' he told Becky.

'My sister has five children. I tried to concentrate and study, but the noise was so bad that I finally decided to come home to London and study here in peace,' he explained. But he didn't say he was curious to see Arnie's cousin before she left.

'There is no need to explain,' Becky said quietly. 'You live in this house. You can come in and out whenever you want. I hope I will find a place to stay soon and not have to bother you.'

'Stay as long as you need,' Alex said, then stood up and headed for his room. 'Now I will start studying for my exam.'

Tactful man, she thought as she watched him walk away.

'I guess we will remember this day for the rest of our lives,' laughed Arnie.

'That's right,' she smiled too. 'I definitely woke up the neighbourhood. You don't need to introduce me to them, they all know me by now.'

'Here they change often—in two months they will have forgotten about you,' he said thoughtfully. 'Will you make it?'

'I will manage. I promise not to scream when I see your other roommate.'

Arnie showed her a picture of Paul to make sure Becky wouldn't be scared if he came home unexpectedly, then asked her to change and come out with him to the park. Becky had a list of things she needed to do in order to recover faster, both physically and mentally. Walks in the park were one of them. The walks would help her not panic around other people and also restore stability in her muscles and joints.

Their first walk didn't last long. After ten minutes of slow walking, she sat down on a bench, exhausted and unable to continue. Arnie waited for her to rest, then helped her home.

Alex watched them from the window and sighed sympathetically. He had no idea how he would feel if something like this had happened to his sister. He would probably find the bastards who did it and shoot them. Alex had always believed that the law should be followed and that the perpetrators should serve their punishment in prison, but, after this morning, his opinion on the matter had changed. He found Arnie had only told him part of Becky's story. After scouring the internet, he realized what a nightmare this girl had been through. He wondered where her parents were and why she had come here. She should be recuperating somewhere where professionals could help her. He watched the young woman and the man supporting her. He could see her physical pain, so severely was she stepping from foot to foot. According to Alex, Becky needed not a few days, but a few months of recovery. After few minutes he heard the front door open, and saw Arnie and Becky walk in. Alex tried to tear himself away from thinking about her, opened the laptop and started studying for his exam.

For the next two days, Arnie and Becky continued their morning walks in the park, then they returned, and she fell asleep for a few hours, exhausted from the effort these short walks took. The stairs to the second floor took a lot of effort to climb. It was difficult for her with each step, so she counted them. There were fourteen steps. She managed to climb the first five faster, but each subsequent one cost her a lot of effort. Sometimes she got tired and sat down on one of them to rest. Arnie watched her from the sofa in the living room. She sensed his concern but refused his help when he offered it. She had to deal with it herself, the doctor had told her.

On Sunday evening, Paul came home, and the house became livelier. It took a while for Paul to understand Becky's delicate situation, but he and Alex didn't mind her staying while she recovered. He even offered Arnie the use of his room when he is gone.

Paul and Alex wanted to help in any way they could and get involved in her recovery. Arnie worked almost every day until late, his work was hard and exhausting, so he gladly accepted his friends' offer to help Becky while he was gone. They made a schedule of who would be free when and what he could do for her. Becky, however, disagreed. The presence of Arnie's two friends bothered her. She didn't want them watching her, let alone touching her and accompanying her anywhere outside the house. It took her a few days to get over her worry about them. After a week, she could stay in the same room with Alex and Paul without worrying. Finally, she trusted them. The three young men helped her with the walks. At first, Becky didn't agree with Alex or Paul accompanying her to the park and supporting her on her obligatory walks, but then she got used to their presence and touch and didn't even notice if either of them suddenly approached. Paul was studying to be a doctor and had studied her injuries. Like Alex, he had read all about her rape on the internet and was shocked by the brutality of her rapists. He knew her wounds hadn't quite healed yet. He could see the bandages on her thighs and one of her shoulders, which she changed often at the local surgery, so he helped her with new physical exercises that would restore some of the injured muscles. Paul was even able to get her into a free two-week program with a physical therapist.

Alex, in turn, contacted Inspector Ramsey and followed the investigation. There was still no sign of the perpetrators. They had several types of DNA, but no match in the database. It was driving him crazy. He didn't want them to get away with what they had done to Becky. The other thing that no one talked about out loud, but everyone was wondering, was where her family was. Why didn't they call her and ask how she was? At every mention of family events and celebrations, Arnie and Becky reacted the same way, their lips smiling but their eyes turning sad. Who leaves their daughter at a time like this, Alex wondered. And she had a family, he was sure of that, he'd read her mother's statement when she'd been found, and he knew from Arnie that Becky had a father and a younger sister. It was amazing to Alex that after everything she had been through, she was able to stand firmly on her feet and not fall into a deep depression. Becky was strong, she wasn't like the other women Alex knew and his respect and admiration for her grew with each passing day. He had mixed feelings about the young woman. He wasn't in love with her, unlike Paul who couldn't take his eyes off her. Becky was beautiful, sensitive, and vulnerable. Alex didn't love her, but he was attached to her, he felt the need to help her and protect her, but nothing deeper. He respected her desire to fight and to get on with her life. What impressed him most was that she didn't grumble, she didn't seek sympathy. She accepted their help, but she didn't whine or beg for it. To Alex, Becky was the most strong and wilful woman he had ever met, and he was sure she would leave them as soon as she felt better and not abuse their hospitality.

Becky stayed with them for a month and a half. Her recovery progressed rapidly after the second week, as soon as she trusted them and started going out to the park with them, and after the two weeks of physical therapy that Paul had managed to get her into. Becky was no longer afraid of any man who crossed her line of sight. She could walk to the park, walk around it quickly, and return without being out of breath. She was better physically and mentally. It was time for her to separate from the three men and live on her own.

Becky didn't know how to thank them for their help, so she promised to come and clean their house once a week. They readily agreed. They would miss her and miss her dearly. Her presence enlivened the house. It also added comfort because while living with them she cleaned, cooked, and created a pleasant atmosphere that was lacking in their male life. All three of them were urging her to stay, but Becky wanted to leave and free Arnie's room. He had slept on the sofa for a long time and all his things were in the living room.

Becky rented a room four blocks from them and found a job in a small coffee shop near the Stratford mall. She was very excited, both with the new accommodation and the new job. For her it was a new beginning, a new life. Her move was quick, as she still didn't have many clothes and belongings. She left most of the books with Arnie, so with only two small bags she found herself in a small room with only one desk and a small wardrobe inside, if the few doorless shelves could even be called a wardrobe. The room she had rented was so small that it was almost impossible for two people to be in there. However, the rent was low. Becky kept everything paid in cash and her name not listed anywhere. She had an instinct for self-preservation and didn't want people to have public information about where she worked and where she lived. Something inside her still made her fear the four men who had hurt her, and she thought for days about every way they could find her.

There were three other women living in the house where she stayed. All three were in their forties. Two of them worked as cleaners, and the third in a care home. When Becky met them, she thought they would live pleasantly, the same way Arnie, Paul and Alex lived, but after only two days in the house she realized that they didn't like her and that the atmosphere in the house would be anything but friendly. At work she found the situation was almost the same. Becky didn't have a passport, she couldn't open a bank account, and so she worked illegally. The pay was minimal, and most of the time she worked in the kitchen washing dishes as quickly as possible. After two weeks at the café, her boss transferred her to one of his restaurants. There she was washing dishes again and the tension was even greater. The restaurant had two rooms, one for normal customers and the other for large parties. All the staff were under a lot of pressure, they were gossiping about each other, playing pranks, and nobody seemed to get along with anyone. Becky worked alone in the large washroom and was constantly harassed by the waiters and cooks. Before they even brought the dirty dishes, they wanted them clean for the next party, whose guests were already arriving. Sometimes her colleagues, annoyed by the bad customers and the ungrateful boss, attacked her, and threw things at her. But she held on. It wasn't anything she couldn't handle.

Someday, she told herself, she would turn eighteen and find a better place to live and a better job. Until then, she would bear it. There was no other choice.

Becky spent six days a week at the restaurant, working from ten in the morning until late at night. The restaurant was near to her house, and she used to run there. She was afraid to walk in the dark, but in time she got used to it. The streets of Stratford were full of people until almost dawn. The street lighting was also good, and, after a while, she felt at ease in the evening as well as during the day. She rarely saw her flatmates, but their presence and negative attitude towards her was perceptible. Sometimes Becky would cook on her day off and not find the box of food in the fridge the next day. There was a note left in the box saying that her food smelled bad, and they had thrown it in the bin. The first time, Becky cried. The second time she tried to reason with them, but she couldn't. It was difficult for her to talk to these women. Becky assumed that their misunderstanding was due to the age difference, but she learned from one of the neighbours that this was how they treated all the girls who rented the room. Becky really wanted to be friends with her flatmates, but with these three women she had no chance of making friends at all. Often her laundry would be taken out of the washing machine and left on the dirty floor just a few minutes before she went to collect it, and her shoes would be left outside the front door on the pretext that they smelled bad. Becky was eager to save up and find another place to live but finding a place to live when you were only sixteen and with no references was difficult. It was a wonder that she had found this one and that she had a place to live, so she gritted her teeth and tried not to annoy the women in the house. When she worked at the restaurant, she didn't see them anyway because she worked till late. Her roommates were already asleep when she got home, so most days the house was quiet.

On her weekly day off, Becky stopped by Arnie's house and cleaned the common areas. The young men had given her a key. She would come in in the morning, make herself a coffee and drink it in the beautiful garden that Paul looked after. Then she would clean the house and leave before any of them got home. Sometimes Arnie would call her and ask her to wait for him and go out to dinner together, but she never did. These men had given enough of themselves to help her. Becky was convinced that if they talked to her for even ten minutes, they would immediately know how miserable she was. It was better not to see them, but only to text each other on the phone. That way, they wouldn't know she was crying when her colleagues showered her with stale bread and salad, and they wouldn't smell the bad smell coming from hastily washed clothes. They wouldn't know how much she missed the three of them. They were all so different. Arnie had turned to finance and started working for a large financial corporation in central London. He, like Becky, had grown up in poverty and his goal in life was to succeed, become rich and have the respect of others. Paul on the other hand, had grown up like them on a farm, but surrounded by a wonderful family who helped him and financed his education.

Paul still had that boyish air that some people don't lose over the years, always smiling and well-intentioned. He was tall, with ginger hair and blue eyes. There were many freckles on his face. The profession he had chosen suited him perfectly. Paul had told Becky that he wanted to be a paediatrician, and she could already see him hovering over sick children and speaking sympathetically to them. He was the most emotional of the three of them and it was almost impossible for him to hide his feelings, whether they were good or bad. It was all written on his face.

Alex, on the other hand, was a bit of a mystery to Becky. He had told her that he grew up in a family of a teacher and a police inspector. His mother had died of cancer five years earlier. That was probably the reason for his sad look. One day he had told her that losing his mother had totally changed his outlook on life and he had gone from a happy teenager to a gloomy man in just a few months. At least that's how his sister defined it. Alex's father was still working for the police and taking care of his family. Unlike Paul, however, his father didn't support him financially, so Alex had taken out student loans to support his education. His training was over, but he had signed up for an additional internship at a law firm, which was unpaid. When Becky asked him why he decided to study to be a lawyer, Alex was silent. Then he told her that one day he woke up and decided that this would be his profession, he just decided that way, but she knew that there was something deeper, something inside him that had pushed him to this decision. Becky didn't insist on learning what it was. She accepted that everyone had things they didn't like to talk about. She really missed the three men. Every time after she cleaned their house, they didn't forget to text to her and thank her for it. She didn't realize it, but the cleanliness and the scent she left behind had a good effect on them, and every time after they got home, they stayed longer in the living room, talking to each other and taking in the comfort she brought in for just one day of a week in their lives. Then they went back to their rooms, each one lost in his youthful anxieties and worries.

5.

Inspector Ramsey called almost every week to hear from Becky and to update her on the progress of the investigation. She didn't have to, but in this girl's case she had to. Becky was afraid, and the inspector, as a woman, felt it. Unfortunately, there was no sign of the four men. Inspector Ramsey assumed they were tourists on a short holiday in Cornwall and felt the investigation was stuck in place. They found nothing about the car, and no one recognized the suspects. Although the sketches drawn from Becky's description were at every police station and published in several regional newspapers, there was no sign of these men. Every time Inspector Ramsey called Becky, she asked her how she was doing and if she was okay.

At first, when she found out Becky was living with three men, she was worried. She didn't think it was the best option for the poor girl, but a few weeks later it turned out to be working well for her. Her recovery progressed rapidly, and Inspector Ramsey began to relax. Becky's case had plunged her into a dark abyss. From the beginning, she had been shocked by the cruelty of the perpetrators. She could not believe that such evil and ruthless people really existed and felt it her duty to put them in prison. If she found them, she thought sadly.

Becky looked forward to the conversations with the Inspector Ramsey, each time answering her call in the hope that they had found the men or the car. And every time she cried when she realized that the men were still out there, somewhere. It was something she couldn't handle. The fear of these men. The fear that they would find her and hurt her again. Or that this time they wouldn't hesitate, they wouldn't leave wounds to remember them by, but they would kill her. This feeling of helplessness plagued her for hours. Sometimes, after talking to the Inspector Ramsey, she could not concentrate, her hands would shake, and she would drop and break some of the restaurant's equipment. Cups, plates, forks, or spoons, she unknowingly dropped them on the floor, and they crashed with a terrible noise that attracted some of the staff. And it didn't lead to anything good. Her boss got angry and threatened to fire her. On days like these, Becky wished she hadn't lived, that she'd stayed there on that rocky shore forever. But then she'd get a text from Paul or Alex, or a call from Arnie, and the grey seemed to turn into bright, beautiful tones. Even if they didn't realize it, the three men kept her alive and kept her willing to go on.

Three months after moving out of their house, Arnie invited her to dinner. He wanted to introduce her to someone who might be able to help her. Becky was excited about the meeting. She hadn't seen Arnie in a long time. They agreed to meet on her day off. She first went to clean their house, did some quick shopping, and then she met Arnie and a woman named Tanya at a restaurant. At first, she thought it was a friend of Arnie's, but then she found she was a private detective.

'I don't have money for a private detective,' Becky whispered in her cousin's ear.

'Paul, Alex, and I managed to raise enough to hire Tanya and her husband for a few months. Let's hope they find your rapists by then.' Arnie looked at her with a smile.

'You shouldn't have done that,' she whispered to him again.

Tanya watched them with interest, but her gaze was most intrigued by Becky.

'They told me you are sixteen years old,' she said.

'That's right,' said Becky.

'Unfortunately, we can't be hired by you Becky, but Paul, Alex and Arnie have agreed to hire us on your behalf. This means they will also have access to the information we find. Do you agree with that?'

'Yes,' Becky said uncertainly. Then she looked worriedly at her cousin. She had avoided talking about what happened to her a few months ago. If they hired a detective, she would have to go through all of this again. And she wasn't ready to do it in front of strangers. The restaurant where they were eating was not a suitable place for such conversations.

'We will need some facts,' Tanya said. 'My husband and I have read everything written in the media, but it would be good to hear the details from you.'

'Do you have an office where we can talk?' Becky asked.

'Yes. After dinner, we can go there,' suggested the private detective.

Becky nodded and focused on the food. Her hand was shaking slightly. Arnie noticed this and patted it reassuringly. After eating, the three headed to the Detective Agency. When they got inside, they found it was mess in the office. A man stood in the middle of the room cursing. Many sheets of paper were strewn about, under the table and desk, and he was crouched down rummaging through them. Receipts, bank documents and statements were displayed on all sides.

'Michael, what's going on?' Tanya asked him.

'Not now. Let me find what I'm looking for,' he said angrily without taking his eyes off the documents.

Tanya made a small path and motioned for Becky and Arnie to follow her. They found themselves in a small kitchen that barely held the three of them.

'Excuse my husband, he is the really good detective in our agency. He's like a dog, he's smelled something, and he won't stop until he finds it. Better to leave him until he finds what he needs.'

Tanya was just finishing the sentence when her husband entered with a big smile. He carried some pieces of paper in one hand. 'I found it,' he said happily, and handed the sheets to Tanya. She looked at them, then looked at her husband uncertainly. He pointed something out to her and this time she understood why he was so happy. Becky and Arnie watched the scene without moving, not that they had anywhere to go, the kitchen was already crowded with people and everyone's shoulders were touching.

'Well done, Mike,' Tanya praised her husband and kissed him on the lips. The two hugged, then Michael left the room and began picking up everything from the floor.

'We have just solved our last case and we will be able to deal with yours right away,' Tanya turned to Becky with a wide happy smile. 'Give us a few minutes to clear up and we'll talk.'

'Okay,' Becky agreed and took the cup of tea that was handed to her. Tanya set off to help her husband while Becky and Arnie watched them with smiles on their faces.

'I like them,' Becky whispered to her cousin.

'I like them too.' He laughed as he watched the two detectives circling like bees around the piles of paperwork.

A few minutes later, the office was cleared, and the euphoria had subsided. Tanya made more tea and put biscuits on a small coffee table in the middle of the office. Everyone sat around the table. At first, Michael asked Becky to tell him in detail what had happened to her, where and how. While she was talking, Tanya and Arnie sighed sympathetically but Michael was listening very intently and even though they were recording he was taking notes and highlighting things. After Becky finished speaking, everyone was silent for a while. Michael then looked down at his notes and turned to her, 'Becky, you said that a couple found you. Do you know their names and where they live?'

'I can ask Inspector Ramsey. She'll tell me where they can be found. I wanted to meet them while I was in the hospital in Truro, but they had already left. As far as I know they live in West Wales.'

'Do you know what exactly they saw? How did they know there was a problem?'

'They heard my cries for help and saw a car leaving the place where I was.'

'Have they seen any of the men?' Michael asked while writing something in his notebook.

'No, I don't think they saw them.'

'Haven't they seen any of them?'

'At least that's what they told the police,' Becky replied and thought she didn't know what those people actually told the police.

'And you say that one of the rapists knew the area and the others did not know where this place was.'

'Yes, the driver knew where he was going. He had certainly been there before.'

'Can you guess where their accent is from?'

'No, all four spoke with an accent. They are not from Cornwall, or so I thought at the time.'

'And with which hand did they hit you?' he asked her.

She unconsciously felt her thighs. The police hadn't asked her that question, but they might have known from the look of the wound who had stabbed her with which hand.

'I only saw the three of them. By the time the fourth man approached, I closed my eyes. All were right-handed.'

'Okay,' Michael said and looked at her sympathetically. 'I'll do my best to find them.'

'I will be very grateful to you,' whispered Becky quietly. Tears welled up again, but she forced herself to hold them back. She shook Arnie's hand and asked him if they could leave.

'We'll call you if we have more questions,' Tanya said and hugged Becky in a tight and strong hug. This calmed her down.

'I didn't know private detectives were so sensitive,' Becky said once they were outside.

'I didn't know they were like that either,' said Arnie. 'Alex's father recommended them to us. He works as an inspector for the police and said that

Tanya and Michael are the best at finding criminals who have escaped from the crime scene.'

'I have to thank Paul and Alex for helping me,' Becky said.

'They are waiting for us at home. They wanted to talk to you.'

'Lovely.' Becky smiled and for the first time in a long time she felt good.

Paul and Alex were waiting for them in the living room, each with a packet of crisps and a bottle of beer in hand.

'You look good,' Paul told her with bright eyes.

Alex, for his part, looked at her, but said nothing. Her pale skin and the dark circles under her eyes didn't escape his gaze. He was the oldest of the three and had experience with victims in his work as a lawyer. He often saw people like Becky. Victims trying to fit into their new lives. She felt his gaze and turned away as if to hide her feelings. Alex pulled her gently to him, hugged her and asked her, 'Are you okay?'

Becky looked up at his eyes, she couldn't lie to him. She wasn't feeling good, and Alex knew it.

'I'm fine,' she answered out loud.

Alex nodded. He handed her a bag of crisps and sat her down on the sofa. Paul sat next to her and Arnie across from her in a chair. Alex stood still, wondering how to react to her lie.

'Becky, what did the detectives say?' Paul asked excitedly.

'They will try to find the four men. They still have a lot of questions, but I'll put them in touch with Inspector Ramsey and she can give them the information they need.'

'I hope they manage to find them. They are a very interesting couple by the way. You'll love them,' Arnie said.

'That's right,' Becky confirmed. 'They are lovely couple. Thank you for doing this for me.'

'This is the least we can do.'

Alex turned to her. He wondered what she was hiding from them and wished she had trusted him more and shared what was going on with her. Becky did, however, look at him, smile a little, and strike up a lively conversation with Paul, asking him about his new internship and his trip to Wales. Arnie and Alex listened to the conversation, each lost in thought. Arnie was horrified by what he had heard in the detective's office. Becky's story was so shocking to him that the beer he was drinking was unlikely to help him calm down that night. He would definitely need a strong drink to fall asleep. He had seen the state these fiends had reduced her to, but hearing everything in minute detail was unbearable. He thought Tanya felt the same way, so she ended up hugging Becky partly for her, partly for herself. Becky had no idea how strong she really was. Alex caught Arnie's sad look and led him to the kitchen.

'What's happening?' he asked.

'You have no idea what she's been through, bro. I'm shocked,' said Becky's cousin and opened another beer.

'We will find them and condemn them,' said Alex.

'These people don't deserve a trial. From what I've heard they deserve to be beaten up and left in some ditch to bleed to death.'

Alex watched his friend and tried to calm him down, but he could feel that he wouldn't succeed. Not tonight. Arnie was going to get drunk that night, and after the second beer his speech started to slur. An hour later, Arnie was already drunk and went to bed. Paul also felt dizzy while talking to Becky, he had drunk more beers than he should have, so he also headed to his room. Only Alex and Becky remained in the living room.

'Will you stay here tonight?' he asked her.

'No. I'm leaving. It's getting late so I better get going.'

'I'll walk you home,' he told her and put on his jacket. Becky nodded, got her bag, went to say goodnight to Arnie, and she and Alex left the house. They walked in silence for a while.

'How are you, Becky?' he asked her. 'And don't tell me you're fine. Although you are smiling, I can see that you are very tired.'

She walked for a while, then stopped and looked at him. 'I am fine. Don't worry about me.'

'Are you sure?' he asked her.

'I'm sure. I have a job and a place to live. I don't need anything else.'

Alex nodded, looked at her for a while, then thoughtfully motioned for them to keep walking. Becky looked at him. His dark hair was dishevelled, a deep crease had appeared on his forehead. He was ten years older than her, but, somehow, she didn't feel the age difference. It was as if they were peers. Maybe it was because he had retained his youthful spirit, or because she herself felt older, but it was as if the decade that separated them didn't exist.

'Arnie got drunk very quickly,' she said to shift the subject away from herself.

'That's right. He said that what you told him terrified him. I had never seen him drink like that before. The three beers were enough to get him drunk.'

'He is the best man I know,' she said.

'Arnie is very worried about you, Becky. He didn't tell me his family history and he hardly talked about his childhood and his family, but he always mentioned you.'

'Really?' Becky was surprised.

'He said that you look alike to him, and you are his favourite cousin.'

'He has only two, me and my sister. My sister was very young when he moved to London.'

'That explains why he is more attached to you.'

'I am glad that he found the strength and courage to move. I suffered a lot then, but I knew it was for his good. And do you have cousins?'

'I have two cousins, one sister and five nephews.'

'So, you have someone to go home to for the holidays?'

'Yes, I have. My father and sister are always happy when I come home.'

'But Arnie told me you don't go to Yorkshire often,' Becky said.

'I have a lot of work, even tonight I had to work on a case, but because of you I refused.'

'You shouldn't have refused. Don't change your plans because of me.'

'I am your friend, Becky, I should support you in such moments, don't you think?'

Becky looked at him. She hadn't thought about it, but she also thought of him as a friend.

'That's right. Thank you for everything you do for me.'

Alex nodded. The two continued on their way in silence. There weren't many people on the street, but some of the off-licences and shops were still open and their windows lit up the pavement. There were several people at the bus stops waiting for the last buses. Alex and Becky passed them and continued slowly on their way.

'Arnie told me that your father suggested that we hire this detective agency.'

'Yes. I don't know Tanya and Michael personally, but I've heard many stories about them. They both worked in the police until one day they decided they wanted more freedom. My father worked with Michael for two years, they were partners, and he told me that if anyone could find your rapists, it was him.'

'Your father must be a good man.'

'He is. One day you and Arnie may come to visit us in Yorkshire, and I will introduce you to him and my sister.'

'That would be wonderful.' Becky smiled. They had reached the house where she lived. 'Thank you for accompanying me. Also, thanks for the help.'

'Take care, Becky. If you need anything call me,' he said as he waited for her to unlock the door. Alex stayed until he was sure she had entered the house, then turned and went the other way. He was worried about her. The others might not have noticed, but he could see the fear and panic in her eyes. It was the same experience as the first time they met, but without the cries for help and the presence of the police. Becky may have recovered physically, but mentally she certainly hadn't made that progress. Alex wondered if she still had nightmares, the kind that kept them all awake during the nights she lived with them. And if she had them, how did her roommates react? He unconsciously stopped and turned to take a closer look at the house where she lived. Then he continued on his way.

Becky watched him go away from the window. Alex was a stable, handsome man with a good job and a good family. She wondered why he wasn't married yet. Was it because of work or that he just didn't want to settle down yet? What woman wouldn't marry a man like him? She learned from Arnie that Alex dated many women but didn't take his relationships too far.

Paul, on the other hand, always fell in love often and quickly, and especially with the wrong woman, and with one in particular who was seven years older than him, with a very aggressive ex-husband. Arnie was also a stable man, despite having lost contact with his family he was a good match for women, according to Becky. He, like his friends, was handsome in his own way, had a good job and was ready for a family. But, according to him, he was still looking for the right woman.

Becky thought about them for a long time that night and a small smile briefly lit her face. Then she decided to take a shower, went into the bathroom, turned on the water and heard someone go out into the hallway and then into the kitchen. Becky was always worried when she was naked in the shower, as if she expected someone to come in at any moment and hurt her. She turned on the hot water, her body shaking uncontrollably with fear. She had just put shampoo on her hair when very cold water flowed from the shower. Becky shivered even more. Fear and the cold water blended into one feeling, and she cried out in fear as she emerged from the jets of water. Her eyes blinded by the foam, she felt for her towel and wiped her face, then quickly dried her shivering body, and dressed in seconds. When she came out of the bathroom, Becky heard hysterical laughter in one of the rooms. There was the sound of running water coming from the kitchen and when   Becky walked in, she realized what had happened. Someone had deliberately turned on the hot water in the kitchen, knowing that she was in the shower. Tears streamed down Becky's cheeks. She couldn't fight it. It was hard enough for her anyway. It was difficult for her to deal with these mean women who inhabited the house. She went into her room, laid down on the bed, wrapped herself in two blankets and cried aloud. Becky didn't care that the ladies would hear her. After ten minutes someone knocked on her door and shouted:

'Shut up, bitch. I can't sleep from your chirping.'

Becky didn't get up to open the door. She left the room locked and the woman at the door to scream as much as she wanted. The other two women joined her and pushed with all their might. Becky didn't want to talk to or see the three aggressive women. She curled up even more in the blankets and continued to cry. She was exhausted and powerless. She didn't feel like living, not like that, in fear and stress. She had to move urgently and find a new place to live. After a few minutes of pushing and shoving, the three women finally went to their rooms and the house fell silent.

Despite being tired, Becky didn't sleep all night. At half-past-five in the morning she got up and packed her bags. Fortunately, what she owned fit into just two bags. She knew that the women had rummaged through her room several times, probably hoping to find money or something else of value. Becky had hidden her money in two places—in a package of sanitary towels and in an envelope in the rubbish bin. She knew that almost no one would think they were there. She had read so in a book. After getting ready, Becky left her room as quietly as possible, locked the door so they would think she was coming back, and left the house. Then she dropped the key into the bin. She had prepaid for a month, so there was no way they were going to come after her for unpaid bills. She had also left a deposit for two weeks. Becky didn't know where to go, so she stopped at the first coffee shop that was open, ordered tea and breakfast, and stared out the window. People were already walking hurriedly through the streets, each deep in his thoughts and problems. She wondered if they had been in a situation like hers. Of course, in her case, there was a solution, she could always go to Arnie and his roommates' house, but she didn't want to abuse their hospitality. She had to deal with her own problems. They had already used a lot of effort and resources to help her. Becky ate and drank her tea and stayed in the café until eight o'clock. She started work at the restaurant at ten o'clock, so she had two hours only to find a new place to stay. Becky remembered the few advertisements left in the windows of one of the Turkish shops and headed there. The owner was just changing the ads and, seeing that she was interested in them, gestured for her to come inside.

'What are you looking for?' he asked. 'Work or accommodation?'

'Accommodation,' she answered quietly.

The man went to the end of the counter where the till was, reached over and handed her some sheets of paper with ads on them.

'Look at these, you might get lucky,' he said and looked at her sympathetically. She wasn't the first to find herself in this situation. He had helped a lot of people in the ten years of working at this store, and this girl definitely had that look, of a wounded animal with nowhere to go.

'Thanks,' said Becky, took the ads and left the store. She found a bench in the small park that was nearby and sat there. Then she looked at the ads one by one, stopping at a house that was close to Arnie. The rent was high, but she decided that if she had to, she would work without a day off to pay it. She needed peace in the house where she lived. Her work and life were already stressful, a peaceful home would bring balance to her daily life. Becky dialled the phone number and waited anxiously for someone to pick up. No one answered, but she left a voicemail. She hoped the woman named Catherine who had left the ad would call her back.

Becky called another girl, but the room there was already taken. Reluctantly and anxiously, she headed to the restaurant where she worked. She left the bags with all her belongings in a corner of the kitchen and started to clean. With each passing hour, her worry about having nowhere to sleep at night grew. Finally, she resigned herself and decided that she would have to go back to Arnie's house again. Two hours before her shift ended, Catherine called her. Her voice was cheerful and happy, as if she had just experienced something good. They arranged to meet each other after Becky finished work. It was as if a warm, nice wind had blown through the young girl's hair. The cheerful mood of the woman she had been talking to infected her, and she smiled for the first time in a long time. The two hours she had left until she was done with work passed slowly, but she finally got out and ran to the address Catherine had given her. Becky didn't look around, she knew where the house was, she had passed by it many times. When she got there, her worry came over her again and she pulled the bags containing her belongings close to her, as if using them as armour to protect her from someone or something. Then she rang the bell and listened to the noises coming from the house. She heard quick footsteps, then the opening of a door. The footsteps continued and finally the outer door opened. Standing before her was a young woman. It was hard to tell her age, but she was between twenty-five and thirty years old. Her hair was dishevelled and dyed several different colours. There were strands of blue, red, and pink. After seeing her, Becky calmed down, dropped the bags on the ground and introduced herself.

'We talked on the phone,' she began.

'Yes of course. You're Becky, aren't you? I'm Catherine. Come in,' she urged.

Becky hesitated for a few seconds, but Catherine ignored her, turning and walking quickly down the hall. Becky followed her.

'I work mainly at night and during the day I sleep,' said Catherine and invited her to sit on one of the chairs in a small, cosy kitchen. 'That's why it's hard for me to find a roommate. Most of them call me during the day and want to see the room then. Two women came yesterday, but I fell asleep and didn't hear the bell.'

Becky nodded in understanding. As Catherine spoke, she looked around the kitchen. The walls were painted white and pale yellow, with a beautiful floral wallpaper in the corner of one of the walls. The wallpaper created the feeling of a garden in the kitchen.

'How many people live here?' Becky asked.

'Just me,' answered Catherine. 'The house is mine, I inherited it from my grandparents. I'm looking for someone to get along with and share the bills with. Come, I'll show you the house.'

Becky dropped her bags and walked around the house with Catherine. On the first floor, in addition to the kitchen, there was also an entrance hall, a small toilet and a utility room. The living room was small, with a sofa, a low table and two armchairs, and led out into the garden, which had probably seen better days. On the second floor, there were three bedrooms and a bathroom. Becky had the option of choosing one of two available rooms. She chose the larger one overlooking the garden.

'Where do you work?' Catherine asked.

'I work in the kitchen of a restaurant,' said Becky. 'I spend most of the day there, so I won't disturb your sleep. I have a day off on Wednesdays only.'

'Lovely,' laughed the young woman. They both liked each other very much. However, Becky wasn't sure how to present her situation to Catherine right now. The only thing she shared with her new landlady was that she was sixteen years old and could not make bank payments. This was no problem for Catherine.

'When do you want to move in?' she asked excitedly.

'I hope you don't think I'm crazy, but can I move in right away? I don't want to go back to my old house.'

Catherine was silent for a while, took a closer look at Becky, and finally agreed.

'Are you running from troubles or from the law?' she asked anyway.

'From troubles,' Becky admitted.

'Okay,' said Catherine. 'You can stay here, though need a recommendation. Is there someone who can give you one or who we can call now and vouch for you?'

Becky looked at her phone. It was eleven at night. Still, she dialled Arnie's phone number, hoping he hadn't fallen asleep. After several unsuccessful attempts to contact him, she decided to try Alex. She had nothing to lose if she didn't stay here tonight, she would go to their place and wake them up anyway. Alex picked up on the first ring.

'Hi, Becky. What's happening?' he asked.

'Sorry to bother you, Alex. I called Arnie, but he must have fallen asleep.'

'Yes, he had a rough day today. I thought he called you to tell you.'

'Right? He might have called. I was at work a while ago. What happened?'

Alex debated whether he should tell her or tell her to talk to Arnie the next day. However, he figured she'd be worried all night and he'd better tell her. 'Today he was fired from the financial company he worked for.'

'Why did they fire him?' Becky was surprised.

'Let him tell you the details. Don't worry about him, he'll find another job. It's just that the shock of being fired has taken a toll on him.'

'Sure,' Becky whispered. Arnie took great pride in his work. What had happened, she asked herself.

'Becky, are you okay?' Alex asked her.

'I am fine,' she said. 'Can I ask you a favour?'

'Of course.'

'I found a new place to live, and the landlady wants a recommendation.'

'Of course. When does she want the reference?'

'Now, Alex. I need it now. Can you come and talk to her? The house is on the next street.'

'Can't we postpone until tomorrow?' he asked in amazement.

'No. I want to move in tonight, that's why I'm calling you now.'

Alex was silent for a moment, as if considering the situation. Then he agreed and asked her for the address. 'I'll be with you in ten minutes,' he said and ended the conversation.

'I hope I'm not delaying you, Catherine. You said you work at night, so you won't be late for work?'

'I have day off today. Who is the person you called?' Catherine had listened to the whole conversation.

'Alex is my cousin's roommate. He works as a lawyer. I hope talking to him will be enough for recommendation.'

'Yes, it will be enough.' Catherine got up and started making tea for herself and Becky. As she moved into the kitchen, she noticed the two plastic bags that Becky had left by her chair.

'Are they all your belongings?' she asked.

'Yes. I will buy everything I need on Wednesday,' Becky said and looked down.

'How long have you been in London?'

'For several months. I lived with my cousin and his roommates Alex and Paul for a while. You will see Alex now, but if you want another reference, I can ask Paul tomorrow to meet you as well.'

Catherine nodded and placed a cup of tea in front of Becky. 'Drink some tea and relax. Even if Alex doesn't come, I won't leave you on the street. Something tells me that the people in the house you came from didn't treat you well.'

'That's right,' Becky admitted and told her what happened the night before.

'Yes, I understand now,' Catherine said. 'I spent five long years in houses like this. It's hard to find good roommates.'

The doorbell rang and Becky assumed it was Alex. When he walked into the small kitchen, she got up and hugged him. Then, for some unknown reason, tears flowed from her eyes.

'I knew something was wrong, but you never told me,' he reproached her, moving her gently away from him.

'Yes, you were right. This job and the women in the house I lived with were horrible.'

Becky stepped back, sat in the chair, and introduced Alex to Catherine. The young woman smiled and offered to make tea for him as well.

'You're the lawyer, right?' she asked as she put a tea bag into a large cup.

'Yes, I am the lawyer. Paul is the doctor and Arnie is the financier.'

'You three obviously get along well.'

'Yes, that's right. We got along from the start. And you, Catherine, what do you do for living?' he asked her, looking at her while she had her back to him.

'I work in musical theatre. I dance and sing.'

'Really??' Becky and Alex exclaimed at the same time.

'Which musicals have you been you in?' he asked her.

'We are currently preparing a new one, that's why I have parrot-coloured hair, but until recently I was in the *Mary Poppins* musical.'

'Fabulous!' Becky was amazed.

'Yes, it looks easy from the outside, but it costs me a lot of time and training. Some of my colleagues have shows until late, so we rehearse mainly at night and sleep during the day. Of course, not all theatres work on that way. For some, the rehearsals are during the day, but this affects the performances afterwards, because most of them are tired. It doesn't matter to me, but for those who have families, rehearsals at night are the better option.'

Alex and Becky listened with rapt attention. None of them had ever encountered someone like her before.

'How long have you been dancing?' Alex asked her.

'As far as I know, everyone in my family is a singer or dancer. It is passed down from generation to generation. And you, Alex, how long have you been in London?'

'Eight years. I was thinking of moving back to Yorkshire this year, but I've started a new placement with a very prestigious law firm and have given up on moving for now. And I want to help Becky...'

Alex sensed that maybe Catherine didn't know what happened to Becky and didn't finish the sentence. Catherine waited for him to continue, but when she realized that he would not, she turned to Becky. 'I'll go find the spare key,' she said then she got up and went up to her room on the second floor.

'Very nice house, and your roommate is cool too,' Alex told Becky with a smile.

'She is my landlady. The house is hers. And yes, Catherine is very cool.' Becky smiled.

'Arnie will be happy to hear that you've moved next door.'

'Yes. I'm sure he'll be glad to know I'm around.'

Alex was about to ask something, but Catherine cut them off. 'Here's the key. I'll give you sheets for tonight,' she said. Then she turned to Alex. 'I know we have seen each other face to face, but would you write me a reference and leave some information on how to contact you if necessary?'

'Of course,' he agreed. After doing so he prepared to leave.

'It's late, I have a case tomorrow and I have to go,' he said.

'Okay,' said Catherine and put the reference in a folder. 'Nice to meet you, Alex.'

'I'm glad to meet you too.' He waved goodbye to her and motioned to Becky to accompany him to the door. 'Are you okay?' he asked her, studying the reactions on her face.

'I am fine. Thanks a lot for the reference.'

'And the work? What's going on there?'

'My colleagues are nervous and sometimes take out their anger on me, but I hope that will change soon.'

'I can help you find another job,' he offered.

'You don't need to, Alex. You have done enough for me. I'll handle this on my own.'

'Okay. But promise me you'll call me if you need help.'

'I promise. I called you today, didn't I?' she reminded him.

'Yes, you called me. I'll tell the boys in the morning that I've been here and that you've changed the house you live.'

'Thank you, Alex. Now go to sleep. Everything will be fine.'

He gave her a quick goodbye hug and left.

'A very handsome man,' Catherine said when Becky returned to the kitchen.

'I don't know if he's handsome, but he's a good friend.'

'And that too. I would like to have such a person as a friend.'

'Don't you have any friends?' Becky asked her in surprise.

'I have, but not those who will get up almost at midnight to write me a reference.'

Becky smiled. In that respect, at least, she was lucky.

'What time do you get up in the morning?' Catherine asked.

'At eight o'clock. I usually have a coffee and go.'

'Okay. Maybe we can have coffee together tomorrow morning.'

'That would be great,' Becky smiled, then left the money for the rent and the deposit on the table, took the two bags with all her belongings and tiredly climbed the stairs to the second floor.

Catherine watched her walk away and thought to herself that nothing about this girl was what it seemed. From the concerned look that Alex gave her from time to time, Catherine could tell that Becky had been through something bad that she was still recovering from. Catherine put the glasses in the sink and, like her new roommate, began to wearily climb the stairs.

6.

Three months after Becky moved into her new quarters, Inspector Ramsey called her. Becky was still working at the restaurant, but on this particular day she was taking a day off.

'How are you, Becky?' Ramsey asked her.

'I am okay. How are you?'

'I'm fine too. I have news. I don't know if it's good or bad for you, but it's still a little progress.'

Becky held her breath waiting to hear the news.

'We found the car in a junkyard. There isn't much left in it, but what we found inside is proof that it was the car we were looking for.' Inspector Ramsey was silent for a moment, someone close to her asked her a question, she answered and went back to talking to Becky. 'We found one of your socks and your underwear in the back seat.'

Becky shuddered, the memories coming back so quickly, she only managed a small gasp of surprise. The car, all those hands on her body. She sat on the bed unable to say anything, it took her a minute to calm down. Inspector Ramsey could sense her worry even from the great distance that separated them. She genuinely felt for the girl, but she had to tell her what they found.

'Becky? Are you okay?' she asked worriedly.

'I'm fine,' Becky said, but before answering she took several deep breaths.

'I will send you a video, I want you to watch it after you calm down and tell me if the found items are yours.'

'Okay. But you said you were sure they were mine?'

'That's the procedure, even though we've confirmed that the DNA is yours, we need to be sure that they were left that night or are from somewhere else …'

'You think I went from car to car, leaving my underwear, right?' Becky said angrily.

'No, Becky, we don't think that. But others don't know you as well as me and my partner do,' Inspector Ramsey said softly. She understood the delicacy of the questions other people would ask, so she wanted to stop them in advance.

'Okay,' Becky said with a sigh. 'Send me the video, I'll take a look and call you back.' Her hands were shaking as she waited to receive the message. She had been trying to forget what had happened to her for several months now, but she couldn't. Something kept bringing her back there. The questions of the inspectors and the detectives who worked on her case fuelled her memories like adding wood to a fire. She wanted this to end once and for all, but she was already convinced that her agony was going to last a long time.

When she got the message, Becky looked at it and shivers ran down her spine. Thin rivulets of nervous sweat went down her entire body. She looked at the video very carefully. She confirmed that the found items were hers and lay down on the bed in despair. The news that they had found the car was good, except that the car had been reported stolen a few days before the rape and the owner was not her rapist. According to investigators, the DNA they found in the car belonged to four people. One was Becky's, the other three were of people unknown to them. The driver's seat was wiped to a shine, and no marks and fingerprints were found there. The man who had driven the car had erased them. That would make it difficult to find him. Becky remembered the man very well, the aggression in his movements, his cold, light blue eyes looking at her with satisfaction as she screamed in pain. Becky vowed to find this man and do everything she could to put him in prison. But there was no sign of him or the other three men. The private detectives assumed that the four had left the country.

'There is no way that people who behave that way have not encountered the law,' Michael had told her. He and Tanya continued to look for any leads, but Tanya had admitted to Becky that they were at a dead end. Finding the car didn't help them much in their investigation. They had nothing to prove who these people were. Even the fingerprints found in the car would not prove their guilt, because the criminals could plead that they stole the car but were not connected to the rape and attempted murder of Becky. The inspectors and detectives were running in circles, hoping at least one of the criminals would show up somewhere soon.

Shortly before Christmas, Alex's family invited Becky and Arnie to visit them for the holidays. Becky was day off the restaurant for three days only, but according to Alex that would be enough time for his friends to meet his family. Catherine was also invited, but she was busy with several performances and couldn't go.

Becky was very excited about the invitation. She had heard a lot about Alex's father and sister and couldn't wait to meet them. Two days before Christmas, Arnie hired a car and the three of them drove to North Yorkshire. The two men chatted animatedly in the front seat, discussing Paul's new crush, a young doctor, a colleague of his, divorced with a five year old child. Becky at that time was looking at the places they were passing through. She had never been to this part of the UK and the buildings and small towns they passed through impressed her greatly. Despite the cold weather, everything around was still tinged with green. In some front gardens rose bushes could still be seen in bloom, and the birds still soared freely in the sky and had not hidden themselves under the eaves. In general, December had been unseasonably warm.

After several hours of driving in heavy traffic, they finally arrived at Alex's hometown. His father, sister and her children had come out on the front door to meet them. Becky wasn't sure how to react to the welcome, she'd never visited for Christmas before and was visibly worried as she got out of the car. Alex's family, seeing her worry, quickly surrounded her and everyone hugged her tightly. Becky and Arnie looked at each other. This family was nothing like theirs. A slight sadness passed through them both. No matter how much they denied it to themselves, it was time to admit that they missed Cornwall.

The family directed the group to the front door and when Becky entered the small house and looked around, she saw a typical family setting. There was a nice aroma of roast potatoes coming from the kitchen and Alex's father invited them in. Ben was a handsome man. Alex looked a lot like him. Alex's dad's shoulders were broad and, despite his advanced age his body was in excellent shape, without the paunch typical of people his age. His eyes watched Becky with tenderness and concern, yet she could feel precision in his gaze. It was as if he remembered every single detail and every word said by her and her cousin.

'Hope your trip was good?' Ben turned to them.

'There was traffic, but while we were talking, the time passed imperceptibly,' said Arnie.

Alex had disappeared somewhere, probably to leave his luggage and change. Three of his sister's children were standing around Becky, asking her various questions. She answered as much as she could and laughed happily with the children. Two dogs also circled the table, waiting for their share of the food that was still cooking on the oven.

'This is Doggy and Doggy,' said one of the youngest children, presenting the dogs to Becky.

'No, Leah,' her grandfather corrected her. 'These are Boggy and Doggy.'

'Yes,' said the child confidently, who Becky thought was about three years old and still struggling with words. 'This is Doggy.' The girl pointed to one of the dogs. 'And Doggy.' She confidently pointed to the second one. Everyone laughed.

Alex reappeared from somewhere, put on an apron and stood in front of the stove. Becky went to him.

'Are you the cook?' she asked him and laughed.

'Yes. My father and I have always taken care of Christmas dinner. Isn't that right, Dad?'

'That's right. We don't cook all year round, but for Christmas we cook Christmas dinner.'

'By the way, as you will see for yourself later, they both cook very well,' said Alex's sister, whose name was Janey.

The two men poked their chins in satisfaction at the praise and began rummaging through the cupboards and checking the dishes on the stove. At this time Janey made drinks for everyone. Becky felt like she was in a fairy tale. She had heard of these Christmas dinners and family events but had never attended one. Nothing was celebrated in her parents' house. Becky could only tell it was some kind of celebration from the smell of alcohol wafting from her father. Now, she watched the smiling happy people and told herself that this is the kind of family she would like to have. If anyone ever agreed to start a family with her.

Alex was cooking and pretending to hide from his sister, giving the children a small part of the already prepared dishes. The dogs also managed to get their part on some food, stealing mostly from children. There was music playing in one of the rooms and some of the children were dancing or chasing each other going from one room to the other. At last, the festive table was set, and although it was not dinner time, everyone was seated around the table. Becky expected to hear a prayer or something, but none came.

To her surprise, everyone started eating the moment their food was placed on front of them. Most of the children were eating and talking at the same time, but no one noticed them. Everyone was in good spirits and laughing heartily. Something Becky had never done in her life. She watched Alex's family in awe and soaked up every moment of the family dinner. After several hours of eating and drinking, Alex's sister and her children prepared to leave. After they left the house, there was silence in the kitchen. Ben and Alex had disappeared and only Arnie and Becky were left at the table, both intoxicated by the happy few hours they had spent. The two looked at each other and smiled.

After few minutes Alex and his father came back and sat down to have a drink with them.

'You have a wonderful family, Alex,' Becky said.

'That's right,' he agreed, and a big happy smile appeared on his face. 'The children are grown up. Sometimes I feel like I haven't been here in years, when in fact it's only been two or three months.'

'Why don't you come back to live here?' she asked him and immediately regretted her question. Something in Alex seemed to break and a sadness crossed his eyes.

'Maybe I'll come back one day,' he answered, but his cheerful mood had left him.

Becky looked at Arnie questioningly, but she could tell from her cousin's reaction that he hadn't noticed the change in his friend's mood.

'Becky, I found out that you live with a theatre star,' Alex's father changed the subject.

'That's right. It turns out that Catherine is famous. Arnie and I went to one of her shows. She is amazing. Next time we will take Alex and Paul with us.'

'Paul is no longer interested in anything but his doctor,' Arnie smiled.

'That's right.' Alex laughed and his good mood returned.

During the three days of staying with Alex's family, Becky visited several nearby towns. The three of them went for long walks in the area and had a wonderful time. Sometimes, his sister and her children joined them. It was fantastic to have all these people around you. Becky and Arnie didn't feel like leaving. Alex's family begged them to stay at least two more days, but Becky had to go back to work, and Arnie had to return the rental car.

'How nice would it have been if we had Christmases like this when we were children,' Becky said to Arnie as they travelled back to London.

'Yes, we probably wouldn't want to leave there,' he agreed. They both tried to imagine their parents hosting such a dinner party. Then they shook their heads, there was no way the two women would do that. Their mothers were sisters and they resembled each other not only in appearance but also in character. They were selfish to the core.

'Arnie, why didn't Alex's sister's husband come?' Becky finally asked. She wanted to ask this question on the first day, but something stopped her.

'Don't you know?' wondered her cousin.

'What should I know?'

'Her husband committed suicide.'

'What?' Becky was amazed. 'But how is that possible? Everyone looks very happy.'

'That's right. Now they are happy, but three years ago it wasn't like that. Alex took a year off from work to help his sister recover.'

'I had no idea. Why did he kill himself?' she asked after a while.

'We don't know.'

'Are they sure it was suicide?'

'Yes, he did it in the town square, in front of many witnesses. Alex's sister was also there. She was six-months-pregnant then.'

Becky opened her mouth in surprise.

'I didn't know that. Why didn't you tell me about this? I almost asked the children at dinner about their father.' Becky was surprised.

'Maybe you'd better ask yourself why Alex didn't tell you? You two are very close. I don't know if you realize it, but you've been spending more time talking to him than me these past few months.'

Becky was about to protest, but then realized her cousin was right. Alex called her every two or three days, and Arnie only once a week.

Unknowingly, Alex had become a big brother to Becky, someone she could completely rely on and share everything with. But the sharing was apparently only on her part. Alex rarely talked about himself and his family. He always steered the conversation to her or to others.

'I suppose you know about his mother's death?' Arnie asked her.

'Yes, she was sick with cancer.'

'They found her cancer almost in the last stage. His mother had been going to the GP regularly because she had a lot of pain. According to Alex, the GP just sent her away for several months without doing any tests on her. When he finally did, it was too late. In my opinion, this is one of the reasons why Alex wanted to be a lawyer. He wants to do justice for people with cases like hers. If the doctor had done his job from the beginning, if the NHS had not restricted the blood tests, his mother would probably still be alive. At least, he thinks so.'

Becky listened to her cousin and thought that was why Alex cared so much about her, helping her, and listening to her whenever she needed it. He took these cases too personally. Unlike Paul, he didn't enjoy life, not in the same way that his friend did. It was as if he didn't want to take any chances. Paul flitted from woman to woman like a bee in a flower garden. He was in love with every girl who paid attention to him and embarked on it like a great adventure. With Alex and Arnie, things were just the opposite. They didn't seem to want to get attached to someone like that. And Becky now realized why. They didn't want to feel that sense of loss that they had felt before. Alex and Arnie were highly emotional, albeit in a different way. They wouldn't love someone just to feel free and in love. With them, emotions are controlled and calculated both for themselves and for the other party. No one should be hurt, in any way. So, they would both go out, see women for a short time and then back off quickly before the feelings got serious. Becky heard about it from her colleagues at the restaurant when they saw such customers. They had called them *butterflies*, moving aimlessly from flower to flower, but at the same time delicate. According to her colleagues, there were *butterflies* both among the men and the women, and they recognized each other.

After returning to London, Becky researched the suicide of Alex's brother-in-law on the internet. Arnie was right, no one had ever figured out why he killed himself. According to the investigators, it was something related to his family, but no evidence was found to corroborate this. It must have been quite a shock to Alex's sister, Becky thought. But now she seemed to have gotten over it, because the whole time they were there, Becky never saw her sad or down. She was as happy at the family dinner as everyone else. Taking care of five children was certainly not easy, but she never complained or mentioned that she was a single mother of many. And Becky envied her. She envied her courage and the ability to turn her back on what had happened. And she wished she could do that too. But she couldn't. Every time before falling asleep she saw their faces. Every time a strange man approached her, she freezes, and her mouth would go dry. And it was as if everything was repeating itself again. She could even feel the pain in her body. Becky knew people could see her confusion and fear, and yet she couldn't hide it. Arnie had mentioned to her several times that she needed professional help. The conversations with him and Alex weren't going to help her get over this. And for the first time she admitted to herself that her cousin was right. Alex had also insisted on talking to a counsellor. He had even offered to pay for a private one in one of their conversations.

'You will regret that you didn't take care in time, Becky,' he tried to persuade her. 'I've seen much tougher and stronger people that collapse from the strain at one point. If you don't put your best foot out there, you will remain a victim and that will eat at you forever.'

Alex tried to talk her into seeing a professional counsellor almost every time they talked, but Becky pushed the subject away. Now she knew it was something serious and she couldn't ignore it. Becky was entitled to free help, she just had to go to her GP and ask for it. Once or twice a week the conversations with a stranger would hardly do her any harm, she thought, and decided at the beginning of January to go and apply for it. She would work until then. The money she was making was barely enough to pay her rent and bills, so she wanted to find a new, better paying job, if possible, although, at sixteen the chances of finding one were minimal. And she only had one day off, completely insufficient to go to job interviews.

'It's going to be all right,' Arnie had told her a few months ago, and he'd been right. At least for now.

At the beginning of January, it was very cold. The cold weather brought snow. London's streets were icy, and traffic was minimal. There was almost no work at the restaurant, and Becky's boss let her take three days off. For her, this was her chance to find another job and visit the GP. Things went quickly with the GP. Becky was on the waiting list for therapy in less than two hours. However, things didn't work out so well with the new job. Becky walked around in the cold weather to restaurants and cafes leaving her CV there, but no one was looking for staff, especially a minor. On the evening of the third day, Becky came home freezing and resigned herself to having to work at the restaurant for a while longer. She was just about to go up to her room when the doorbell rang. When she opened it, Alex, Arnie, Paul and the two private detectives were standing in front of her.

'What's happening?' she asked as they all entered the small kitchen. Everyone sat down, only Michael and Becky remained upright.

'We found one of the rapists, Becky. He's here in London,' Michael told her.

'Right?' she asked and unconsciously took a step back towards the door. 'Where in London?' she asked quietly.

'Here in Stratford. He works at the Tube station and lives in Stratford,' Michael said.

Becky felt sick, her blood began to drain from her face and her skin turned pale. Tanya was the one who caught her before she fainted.

'We should have told her to sit down before we told her the news,' Paul said guiltily. Becky could hear him whispering. Then she felt someone massaging her legs and arms and little by little she recovered. Everyone was leaning over her, and Paul was busy massaging her and talking to her soothingly. Becky had never imagined that she would faint from such news, but it further confirmed her feeling that she needed therapy. Something to normalize her and stop her nightmares. When she finally stood up everyone backed away.

'I'm sorry, I don't know why I passed out.'

Almost everyone nodded in understanding, only Alex watched her shrewdly. He didn't need to tell her he was right. She already knew it.

'What's his name?' she asked. To the surprised looks, she added 'the rapist. What's his name?'

'Albert Levy. Twenty-six years old,' Michael said. Then he added, 'He has no criminal record. He has not been in the country in the last three years. He was in France. He returned two days before the rape.'

Becky nodded.

'What does he look like?'

Tanya handed her a picture of him from her smart phone. At the sight of the man, Becky's blood began to drain from her face again. Paul quickly stood beside her and asked her to breathe evenly.

'Everything will be fine,' he said and took one of her hands. Becky calmed down. She looked at the picture again, then handed the phone back to Tanya.

'He was sitting in the back seat, in the seat behind the driver.'

Everyone in the room was silent, waiting for her to say something else, but she was silent, lost in thought.

'Becky, Michael, and Inspector Ramsey have some questions. Do you think you can come with us to the nearest police station?' Tanya asked her.

'Yes, of course.'

Alex, however, was shaking his head in displeasure.

'It is best if one of us accompanies her,' he said. 'I've seen people in her condition. I don't think she is stable.'

Becky looked at him in disbelief. Steady or not she had to go and identify this man.

'Do you want to come with us, Alex?' Tanya asked him. 'It would be nice if you were also present as a lawyer.'

Becky and Alex looked at each other. No one had thought she would need legal protection, but now it seemed like a good idea. Alex nodded, so did Becky. Arnie walked over to his cousin and hugged her.

'If I wasn't on probation at the new company, I would come with you, but if I'm absent all day, I'll probably lose my job,' he explained.

'No problem. If Alex comes with me, I will feel safe.'

'I'll call Inspector Ramsey,' Michael said and went to talk quietly in the corridor. Becky went up to her room to change while the others stood in silence in the kitchen.

'Inspector Ramsey will send a police car to pick you and Alex up. We will follow you.'

'Do we want to attract attention with a police car?' Becky asked.

'They are obliged to protect you as an important witness. It's better to accept the help,' Tanya advised her.

Becky nodded. Everyone prepared to leave when the outer door opened, and Catherine entered.

'What is going on here?' she asked, surprised by the many people in the house. At the same time, the police car arrived. Becky started to explain to Catherine what was going on, but the police were in a hurry.

'We don't have time,' they said and asked Alex and Becky to get into the car.

'Calm down,' called Paul. 'I will explain to her. Arnie, go to work so you don't get fired,' he urged his friend. Then he followed Catherine into the house.

Becky and Alex didn't travel for long. It took the police officers on duty several minutes to drive them to the police station, where another officer was waiting for them. Becky, Alex, Tanya, and Michael were placed in a room and waited for someone to explain to them what they were expected to do.

'Since the investigation is not theirs, maybe they will connect us to Inspector Ramsey,' suggested Michael.

Half an hour later their statements were taken, and Inspector Ramsey questioned Becky about details of Albert Levy's involvement in her rape and attempted murder. Becky confirmed again that this person was in the car and was in behind the driver's seat.

'Becky, I know it's hard for you to remember, but from the wounds that were inflicted on you with the knife, what exactly was the wound that Albert Levy inflicted on you?'

Becky was silent for a moment, then gestured to her left shoulder. Everything passed before her eyes like a movie, as if she were there again, lying and drowning in her own blood. And she saw him swing his right hand and stabbing her. Becky's head drooped at the memory and Alex caught her. He pressed her tightly to himself and asked the inspectors if they could take a break. 'It is best we come again tomorrow,' he advised. 'This is her third seizure in two hours. Becky needs medical attention and medication to calm her down.'

'Okay,' agreed the inspector. 'Tomorrow morning you must come for the identification of Albert Levy.'

'Is he here?' Alex asked as he supported Becky.

'No, we are looking for him, but I think we will find him by tomorrow.'

Alex nodded and asked for a taxi. Becky was right, the police car was attracting attention she didn't need right now.

When they got back to the house Paul was still there. He called Becky's GP and after a long consultation over the phone she was given weak sedatives.

'I think it's best if Becky comes to us for a few days,' Alex turned to Catherine. 'You won't be here at nights, and she will be afraid and worried.'

'I completely agree. I never imagined that she went through all this,' she added sadly.

'Yes, it is not easy for Becky to recover. I think she needs professional help.'

'She told me she was going to apply for therapy, but I thought it was because of her family.'

'Right? Did they approve it?' Paul asked.

'I have no idea. You should ask her. A few days ago, there was a letter from NHS for her. It might have been about that.'

'Okay, we'll ask her,' said Paul.' It was nice to meet you, Catherine.'

'Me too,' she answered. Alex noticed a glint in her eyes. Apparently, his friend the doctor had managed to charm Catherine.

Paul gave him a knowing look and smiled.

'Let's prepare Becky's luggage and settle her in our house. Arnie will have to move to the sofa downstairs again.'

'One of you can move in here temporarily until Becky gets better,' Catherine suggested. 'I don't like to be alone, and it will be overcrowded at your house.'

Paul and Alex looked at each other. Alex already knew who would want to move in with the beautiful blonde lady.

'Thank you, Catherine. We will discuss it and call you. And you are always welcome in our house.'

Catherine nodded and went upstairs to help Becky get ready.

'I thought you were in love with the doctor?' smiled Alex.

'The doctor is ancient history. I didn't know Becky had such a beautiful roommate,' Paul said, grinning. 'She is the right woman for me.'

'This is the fifteenth woman that you claimed is the right one for you,' said Alex as he sat down tiredly on the chair. The next few days were going to be difficult for him. He had to prepare for two cases, appear in two others, and accompany Becky to testify and identify Levy, if they could find him. As long as Becky stays mentally stable until then, he thought, staring at his friend's grinning face. At least Paul had a good day, Alex thought.

After half an hour, Becky finally came down from her room, carrying a small suitcase that Catherine had given to her. Alex took her by the elbow, then by the waist, and helped her to the door.

'Thank you, Paul.' Becky turned just before leaving.

Paul gave her an encouraging smile and nodded.

Alex didn't take Becky to their house right away. He led her into the first cafe they saw. 'I think some food and a cup of coffee will do us both good,' he told her. But he actually wanted to talk to her without the presence of other people around them.

Becky's face was still pale. She was surprised to find that she hadn't eaten all day and assumed that this was one of the reasons why she felt sick so often. She and Alex ordered the food. He watched her as she sipped her coffee but said nothing. If he didn't know her, he would never have guessed that she was only sixteen years old. He would have thought she was between twenty-two or twenty-four years old. Her air was that of a post-teenage woman. Her thinking was like that, she was not frivolous and spoiled. Alex wondered if she had always been like this or if what she had experienced that night had changed her like this?

'What do you want to ask me?' she asked.

'Why do you think I want to ask you something?' he answered.

'That's how you look at me when you want to ask me something. Ask, don't worry. I have no secrets from you.'

'You don't?' he looked at her in surprise. 'Everyone has secrets.'

'I don't have any, not from you either, so ask,' she urged him.

'Albert's photo incapacitated you for a few hours. How do you feel now?'

'I am fine. I guess I was shocked when I saw his face.'

'Will you be able to handle it tomorrow if you have to see him in person?'

'Does that bother you?' she asked him and raised her eyebrows questioningly.

'Yes. I need to know if you're afraid of him and you don't want to testify.'

'Nothing will stop me from testifying, Alex. And yes, I'm scared. But that won't change my mind. I'm going to take some sedatives tomorrow and go find out if it's him.'

'Okay,' Alex nodded and looked at her again.

'What?' she asked.

'You need therapy.'

'I know. I have an appointment. I start it in two weeks' time.'

'I'm glad you listened to my advice.'

'I know you mean well, Alex. It just took me a while to realize you were right.'

Alex nodded and focused on the food. Becky wasn't as strong as she thought she was. He had seen far more stable people break down with nerves in the courtroom.

'There is something else I wanted to talk to you about,' he told her after they had eaten. 'Your case is more special than other cases of rape and attempted murder.'

She looked at him questioningly.

'In your case, there are four perpetrators. If you recognize one tomorrow, the other three will know about it and the probability that they will start looking for you will be very high.'

Becky stared at him for a while, then she realized what he was trying to tell her. She would become a target for the other three perpetrators. The skin on her face paled again and when Alex noticed it, he moved and sat in the chair next to her.

'Calm down, everything will be fine. But I think it's good for you to be prepared for a big fight. You might also have to seek police protection.'

'And if they decide not to hurt me, but to hurt one of my friends?' she asked.

'Personally, I don't think they will hurt someone else. They will attack you to break you mentally, so you refuse to continue with your testimony.'

Just the thought that these men might start stalking and threatening her made Becky's body shudder. Her arms and legs were shaking so badly that she had to cross her legs and put her hands between her thighs to stop them from shaking. Alex walked over to her and put his arm around her shoulder.

'Don't worry. I'll be there for you. Paul and Arnie too. I also assume that the police will be watching over you as well. However, for your peace of mind, I suggest that we order you a panic button now, which is connected to the three of us and the police.'

Becky nodded but was still unable to speak. Her lower lip was trembling, her eyes were watering. Alex hated to see her hurt like this, but he had to tell her what awaited her and prepare her for a possible confrontation with her attackers. Becky clearly hadn't thought about that before. She stared ahead for a while, then her gaze met his eyes. They had turned a dark blue colour and looked at her sadly and with understanding. There was nothing more soothing to Becky than his eyes. When he looked at her like that, she could trust him with her whole life. She slowly calmed down and they both got up and headed for the house. When they got there, they found Paul smiling and packing up. But when he looked at Becky, his smile faded.

'Are you okay, Becky?' he asked her.

'Yes. I am fine. Thanks for doing this for me.'

'I'm not doing this just for you,' he smiled at her friend. 'It will be a pleasure for me to stay for a while in Catherine's company.'

Becky smiled too.

'You can help her with the garden,' she suggested.

'Great idea,' Paul said. He approached her, kissed her on the forehead, and started to leave.

'Your room is free. Call if you need anything,' he said, then said goodbye and left the house whistling.

Alex and Becky waved him off with a smile. They would miss Paul. Becky went into his room and started unpacking her things. Alex, on the other hand, entered his room, liad down exhausted on the bed, and fell asleep almost instantly.

Becky cleaned her new room. After hearing Alex's light snoring, she decided to have a cup of tea in the beautiful garden. Although the weather was cold, she went out, wrapped herself in a blanket and stared at the frosted leaves on the bushes and trees. It calmed her down. Her thoughts turned to her abusers. What would they do when they found out she recognized one of them? Were they going to hunt her down or were they going to attack her friends and Arnie? After moving in with Catherine, she began searching the internet for cases like hers. The criminals had done everything possible not to be convicted. There was a case that even ended with a witness being killed. All of this bothered Becky. After her conversation with Alex, she no longer feared for herself as much as for her loved ones. How was she going to protect them? Was it not better to forget about the case and not recognize the criminal tomorrow? What if someone else got hurt too? What if they hurt other women the way they hurt her? Becky got lost in the thousands of questions she couldn't find an answer to within herself. Her thoughts were interrupted by Arnie coming home from work. He smiled sadly when he saw her.

'How are you?' she asked him.

'I am fine. I got back to work just in time. Sorry to leave you behind, but I can't lose this job either.'

'No problem. Alex and Paul took care of me. Paul is smitten with Catherine and has offered me his room until I start to feel better.'

'Great idea. And where will he live?' Arnie was surprised.

'In my room.' Becky laughed. 'He didn't mind sharing his days with Catherine.'

'Our Paul turned out to be a great trickster.' Arnie also laughed. 'And how are you?'

'I feel better. Tomorrow I should recognize Albert Levy, if they can find him.'

'Are you worried?'

'No,' she lied. The last thing she wanted was for Arnie to worry about her. She had had enough of Alex for now. If there was a problem, she would share it with him.

'How is Alex?'

'Asleep. In my opinion, he is very tired. My case seems to be more than he can take.'

'We're lucky to have him, Becky. Alex is one of the best people I know. Do you know half the time he works for free? And people trust him. They only pay him if he wins the case, and ninety percent of the time he wins.'

'Why am I not surprised?' Becky hugged herself even tighter with the blanket. She thought about how her life would affect the lives of the three men and possibly Catherine as well. Maybe she should have prepared them for what was to come. Perhaps she should have told them that by standing up to these men, she was putting their lives at risk and danger, and they should be careful.

'What's up, Becky?' Arnie asked her. 'What are you worried about?'

'Losing one of you,' she answered, and tears flowed from her eyes again. Arnie didn't know how to calm her down. Alex seemed to be better at it.

'You won't lose us. Everything will be fine.'

'And if it isn't? If one of these monsters hurt you, or one of the others? They will stop at nothing, Arnie. I am convinced that they will use all means and ways to stop me.'

'You know they can't buy Paul and Alex, right? We are not like your parents.'

Becky opened her mouth to say something, then turned to Arnie and gave him a horrified look.

'What do you mean? Did they pay my parents? And if so, how do you know about it?'

Arnie wasn't looking at her. He had looked away and was cursing himself for not being able to keep quiet. Becky didn't let him go though, nudging his elbow to get his attention.

'Arnie, tell me the truth, whatever it is. I need to know everything, do you understand?'

He didn't turn to her. He couldn't. Somehow, he kept forgetting how smart she was, and the words just came out of his mouth.

'Please, Arnie, tell me. Why do you think my parents were bought? Who paid them? How much?'

Arnie turned to her. His eyes said it all. Someone had paid them, and he had found out about it. But how did he know, she wondered.

'Someone paid them, and then they paid you to shelter me,' Becky finally said.

It was not a friendly gesture. It was a deal. Becky got up, walked past him, and went up to her new room, where, out of breath, she cried quietly. She didn't want to wake Alex. He didn't need to know about it. Her mind raced, she wondered if she should leave and return to Catherine. But how would she explain her behaviour? And she would bring Catherine into this story as well. She had better spare her that.

Becky lay exhausted, tears still flowing and dripping onto the pillow. She expected anyone else to betray her, but not Arnie. This she could not bear. If she couldn't trust him, then who, she wondered, and a small moan escaped her. Which of the four had paid? And how did he actually pay them? He met with them and gave them cash? Becky remembered the envelope of money her father had left at the hospital. She had only taken three hundred pounds of this money, the rest being in the envelope intact. What if there were fingerprints on the envelope and the money?

While she was asking herself all these questions, Alex had woken up and was drinking beer in the kitchen. He picked up his laptop and was going over the information for one of the cases he had taken on. Arnie joined him, dejected.

'Everything will be fine,' Alex tried to calm him down.

'No, it won't be fine,' said Arnie quietly.

'Take it easy. I'll take Becky tomorrow and help her with the police.'

'No, it's not that. I betrayed her, Alex, and she just found out.'

'What do you mean? How did you betray her?'

'Her parents paid me to take care of her here.'

'So what? My father would send you money to take care of me if I had a problem.'

'It's not the same,' Arnie said and looked away. 'Someone paid Becky's parents to send her away and they paid me to take care of it.'

'What you mean?' asked a surprised Alex. 'You mean you knew about it from the beginning? And that one of the rapists met any of them in person and paid them?'

'Yes. And I'm not proud of it. I thought someone was going to scare her. After I received the money, I read on the internet exactly what happened. But it was too late to turn back time. And if I hadn't accepted her, who knows where they would have sent her?'

Alex looked at his friend and couldn't believe it was the same person he knew. The Arnie he knew wouldn't take money from Becky's parents. He would not allow himself to be bought.

'Before you judge me,' said Arnie 'let me remind you that my family is not like yours. I have neither their moral nor financial support. To help Becky I needed money.'

'But why didn't you tell us? Me and Paul were going to help you.'

'As I already told you, when I accepted the money, I did not know what exactly had happened to Becky. I thought she had just broken up with a boyfriend, at least that's how her mother presented it to me. I thought I just had to find her a job and a place to live. A few days later I found out from a friend in Cornwall what had happened to her. I didn't even think the money was from one of the rapists because I didn't know about it until then.'

Alex nodded in understanding. But how had Becky taken this information? He got up, patted his friend on the shoulder, and went up to the second floor. He knocked on Becky's door and, upon hearing an invitation, he entered. Her eyes were red from crying, her lips trembled slightly, and her gaze was nervous. Alex didn't know what to do to help her anymore. He pulled up a chair and sat beside her without speaking. He reached up and brushed her sweat-drenched bangs from her forehead. Her tears continued to fall softly. Her bitterness and disappointment had broken her. Neither massage, nor tea, nothing could soothe her, so he remained silent, empathizing with her anguish. After a few minutes, she removed his hand and squeezed it tightly.

'You won't betray me, will you?' she asked him.

'I'll try not to, Becky. But I think you should forgive Arnie and talk to him again.'

'But he accepted money from them.'

'He didn't know where the money came from and what happened to you. He thought he was helping you find a job and a place to stay after a break-up. Talk to him. He will be able to explain it to you. He didn't betray you, but he feels like he did.'

Becky shook her head. She couldn't talk to Arnie today. Tomorrow, perhaps, they would clear things up. Alex stroked her hair again, then advised her to sleep and left her room.

7.

The next day, Becky identified Albert Levy as one of her rapists, and he was charged. Alex had warned her that by doing this she would start a long process to prove his guilt, and, with more evidence, it could quickly end up in court. Becky and Inspector Ramsey agreed to meet in two days when Alex would be available. Until then, Becky's life would go on as before. Going to work and coming home to Alex and Arnie's place. They had ordered a panic button for her, and a police car would pass by the house in the evening. This somewhat calmed Becky. After leaving the police station, she went to work thinking all the time about Albert Levy and about Arnie. Albert didn't look so cocky when he wasn't stoned and drunk. He was nervous, but not aggressive. Watching him at a distance, Becky couldn't believe this was the same person who had hurt her. He had no previous convictions, and it was surprising to Inspector Ramsey that Michael had found him. The private investigator hadn't said exactly how he had come across the information about Albert, but there was no doubt that it was him. His fingerprints and DNA also confirmed it. Albert would remain in custody for several days, where he would be questioned in the presence of a lawyer. Everyone hoped he would betray his accomplices. Becky hoped so too. That way she wouldn't have to wait long for them to be convicted.

Becky's thoughts then turned to Arnie. What had her mother told him, she wondered. How exactly had he agreed to help her? And how could her mother call rape and attempted murder boyfriend trouble? Did she consider her guilty? After all the injuries she had sustained?

Becky couldn't wait to get back to their house and talk to Arnie. However, he surprised her and came to pick her up from work. He was waiting for her outside the restaurant with hunched shoulders and an absent-minded look. He nodded at her when he saw her but didn't give her the friendly smile he usually did.

'Hello,' Becky greeted him. 'I didn't expect to see you here.'

'I wanted to talk to you somewhere in peace,' he explained.

'Okay,' she agreed, and they both walked towards the house.

'I didn't know who the money was from, otherwise I wouldn't have accepted it,' he told her.

'I know.'

'And I didn't know what they did to you. Your mother called me, I don't know how she got my phone number, probably from a friend. She told me that you were desperate and that you needed to get out of there. You had trouble with your boyfriend. She promised to send me money so I can help you find a job and a place to live.'

'Why didn't you tell me?' Becky asked.

'I wanted to, but I didn't know how. Do you remember my friend, Brian? When I spoke to him a few days after your mum's request, he told me what was being said in the area. That someone had raped you and that you almost died. I didn't believe him, but I dug around on the internet and that's how I found out what happened to you. But I had already taken the money. I needed it so I could help you, do you understand Becky?'

'I understand. But how did they pay you?'

'I received an envelope addressed to me, which contained a thousand pounds. I assumed they asked someone to deliver it to me, but since they didn't find me at home, they just dropped the envelope in the mailbox.'

'My father also brought me an envelope of money to the hospital. Inside was twelve hundred pounds.'

'Do you think both lots of money are from the same person?'

'I don't know. But I can give the envelope and the money to Inspector Ramsey to check for fingerprints. Did you keep your envelope?'

'Yes, the money is still inside. I never used it. I can't tell you why, I just felt like it was dirty money.'

'I see,' Becky said.

Arnie admired his cousin. It would never occur to him to send the money and the envelope for fingerprints. Although it appeared that both had taken a ransom for their silence, this was not the case. Arnie was conned, and Becky's money was given to her by her father. Yet it was clear to both of them where the money had come from. When they got home and compared the envelopes, their suspicions were confirmed. Becky told everything to Alex, who in turn called the inspectors and private investigators to tell them what they had. After a few minutes, a police officer rang the doorbell and the envelopes containing the money were handed over to him as physical evidence.

Two days later, Becky and Alex went to the police station. Albert had not betrayed his accomplices. He was silent and didn't admit anything. Inspector Ramsey had checked his financial situation, the man had no savings and was living on credit. He could hardly have paid Becky's parents for their silence.

There were also none of his fingerprints on the envelope or the money. The fingerprints were different and not in the database.

'I'm sorry, Becky. There are no signs of the other three men and Albert remains stubbornly silent. I think he's afraid to talk.'

'Did he make a confession?' Becky asked hopefully.

'No. He's quiet, he hasn't said anything since we got him.'

'We have to find the others,' Alex said. 'That way we will have more opportunity to negotiate.'

'Everyone is looking for them. I even made an official inquiry to the French authorities. If Albert was in France for a long time, the others may have been there or still be there.'

Becky and Alex nodded, then left, stopping by Michael and Tanya's on the way. They hoped they would have some news.

'I have no new information at the moment, but I am working on it,' Michael said.

'If you need more money...' Alex began.

'No, we don't need money. We failed in this case, and it is a matter of dignity to continue to search,' said Michael. 'There's something strange about not having any trace of all these men. It's like someone is covering their tracks.'

'What do you mean?' Alex asked.

'Every time I get close to a trail, and I'm an old dog and I can smell that I've found something, the trail just disappears.'

'Do you think someone from the police is involved?' Alex was surprised.

'It wouldn't be the first time, would it? But no, I don't think it's from the police. It's someone else, someone surrounded by influential people. You two have to be very careful. Whoever he is, you're already a target.'

'Good to know. I'm not worried about myself, but about everyone around me. I put them in this situation,' Becky muttered disgruntled.

'You are the only one who can put these people in prison. They will chase you, so be careful, Becky. If you ask me, quit work for a while and seek police protection.'

'If there are police officers around me, they will find me even faster. No, I will go to work, but I will work fewer hours. Let's say from ten to six. That way I won't be home too late.' Becky looked at Alex questioningly.

'Fine, if that's what you want. I'd rather you stay in the house, but since Arnie and I won't be there during the day, I think it'll be safer if you're around people.'

'You can always call me if you want to talk to someone,' Tanya offered.

'Thanks! I might take advantage of your offer.'

'It's the least I can do for you.'

Becky thought she had inadvertently made two more friends. People who understood her.

For two weeks life continued as before. Becky, Alex, and Arnie went to work and got together for dinner at home. Sometimes Catherine and Paul stopped by the house. The two had already declared themselves a couple and were almost inseparable.

'Finally found her, huh?' Arnie said.

'Who have I found?' asked Paul.

'The special woman.'

'That's right. I met her thanks to Becky.'

'You probably won't want your room back anytime soon,' Becky smiled.

'No, I don't want it. You can keep the room,' Paul winked at her happily.

One evening on the way home from work, a man pushed Becky down a side street. She thought at first that someone had accidentally pushed her and started to continue on her way, but the man pushed her again and pinned her against the wall of one of the houses. He was the Driver. Becky's breath caught in fright. He stood across from her, then clung to her body. From the side they looked like a couple, alone by the corner of a house. Becky tried to scream, but he quickly covered her mouth with his hand, leaned down and whispered in her ear.

'Retract your testimony or I will find you and finish you off. You understand?' His hand still held her tightly. Becky could smell his breath. He smelled of cigarettes and alcohol. The man wasn't drunk, but his look was menacing, as if he wasn't himself. Two women approached them, he quickly removed his hand from her mouth and ran in the direction of the crowded street. Becky was stunned for a while by what had happened. He had found her, it hadn't taken him long. Whoever it was, he had no qualms about pursuing her. Despite her fright, Becky managed to study him, as Tanya had advised her in case one of them threatened her. His clothes were expensive, so was his cologne. This man was of a different social status than Albert. Becky tried to calm herself, then called Inspector Ramsey, told her what had happened and where she was. The man was leaning with one arm on the wall behind her. Maybe he had left fingerprints, she thought. The cops came in a few minutes, followed by forensics who took the fingerprints Becky told them about and took samples of the skin near her mouth. They could be lucky and find DNA. After it was all over, Becky went back to the house and called Alex and Arnie.

'There's a police car in front of the house,' Arnie said when he got home. He expected to find Becky upset, but she wasn't. She had started cooking and greeted him with a smile.

'Okay,' he said. 'That's strange. You should be scared, right?'

'Yes, but do you know what this person did today? Set me free from fear.'

'How so?' Arnie was puzzled.

'All these months I was afraid of these men, but today I found that I had nothing to be afraid of. He was trying to scare me because he is afraid of me. Our roles have reversed.'

Arnie sat down in a chair and stared at her in confusion. 'What do you mean?'

'His eyes, Arnie. He was scared. He smelled of alcohol, the same way my father smelled when he drank a few for courage.'

'Don't underestimate him, Becky. This man is dangerous.'

'He's just human after all, isn't he?'

Arnie didn't want to argue with her. He was going to leave that to Alex. Her rapists, especially the driver, according to her cousin, were psychopaths. Even if they looked like 'just people', they weren't.

'Everything will be fine,' she said, and that made him even more worried.

'Becky, you have to be careful. Lack of fear is not a good thing.'

'Right? How do you know? Every day, every hour, every minute I was afraid of these men. And you know what, I'm fed up. I'm sick of being a victim. I'm sick of crying. I'm tired of bothering everyone around me and being treated like a fragile doll. I want my life, Arnie. I want to walk the streets without turning around. Entering the shops without looking around.'

'What is going on here?' asked a surprised Alex, who had just entered the kitchen.

'I don't know, bro. Speak to her. I hope you manage to make her understand' said Arnie and left the room.

Alex looked at Becky questioningly. And he, like her cousin, was surprised that she wasn't upset by what had happened.

'I told Arnie that I was no longer afraid of these men, and I don't know why he was worried about that.'

'Not to be afraid can be dangerous, Becky.'

'That's what he told me too, but I'm tired of worrying about everything and all of you looking at me as if I'm going to pass out at any moment.'

Alex, like Arnie, sat down in the chair and stared at her in amazement. Something had unleashed that anger in Becky. Unlike Arnie, he didn't want to argue with her. Rather, he wanted to send her to therapy right away. She needed to talk to someone who wasn't close to her and didn't see her as a victim. He knew two or three good specialists, but he had to convince Becky to talk to one of them.

'Aren't you going to say something?' she asked him while mashing the potatoes.

'Whatever I say right now will be wrong.'

'You sound like a lawyer,' she teased him.

'No, I sound incompetent in your field. I have never met anyone who claimed that they were not afraid of the person who tried to kill them.'

'Well, I don't just say it, I really mean it. I saw fear in his eyes, Alex. He's afraid of me and that's good, right?'

Alex shook his head. 'No, Becky. That's not good. He is a dangerous man, and you should not underestimate him. He may be afraid now, but tomorrow he will find a way to subdue you.'

'You didn't see it. He tried to scare me, but I felt his fear.'

'Don't be under any illusions, Becky. Next time, that person might not just let you go.'

Becky threw up her hands angrily. 'Why don't you leave me alone, huh?' she screamed, and pieces of potatoes flew out of the masher in her right hand.

Alex was startled. He tried to pull her closer and calm her down, but she pointed the masher at him and motioned for him to get out of the kitchen.

'Okay,' he agreed. 'If you need me, I'm in my room. And don't call me for dinner, I don't want to eat these potatoes.' He pointed to the food scattered in the kitchen. Then he hurried up to his room. Shortly after, Arnie joined him.

'What are we going to do?' he asked.

'We'll give her some time. My sister had those moments after my brother-in-law killed himself. After two hours, she acted as if nothing had happened.'

'I hope you're right, Alex. Now I understand why some men are afraid of their wives. Even with just a masher she scared me but imagine if she was holding a knife.'

Alex smiled slightly, but inside he was trembling. He was worried about Becky. After a moment's hesitation, he called Inspector Ramsey to find out exactly what had happened. He needed her point of view.

'This is not normal behaviour,' she agreed. 'Longer therapy is also needed, otherwise she will collapse.'

'How do I get her to volunteer to talk to someone? We are not her parents, and she is a minor.'

'She needs a female friend, Alex, who understands her. No offense, but you and Arnie as men have no way of understanding her. Is there a woman, a friend of yours, to talk to.'

'There is one,' Alex said thoughtfully. Then he thanked Inspector Ramsey and contacted Paul. He invited him and Catherine to dinner, then informed Arnie of their plan. As the two talked, the sounds of objects falling from a height and Becky's swearing could be heard from the kitchen. Neither of them dared to go down to the kitchen to see what was going on. They were afraid that one of these objects would fly towards them.

As Alex had predicted, after two hours Becky calmed down. She was sitting on the sofa in the living room with her hands on her knees. Her euphoria had evaporated and been replaced by sadness. Becky watched out the window as two pigeons did their love dance. Alex walked quietly over to her, made enough noise to let her know he was there, and sat down on the sofa next to her.

'Paul and Catherine are coming to visit us,' he said.

She kept her eyes on the birds.

'If you don't want to see them, I will call them not to come.'

This time she looked away and looked at him and nodded. They stared outside for a moment, then Alex picked up his laptop, sat back down next to her, and started working. Becky watched him and realized that if it wasn't for him, she wouldn't have survived. She didn't know where he got the intelligence and strength to help her and understand her. But she was grateful he did. She got up and went to clean the messy kitchen. When Paul and Catherine arrived, there was no sign of an angry Becky. Everything was back to normal.

Paul and Catherine were so in love that they paid attention only to each other. The two hugged, kissed and courted each other at every possible moment. Not that Arnie, Alex, and Becky weren't happy for them, but somehow, they felt like they were unnecessary. After starting a three-hour dinner, the couple had not exchanged five sentences with the hosts. It was as if a veil had been lowered around them and they could see only themselves. The dinner had not gone as Alex had expected but it still left a nice romantic mood.

'There will be a wedding soon,' he said after Paul and Catherine left.

'How can you be sure?' argued Arnie. 'You know Paul, tomorrow he will be with someone else.'

'Are you blind? Can't you see how bewitched he is? I've never seen Paul like this. And don't forget they live together. If it was just an infatuation, Paul would have been tired of Catherine by now.'

Arnie smiled. Alex was right, as always.

'Why don't you have any girlfriends?' Becky asked them.

Her question seemed to surprise the men. Before she'd moved in their house, they'd often brought women home, but since she'd been in the next room, they'd both stopped doing that.

'No, don't tell me it's because of me. If you want to bring your girlfriends home, I don't mind. What happened to me shouldn't change your lives.'

The two men were still saying nothing. Not because they had nothing to say, but because they didn't know how to say it.

'You mean if I bring my girlfriend on Friday night you won't mind?' Arnie asked her.

'Of course, I wouldn't mind,' she confirmed.

'Are you sure about this, Becky?' Alex asked her as well.

'I am not ten years old, and I spent my childhood in Cornwall, a romantic hotspot. I've said it before today, but I'll say it again, stop tiptoeing around me. If you have a girlfriend, bring her, just do it.'

Arnie and Alex looked at each other. They expected Becky to scream again, but she didn't. She was calm and serious in what she told them.

'Okay,' Arnie said. 'I'll keep that in mind.' Then he left the room whistling to himself. Alex took his laptop and left the kitchen as well. Becky was left alone. Her hands were shaking. She thought about cleaning the kitchen and washing the dishes but decided she had broken enough dishes for the day. And she, like the two men, retired wearily to her room, and, for the first time in several months she had no nightmares. When she shared this with her new counsellor the next day, she said that sometimes it's good to get your anger out and tell others what you're thinking.

'You have to learn to live with it, Becky. People who know what happened to you will always try to be nice to you and protect you. You should not be angry with them but be grateful that you have such people around you.'

And Becky was grateful. But she never told them.

8.

For several months, investigators searched for clues and evidence of Becky's rape. Albert Levy was left in custody and the case against him would soon be underway. The problem was that there was no sign of the other perpetrators, and it was not beneficial for there to be only one defendant. After assaulting and threatening Becky, the driver disappeared, and no one knew where he was. Forensics were unable to obtain any DNA or fingerprints. Becky was very disappointed by this and there was nothing she could do but hope that something would come up soon.

It had been over a year since she had been raped, and Becky was about to have her birthday and turn seventeen. She still lived with Alex and Arnie and worked at the same restaurant, except she was now working as a waitress and her shifts were shorter, mainly during the day. Her life seemed to be in order for a while, and, if it wasn't for the police car that regularly drove past their house, she wouldn't think of what had happened a year ago. The new therapy she was going to, and Alex's care were helping her, at least for now. Becky was glad she had started it. There was more trust in people now. Not only to the people close to her, but in humanity as a whole.

Arnie had organized a small party for her birthday. Becky had never had a party in her honour before, and, as she walked down the street, she wondered what she was expected to say or do. The invitees were not many—Alex, Paul, Catherine, Michael, and Tanya. They were all settled in the beautiful garden that Paul came over to tend to from time to time and got up when they saw Becky enter. It was all kind of surreal for her, she had never been sung a birthday song before, nor had she received any presents before. It was as if the person she was now was not her, but some new person, a new personality hidden beneath the surface of the old one. She looked in the mirror and saw a beautiful slim brunette with bright blue eyes and almost didn't recognize herself. Last year's teenage girl had disappeared somewhere, and a beautiful young woman had appeared in her place. Becky smiled to herself and looked around at her friends. Paul and Catherine stood pressed together again. Alex was smiling at her, and Arnie was happily handing her a cake. Michael and Tanya raised beer glasses to her.

'I don't know where I found you,' Becky finally said. 'But I'm happy to have you.'

'Happy birthday, Becky!' they all shouted in unison. Becky laughed and felt light and happy like never before.

The gifts worried her, she hadn't received birthday presents before and she didn't know how to react. Arnie helped her by carrying them into the kitchen. It was such a strange feeling to be the centre of attention for her birthday. She was both glad that everyone was there for her, but she wanted everything to be over quickly and to divert attention away from herself. The party didn't last long anyway. Catherine had to go to work and of course Paul accompanied her, and Michael was on the trail of something and was also in a hurry to leave with Tanya. In the end, there were only three left again in the house, eating birthday cake and talking.

'Thank you, Arnie,' she said as she went into the kitchen to open the presents. Her hands were shaking with excitement as she tore up the wrapping papers. Alex watched her amused.

'It's like it's your first time,' he said.

'That's right. It's my first time. These are the first birthday presents in my life and I am so excited,' she answered, and her face lit up at the sight of the first gift. Arnie also circled around her, caught up in her excitement. As he looked at them, Alex thought that one day he would have to thank his father for the good childhood he and his mother had given him.

After all the presents were unwrapped Becky, Arnie and Alex sat down in the garden again. It was the most beautiful day of Becky's life. At least for now. Hopefully it will be not the last one, she thought.

Two months after the party, Michael called Becky.

'I found the other two rapists, Becky. The police will come to get you in half an hour. Alex is on his way to you, too.'

Becky sat on the couch, unable to process the news. She hoped it really was them. So, there would be three defendants in court, not just one. One part of her was satisfied and happy that they had found them, but the other realized that her peaceful life would soon be over, and she would have to prepare for a tough battle in court.

Alex and the police arrived almost at the same time. When they arrived at the police station Becky had a feeling of déjà vu. It was as if everything was repeating itself, this time in a double dose. She had no idea how Michael had found the two men, but it really was them. And despite the therapy, despite the time that had passed, Becky froze with fear when she saw them. She felt with her body every pain the two of them had caused her and it was as if her life had crumbled again. Her blood drained from her face, her skin turned pale, and

Becky was on the floor before everyone else knew what was happening. This time she didn't come to her senses easily. It took them half an hour to stabilize her and get her to the hospital.

No one had expected this, not even Alex. Becky's fainting shocked him. He stayed with her as they wheeled her into the ambulance and then sat on a bench with his head in his hands. What happened to her must have been so horrible that her mind couldn't accept it every time she went back to it. That's what the counsellor had explained to him after her first seizure upon recognizing Albert Levy. Alex didn't know the details of her rape and attempted murder. He was only familiar with the facts that were in the reports, and there were no emotions, only findings. It was time for Becky to have the conversation between client and lawyer and for him to understand who and what he was up against. His life somehow revolved around her and even now he couldn't explain this affection he had for this girl. It wasn't just the pity and sympathy he felt for her. Nor was it romantic love, although he did feel a slight infatuation. It was more respect and honour, and also a desire to support her, to replace the family that had not stood behind her in this difficult moment.

A few hours later, Becky woke up in the hospital with a severe headache. After a thorough examination, the doctors discharged her. She needed to rest physically and emotionally; she had been advised. Becky went home, laid down on the bed and tried not to think about the two men she had not been able to identify before passing out. She had to find the strength to go there again, but she didn't have the strength. In front of her eyes were all of them, leaning over her, drawing lots as to who would be first. And then nothing, as if the memory ended there, right before the intense pain, before the injuries and blows. She didn't want to remember and didn't want to relive that even for a moment. Before, all this was hidden somewhere deep in her mind, her nightmares had stopped, her fears too. She didn't want them back. She wanted them to stay buried deep there. But if she went to the police station again, if she met the eyes of her rapists again, her memories and nightmares would return. Becky had to make a choice to go there again or try to put everything back deep in her mind and not take it out of there anymore. She held her breath trying to make up her mind, her head ached, her hands were shaking, and she unconsciously pulled them away from her body and gripped the sheet with them tightly. Her knees buckled and her body curled into a foetal, protective position. That's how Arnie and Alex found her a few hours later.

'Are you okay?' Arnie asked her.

She opened her eyes. Her gaze was tired and desperate. She hadn't made up her mind yet.

'Let's let her rest,' Alex said. 'I'll order something for dinner. If you feel better, come downstairs and we'll talk,' he said to Becky, leaning down and kissing her on the head.

Arnie did the same, and she was left alone with her thoughts again. Becky fell asleep, exhausted from the tension she kept inside her. When she awoke it was dark outside and no muffled voices could be heard in the living room. When she got up, she saw that it was almost midnight. She had slept for almost four hours. She felt the urge to take a shower and wipe off the nervous sweat. Then, starving, she went down to the kitchen looking for something for dinner. To her surprise, Alex was still sitting there, engrossed in some paperwork he was looking at on his laptop.

'I thought you were already asleep,' she told him.

'I couldn't sleep, so I decided to work,' he explained.

She took a slice of pizza and sat down close to him. When she looked at his laptop, she saw her name and gasped.

'You are working on my case,' she was surprised.

'I want to examine documents and facts,' he said and looked at her questioningly.

'Alex, what if I don't go to the police station tomorrow?'

He looked at her, surprised by her question. He didn't say anything to her, he waited for her to eat, and though she expected his answer, he didn't give it to her. He had to find out what was going on in her head. She swallowed the last two bites with difficulty, his look bothering her and the fact that he hadn't answered her question made her even more nervous.

'I was thinking,' she said, putting the empty plate in the sink and turning her back on him, 'that it would probably be best if I do nothing. If I don't testify, then these men will leave me alone and none of my friends will be in danger.'

Becky continued to speak, turning to the tap, pretending to wash the already clean plate. She didn't want to look Alex in the eye. He, for his part, remained silent. He didn't know what to say or what to advise her. The decision should have been hers, but the fact that she seemed to have surrendered surprised him. He hadn't expected such a turn of events, not from her.

Becky finally turned and sat down close to him again. And when she looked at him, he understood what was going on. She was numb with fear. Her lips trembled and her eyes were nervous. All the symptoms of a frightened witness, he thought. Alex reached over and wrapped his arms around her shoulders. She leaned against him and wept bitterly.

'Everything will be fine,' he told her and stroked her hair.

'I don't know what to do, Alex,' she cried. 'I'm afraid.'

'I know, Becky, and it's normal to feel that way. But if we let them go, you'll be scared for the rest of your life.'

'I can't go through with this, Alex. I don't want to remember what happened. I just started feeling better and not having nightmares.'

He didn't say anything, just left her pressed against him until she calmed down.

'Do you want to talk about it tomorrow?' he asked her. 'Maybe you'll feel better in the morning.'

She pulled away from him, seeing his tired look and nodded in agreement. Then she went up to her room and thought for a long time about what to do tomorrow. Becky didn't sleep until morning. She woke up to a noise in the kitchen. She became quickly frightened, opened the door, and peered down. Tanya, Michael, and Alex were sitting drinking coffee in the living room. Arnie was nowhere to be seen and she assumed he had gone to work. There was no point in him standing around guarding her either, Becky thought, changing quickly and joining the others.

'I wasn't expecting you this morning,' she told the detectives.

'Alex invited us. He wanted us all to talk together. Arnie is here too. I think he's in the kitchen,' Tanya explained.

'Okay. And what is this meeting about?' Becky asked as she walked over to the coffee machine.

'We all want to talk to you together,' Alex shouted from the far corner of the room.

Becky hugged her cousin when she saw him in the kitchen, then poured herself some coffee and went back into the living room. Arnie followed her.

'I'm listening to you,' she said resignedly and waited for someone to start speaking.

'Actually, the idea is for you to talk,' Alex said.

'Why me?'

'Because you are afraid, and you certainly have questions,' he explained.

She looked at him, unpleasantly surprised that he had shared her fears with others. 'I didn't know you were going to tell everyone.'

'Everyone in this room is involved in your case, Becky. Paul and Catherine aren't here just because she's on tour and he's accompanying her. You have to accept the fact that you are not alone, we are with you and by your side and we will help you in whatever decision you make.'

'Then first tell me what decision you think I should make.'

'It doesn't work like that,' Michael said. 'No matter how much we want to, we cannot put ourselves in your place. The decision must be yours, and, although you are only seventeen years old, I would prefer that you make it without regard for the opinions of others.'

Becky looked at each of them trying to understand what their thoughts were. Everyone was tense, Alex was overtired, Arnie was tight-lipped, but nothing told her exactly who was thinking what. She sipped her coffee and remained in her thoughts for a while.

'It's hard for me to make a decision, mostly because I know how dangerous these people are. All night I didn't sleep, thinking and considering. The best option is for the police to find evidence without my having to participate in any trial, without even having to set foot in a courtroom. But after looking into things, I guess Alex will confirm, even if he is not my defence attorney, the prosecution will find a reason and I will be called as a witness. So, I don't think I have much of a choice and I have to participate from the start until the end.'

Becky looked at the people around her, still not seeing any reaction from them. 'Don't you agree with me?' she asked.

'On the contrary,' said Alex. 'However, there is one small detail that you forget about.'

'And what is it?'

'Your parents.'

Becky looked at him in surprise. She opened her mouth to say something, then blinked as she understood what Alex meant. 'Can they stop me from hiring you?'

'I don't know them, Becky,' said Alex frankly. 'However, we must prepare for them to intervene at some point. You are a minor and whether you like it or not, they are still your parents and can make decisions on your behalf.'

Becky looked at Arnie.

'I agree with Alex. As far as I know my aunt, if she finds out that she can get some amount of money, she will immediately join the process.'

'But they paid her to keep quiet, didn't they? Didn't you say it yourself?'

'We have no evidence of this,' confirmed Michael.

'And the envelopes with the money?'

'The money doesn't prove anything. They can say they found it or come up with something else.'

Becky couldn't believe it. Her life still depended on these people. She was counting down the days until her next birthday to finally cut off all contact with them.

'So, you have gathered here to prepare me for all kinds of surprises, right?'

'No, Becky,' said Alex. 'We are here to support you. Whatever happens, we are with you, for you and by your side.'

Becky nodded her thanks.

'It is best to act before your parents have guessed that they can take advantage of you,' Tanya advised her.

'What if we delay the process until she comes of age?' Alex asked.

'Can we?' Becky asked with hope in her voice.

'Nothing prevents us from trying. Either way, the police investigation will take a few months, then we may ask for an adjournment.'

'Nine months and twenty days is a long time to delay.'

'It wouldn't be the first time they delayed a case for so long,' Alex said, and Michael confirmed it.

'Until then, what will we do?' Becky asked.

'We will go with the flow,' said Alex and smiled for the first time. 'We will play them. No one should know about it. Once they understand what we are after, they will find a way to tie our hands. Becky, if your mother tries to contact you, don't answer her. This way we will avoid a direct conflict. You'll have to talk to her at some point, but we need to delay that as long as possible.'

'And won't those who paid her cause trouble for them?'

'They probably will. They will try to stop you from testifying,' Alex said. 'There are many unknowns, Becky, and none of us will give you an exact answer to what lies ahead, but one thing is clear, if you don't go against them yourself, someone else can make you do it. Therefore, although I don't want you to take this as advice, but rather as an opinion, I would say that it is better for you to go today and identify the two men if they are your abusers. You have nothing to lose, at least for now.'

'Okay,' Becky agreed. 'But I hope no one gets hurt because of my decision.'

'Whatever happens, even if we are threatened, hurt, or even killed, this is the better option. Otherwise, what we will be left with is only fear.'

Becky nodded, put the coffee cup down and went up to her room to change. She wouldn't forgive herself if these criminals threatened or hurt any of her loved ones, but no matter how hard she thought she couldn't protect them or herself until her abusers went to prison. And she would do her best to get them where they belonged, with the rest of the criminals.

After changing, she and Alex headed to the police station and the others to work. A few hours later, Becky recognized Vincent Geer and George Bell as two involved in the crime. They were taken into custody, and Becky was forced to testify as to who had raped and stabbed her, when and how. She gave detailed descriptions that shocked Alex. Every time Becky talked about the details of the rape, her lips trembled, her eyes watered, her hands in her lap also shook, but she didn't stop talking. She described everything in the smallest detail, the words, the gestures, the things they had done to her. Her testimony was shocking. She was going back there in her mind, first to the road where she had been chased, then to the car where she had been stripped, finally to the place where she had been raped and almost killed. There was no doubt to anyone in the room that she was telling the truth, but everyone wondered how she was even experiencing all of this.

After several hours of testimony, Becky and Alex finally left the police station. The two stopped by the park next door, as if to let the wind blow away what had happened inside the police station. They sat on a bench and were silent for a while.

'You did well,' Alex told her.

'Yes. I feel better now.'

She sighed and took a deep breath of the fresh air in the park. She looked at the birds pecking at something in the grass and the squirrel running from one tree to another. Becky was surprised to find that she missed the beautiful sights of Cornwall. And for the first time she admitted that the tourists were right. It was like a corner of heaven. She hadn't thought about how beautiful the place she actually came from was. Becky wasn't sure she wanted to go back there now, but she missed the ocean and the waves and the breeze. An urge came over her to go and swim freely, just her and her surfboard. She missed that feeling here in London, the feeling of being alone in the nature. And somehow, while she was telling today what and where it had happened to her, all this brought her back there, but with a mixture of a new note, the memory of the sunrises and sunsets, the storms and the elements that were in her birthplace. Also the smiling people, whom she didn't understand at the time. But now she understood that, and small smile appeared on her face.

'You're smiling,' said Alex and infected by her mood, he also smiled.

'Yes, I remembered the good times of my childhood. The ocean, the wind, the waves... I wondered why the tourists envied us for living in this place and now I understood. Perhaps the atmosphere in the park brought me back to that feeling of being in nature.'

'Yes, it's nice, isn't it?'

'It's wonderful,' she agreed and looked at the forest and the animals that were walking in front of her.

The two of them stayed in the park and then went back to the house where they rested. After the sleepless night of the tiring day, Becky and Alex fell asleep, enraptured, and captivated by the atmosphere of the peaceful park where they had spent the whole afternoon.

9.

The summer passed quickly and imperceptibly. There was no change in Becky's life. The fourth suspect was still being sought. His three friends were covering for him and not giving any information about him. Becky was sure they wouldn't find him. Of the four, he was the evillest. Becky was afraid of him, looked around every time she was on the street or in other public places. She expected him to attack her again, but he didn't. Apparently, he had gone into deep hiding or left. She never found out how Michael located the other three. He didn't talk about it with her, he told her that everyone leaves traces, and he just followed the traces. Except Michael couldn't find anything for the driver. It was as if this person did not exist, and that caused problems. The trial against her rapists was being deliberately dragged out, awaiting expert reports, seeking more evidence, and Inspector Ramsey and Alex were doing their best to delay it for a few months until Becky came of age. As everyone had guessed, her mother tried to contact her and stop her from testifying. Becky didn't talk to her, let Arnie do the talking. It was hell for the two cousins. Arnie's mother and Becky's mother attacked them from all sides. They called every possible phone, even sending Becky's father to talk to her. To talk her out of it, like her mother had said. Fortunately, Becky was at work when her dad had gone to their house. Alex had invited him, talked to him, and then sent him to the station.

'What did he say?' Becky asked after she got home.

Alex didn't answer right away. He had to choose the right words, but for the first time, they didn't come to his mind. He was confused by Becky's father's behaviours. 'First he said he was sorry for everything that happened to you and is happening to you now.'

Right, thought Becky. 'Is he really sorry?'

'I think so. He was sincere when he said it. But then he said that they are still your parents, and you have to do what they tell you.'

'What if I don't?' she asked with a crooked chin.

'If you don't, they will send you home.'

'What? They can't do it, can they? Can they?' Becky was horrified.

'They can, Becky. You are still their daughter. They can do more than that.' Alex paused for a moment. 'They said that if you testify, they will file a case against me and your cousin because we live in the same house with a minor, without her having a guardian in the house.'

'What?' she shouted. 'They sent me here. They kicked me out and sent me to Arnie.'

'We can't prove it, Becky. They are right, they can give us a lot of headaches.'

Becky shifted on the sofa in the living room, her shoulders relaxed, her head as well. Her whole body betrayed the impotence and frustration that had overtaken her. Alex left her for a while to collect herself and make sense of things. Then he handed her a glass of water and sat down next to her.

'We all forgot and maybe we didn't expect such a turn of events, Becky. You are underage, I am ten years older than you. Your cousin, although related to you, is in the same position.'

'I don't want to move in with Catherine again,' she said.

'Maybe it won't be necessary. I will seek help from my colleagues, maybe they can advise us on what to do until you come of age.'

'I only need a few months, Alex.'

'I know. But for now, we will agree to your parents' terms because we have no other choice.'

'Does Arnie know?'

'I don't know, I didn't talk to him, but they maybe had the same conversation with him.'

'I don't want to cause you any more trouble. Maybe I'd better move somewhere else.'

'You won't move. There's a criminal out there who I think is dictating the rules of the game right now. I think the best for you is to stay here where you are safe.'

Becky nodded in agreement. She had to last a few more months, she told herself. But the anger towards her parents grew tremendously. She wanted to buy a gun and go shoot them. How can you even call yourself a parent if you harm your child, she wondered. But this would be over soon, she thought. It wasn't worth going to prison for them.

While she was lost in thought, Alex was on the phone. He talked to his colleagues who had more experience with juvenile cases. He had just finished talking when Arnie came home. His face was red, his eyes angry. There was no doubt in Alex and Becky's mind that he had had the same conversation as Alex.

'They trashed her last year, just when she needed them the most, and now they want to bring her back to Cornwall.'

'If she does not testify in the court, they will force her to go back,' said Alex.

'No, Alex, this condition has been dropped. They decided to take her away for safety.'

'What?' Becky exclaimed. 'They can't do that, can they?'

'Unfortunately, they can,' said Alex.

'But how?' Becky objected.

Alex didn't answer. There was still a way to get out of this mess. He needed a few more hours to study things better.

The three sat in silence in the kitchen, each lost in his own dark thoughts.

'I don't want to go back there,' cried Becky.

'I will do everything legal to stop them, but if we don't find a way you will have to stay with them for a few months.'

'I won't last a few months on that farm, Alex. Can't I offer them some kind of deal or pay them or something?' she asked.

'I think someone has already paid them,' Arnie intervened.

'I think so too,' said Alex. 'A friend of mine will investigate them, investigate their finances and if there is any trace of anything illegal, we will know. By tomorrow morning she said she will be done with the investigation.'

'So, there's nothing we can do for now, right?' Becky asked.

'At the moment, we have nothing to stop them from taking you away.'

Becky sighed tiredly, wrapped her arms around her knees and stared out into the garden. Alex and Arnie stayed with her for a while then went to their rooms.

Becky didn't know what to make of her parents. On the one hand, they had not completely abandoned her, they took care of her while she was little, they wanted her to get an education. On the other hand, she had been bullied since she was four years old. She was forced from a young age to work on the farm, take care of the cows, chickens, and horses. Very early in the morning and while her mother was in bed, Becky would go around the barn taking care of everything. She did everything in quick succession, then went to school where her classmates could smell the animal smell coming from her clothes. It was humiliating and Becky had nothing else to do but listen to the innuendos and taunts at school. She was nine years old when she first wanted to leave home. Now, she had finally done it and they want to take her back there again. She would not be able to bear this. After a moment's thought, Becky called Inspector Ramsey and explained what was going on. Ramsey cursed at first, then composed herself, considered what Becky had said, and tried to calm her down.

'I won't let them take you. You are an important witness, and you need police protection.'

'You don't understand! If I refuse to go, they will make Arnie and Alex's life hell. They will file a case against them.'

'We'll find a way, Becky. Don't despair, I'll go and talk to them right now. I'm only a few miles from the farm.'

'Good,' desperation was felt in the young girl's voice.

'I'll call you later. Don't worry, everything will be fine,' said Ramsey and hung up the phone.

Becky remained curled up on the sofa until her phone rang. It was a call from Inspector Ramsey.

'I have bad news,' Inspector Ramsey said sadly. 'Your parents are adamant—they want you on the farm as soon as possible. From what I understand, someone is coming to pick you up tomorrow.'

'No, no...' Becky shouted, drawing the attention of the two men in the house. 'I won't go back there. I would rather kill myself than return to that place.' This time Becky was crying. She was desperate.

Ramsey felt like breaking something, she was so angry at what the girl's parents had done. 'You only have to stay with them for a few months, Becky,' the inspector tried to calm her down.

'You don't understand. I don't want to go back there. I can't, do you understand?'

'I understand, sweetheart, but we have no choice,' Ramsey answered, and by the tone of her voice you could tell she was crying too. 'The moment I can do something I can get you out of there I will. I promise.'

Becky was crying, she couldn't even speak. She had put the woman on speakerphone and both Alex and Arnie, albeit from a distance, were in tears. They didn't know what to say or what to do. Helplessness was written on their faces. Becky was curled up on the sofa, her hands clutching her knees tightly. Her head was resting there, and her tears were dripping and soaking her jeans.

After Ramsey hung up, Alex and Arnie approached the crying girl and tried to calm her down. They were both angry and furious and didn't know how to react themselves. Becky didn't deserve to go through this. Her life was complicated enough.

'We'll find a way to get you back, Becky,' they told her, but she didn't believe it. She had stopped believing in miracles a long time ago.

When she woke up the next morning, the sun had not yet risen. Becky was asleep on the sofa. She slept less than three hours, but for some reason she felt rested. It was as if the new day had given her hope and warmth. Becky changed, made herself some coffee and waited for Alex and Arnie to wake up. She took a blanket and sat down in the garden. The sun slowly rose, the day overcame the night, and soon its rays illuminated the autumn flowers.

Arnie woke up first. His eyes were red, his face puffy, as if he had been drinking and hadn't slept all night. He joined her in silence. He looked at her and was surprised to notice that there was no sadness in her smile. Quite the opposite, as if there was some freshness, some hope that Arnie didn't know about. He looked at her in surprise, but she remained like that, saying nothing, just looking ahead and smiling. Arnie didn't know what to think, be happy or be worried. He looked at her once more and, seeing no change in her mood, focused on his coffee. Alex also noticed Becky's good mood. He raised a questioning eyebrow at Arnie, but he shrugged. He didn't know what to say. Alex sat down in the chair next to Becky and looked at her, expecting her to say something.

'What are you up to?' he asked her.

She smiled again and handed him her phone. Her mother had texted her that she was okay with Becky staying with Alex and Arnie.

'But how?' the two men were surprised.

'My mother received benefits that were meant for me. Child benefit and all the others for which she managed to apply. I looked at charities' campaigns. She gave few charities in my name and an account to transfer money to for my recovery. She also took money from charity by submitting false documents for several therapies, treatments, and things that I had not even thought of that could help me in my recovery.'

'Did you threaten to betray her?' Alex was amazed.

'Yes.' Becky smiled contentedly. 'I threatened to talk to the social services and all the institutions that granted her the funds.'

Arnie chuckled. Becky had played her cards right.

'I made her send me a written consent to stay with you,' Becky face beamed. Her eyes shone with satisfaction. Alex and Arnie sat back in their chairs with relief, and both looked smiling at the garden and the rays of the rising sun. It was going to be a nice day, they thought.

'So, you managed to buy us some more time,' Alex said happily.

'Yes, until the next round.' Becky was not stupid. She knew that this was a very small victory and that her mother would not give up. She would find another way to prevent her daughter from testifying. Until then, everyone could relax and take a few days off.

'Let's go to Yorkshire for the weekend' suggested Alex. 'I've been meaning to go see my father, my sister, and nephews for a long time. Come with me.'

'I can't,' said Arnie. 'I have an important meeting on Saturday, but Becky can come with you. Right, Becky?'

'Yes, I would be happy to,' she said with a big smile.

Alex postponed all of his commitments, Becky took a few days off, and they both went away for the weekend. This time, Alex's father was more reserved in his reception. Becky didn't know what was causing this, but she assumed it had to do with her. However, his sister and her children welcomed her warmly. They invited her to their house and Becky spent almost a whole day with them. When she returned to Alex and his father there was an argument between the two men. They didn't even realize she had entered the house.

'Leave her, Alex, she is not your responsibility and never was. And I must remind you that she is a minor,' shouted his father from one corner.

'I don't want your opinion and it's none of your business who I help and who I don't,' answered Alex.

'It's my job when it concerns my son's future. You are almost thirty years old; she is not yet eighteen. I won't tell you how this looks like from outside.'

'What does it look like?' Alex shouted angrily.

'It's like she has you wrapped around her little finger, it seems. And it's like you're taking advantage of a minor.'

'I don't sleep with her, Dad. I help her.'

'That may be so, but no one believes it.'

The two men glared at each other. Becky moved and they were surprised to see her.

'Sorry, Becky,' said Ben. 'Nothing personal, I just want to protect my son from troubles.'

'I do not need protection,' shouted Alex angrily.

Becky stood in front of the two men who looked like they were going to fight at any moment.

'Enough,' she cried desperately. 'Alex, your father is right. I shouldn't have come with you. I was supposed to stay in London with Arnie.'

Alex tried to protest.

'Listen,' she said. 'I don't belong here. Just as I don't belong in the house in London. As soon as I'm of age I'll be moving somewhere else. I don't want to stop you from having your own life, and I don't want to tie your life to mine.'

'No, Becky. You don't understand,' he tried to calm her down.

'No, Alex. I was thinking about it a few days ago. You don't go out, you don't meet friends anymore, you don't have fun and it's all because of me.'

'It has nothing to do with you,' he protested.

'On the contrary,' called his father.

'All I want is to help you,' Alex turned to Becky, ignoring her father's comment.

'I know. And I am grateful to you. You are my best friend. And as my friend, I want you to be happy. My presence doesn't make you happy, it makes you restless and puts you in danger.'

'Here she agrees with me,' his father called again.

'You shut up!' Alex attacked him again.

'Alex, please calm down,' Becky stepped towards him. 'Come outside and talk,' she suggested, motioning for his father to step back. Alex glared at his father and followed Becky into the garden. She walked by the flowers, pulled out a rose, and breathed in its fragrance. She acted as if he was not there. Then she turned to him with a sad smile. 'Your father is right, and you know it. From the outside it looks like we both came here as a couple in love.'

'That's right,' he admitted. 'Except we're not in love. All I wanted was for us to come and rest for a few days.'

'People won't think like that, and you might get in trouble. I don't want you to get in trouble, and neither does your family. I will go back to London today and find somewhere to stay there.'

'You don't have to leave. You can stay with my sister.'

'It's better that I leave now, Alex, and you stay and fix your relationship with your father.'

Alex once again marvelled at her maturity. Becky didn't seem to be a minor. Her words and actions were those of a mature woman who had been through a lot. He nodded in agreement, then sat wearily on the garden bench and stretched out his legs. 'Arnie had told me about you before you came. He told me you were the nicest and smartest person he knew and even though he only remembered you as a ten-year-old he was very impressed with you. As he was telling me, I thought he was talking about you like that because you were his favourite cousin. But now, I don't know, it's like you're justifying his words. I shouldn't have reacted like that and yes, my father is right. We might be in trouble. Sorry Becky, I didn't think of that.'

'Nor did I. Fortunately, we have your father to help us judge some things.'

Alex nodded, smiled as if to himself, and went into the house to arrange for Becky's safe return to London. His father was still standing in the kitchen sulking, but Alex decided to deal with his mood later. He bought Becky a train ticket, and they took her luggage and left for York station. Although it was almost nine in the evening it was still light outside. The two travelled in the car in silence. From time to time, Alex looked at her, expecting to see some reaction from her, but Becky sat calmly in the passenger's seat, looking at the scenery along the road. When they reached the station, she hugged him before entering the platform and told him to talk to his father. Then she was out of sight.

Becky only pretended to be calm, not wanting to show the pain of what Alex's father had said. She sat close to the window and when the train started, tears flowed from her eyes. Although she agreed with Ben, what he said made her feel ostracized. As if she had gone back in time, her memories returned, and she remembered her last train journey to London. Alex's family was justifiably worried about him. She burdened him, prevented him from living, as if she were a weed wrapped around him. She needed to free him, but she didn't know how to do it without hurting him. Maybe she should talk to Arnie when she got home and ask his advice. She and Alex tried to contact him and warn him that Becky was coming back but were unsuccessful. Becky tried to call Arnie again, but the phone went to voicemail. Shortly before the train arrived in London, Becky received a text from Alex. He had not contacted Arnie and had asked Paul to go and meet her.

Paul was waiting patiently for her on the platform. When he saw her, he noticed that she was upset, but he didn't ask what happened. He took the suitcase from her hands and directed her to the parking lot where he had parked the car. 'It's been raining for two days,' he said when they had to jump over a large puddle.

'The weather is fine,' Becky replied, grateful that he wasn't questioning her. 'How is Catherine?'

'She sprained her leg and is now resting at home.'

'Is it serious?'

'No, but with her job she has to be careful. She is not pleasant company these days. She is bored. Perhaps you should come and see each other tomorrow.'

'Okay, I will come tomorrow. I have no other plans anyway.'

Becky and Paul talked on the way to her house. When they arrived there, there was a surprise for them. As soon as they opened the front door, they smelled a woman's perfume. Then they saw women's shoes, scattered clothes, and socks on the floor. Paul quickly pulled Becky out into the street.

'Arnie is with his girlfriend,' he grinned. 'Apparently, he's not expecting you. You'd better come sleep with us tonight. There are two rooms available, and Catherine will be glad to see you.'

Becky nodded. For the second time that day, she felt redundant. It was as if someone had slapped her twice. She tried to hide her mood from Paul but failed. As they entered Catherine's kitchen, he whispered something softly in his girlfriend's ear and Becky had no doubt that he had mentioned her. Catherine hugged her.

'Come here. We'll cook something and cheer you up.'

Catherine hobbled to the refrigerator, opened it, and rummaged inside. She took a pan and started cooking.

'Will you tell me what happened?' she asked as she stood with her back to Becky, chopping something on the kitchen board.

'Alex's father doesn't think it's a good idea for me to visit them.'

Catherine turned around with a surprised look on her face. 'Are you sure?' she asked.

'Yes, I found them arguing. And I agree with him, people could get the wrong impression and Alex could get in trouble because of me. It's also probably preventing him from living his life, having fun, you know what I mean?'

'I know. Paul and I wanted to talk to you about this, but we didn't know how to broach the subject.'

'Well, I'm here now. And we're on the subject,' Becky said sadly.

Catherine turned, put down the knife she was using to chop the spring onion and sat down in the chair next to Becky. 'You didn't do anything wrong, Becky. But men are men. They need female company.'

'So, you think I stopped them going out, right?' Becky asked.

Paul walked into the kitchen.

'Try to explain to her,' said Catherine. 'After all, you're a man, Alex and Arnie are your best friends, and you know what it's about.'

Paul looked at Catherine helplessly. He didn't want to have this conversation with Becky, but the two women stood across from him, looking at him, waiting for him to speak. 'Let me start by saying that I am not surprised that Arnie is with a woman in the house. He has been dating a colleague of his for some time. They usually see each other at her house, but after you left for the weekend, he apparently decided to take advantage and spend two days with her alone.'

'Why didn't he tell me?' Becky asked.

'Because he's worried about how you'll react,' Paul turned around in his chair, feeling uncomfortable that he should be having this conversation with Becky.

'But I already told them before that I don't mind them bringing their girlfriends home.'

'You are a minor and you were raped,' Catherine intervened in the conversation. 'That's why they wonder how you will react.'

'I still don't understand. How is this relevant?'

'They don't want to upset you in case you find them in an awkward...' Paul began to explain again, this time visibly stuttering with worry.

'Okay, I understand,' said Becky.

'There is one more thing,' said Catherine. She took the scrambled eggs out of the pan, put them on a plate and added salad. Then she placed the plate in front of Becky. 'Eat, you must be hungry,' she said and hobbled back to the stove.

Becky began to eat, but watched Catherine, waiting to hear what else she wanted to tell her.

'Arnie never stopped going out and having fun. Alex, for his part, stopped going out a month after you came to London. He used to not stay home on Friday nights but go out, he had a girlfriend and not just one, not that he was a womanizer, he just liked female company. He went to bars and clubs, had fun even after the death of his brother-in-law. But since you showed up, he doesn't go anywhere. He behaves like a married man—from work to home and from home to work,' Paul said.

Becky listened, opened her mouth to object, to say something, but found no words. She looked at the plate and pushed it towards the middle of the table. She didn't feel like eating anymore.

'What do you mean? You don't think it's my fault, do you?'

Paul and Catherine said nothing. They looked at each other visibly nervous. 'We don't think it's your fault. But you are the reason for his behaviours.'

'Do you think he is attracted to me as a woman or...'

'This is exactly the problem,' Paul tried to explain. 'Neither we nor his family are aware of what exactly is going on in Alex's head. And it has been that way for a very long time.'

'You probably have an idea what's going on?' Catherine asked.

Becky thought about it. She didn't know what to say. 'If you're asking me if he gave me looks or proposals, no, he didn't. Alex and I are very close, but more like brother and sister. I never felt any other attraction between us. According to Arnie, losing his mother and brother-in-law made him who he is, and his only desire is to help me out of the mess I'm in. He is a kind of protector, patron to me.'

'But that doesn't explain why he doesn't go out and have fun,' Paul tried to explain.

'Did you talk to him? Have you asked him why he doesn't come out anymore?'

'Not exactly.'

'Maybe if you talk to him, you will find the answers you are looking for. Even if I am a minor, I am not blind and unfeeling. If Alex was in love with me or had any sexual desires, I would feel it. But I don't think that's it. We are just close, like kindred spirits. I don't really know how to explain it. But you're right, I'm probably suffocating him for some reason and preventing him from living his life to the fullest, and in a few months, the moment I come of age, I'll be leaving the house.'

'Becky, don't take it that way,' Catherine tried to calm her after seeing the tears streaming down her friend's face.

'Don't mind me. I'm just emotional. Sorry, I didn't mean to spoil your evening.'

'Everything is fine,' said Paul. 'Eat your dinner. Calm down, you didn't do anything wrong.'

'That's right,' said Catherine. Then she took one of her friend's hands and gave it an encouraging squeeze. 'Everything will be fine, don't worry.'

Becky stayed with Paul and Catherine until Sunday evening. They watched movies, ate popcorn, and had fun like they hadn't in a long time.

On Sunday, Paul accompanied her to her house. The women's clothes were gone, as was Arnie. Becky entered the empty house and threw herself desperately on the sofa. She had suppressed her emotions for hours. She curled up and cried quietly. She only caused trouble for her friends. The best decision was to leave. But she couldn't do it now. The ringing of the phone brought her out of her thoughts.

'How are you?' Alex asked her.

'Okay. I am resting. How are you?'

'I will stay here tonight as well. I'll be back tomorrow, and we'll talk in the evening.'

'Okay.' She wanted to ask him what they were going to talk about, but she didn't ask the question.

'Okay,' he said, silent for a moment, then hung up. Becky stared at the phone, then tearfully went up to her room. She couldn't sleep until late at night. A little after midnight, she heard Arnie coming home, but Becky didn't get up to talk to him. She left the conversation for the next day. Finally, exhausted by thoughts, she fell asleep.

Becky woke up late in the morning, for the first time in her life she had overslept and was late for work. She got ready quickly, ran down the street and entered the restaurant just in time.

Becky's day was slow. There were not many customers in the restaurant during the day and it was as if the clock had stopped. She didn't know what Alex wanted to talk to her about. This whole situation, the conversations with his father, Paul and Catherine were bothering her. She didn't know how to act or how to react. But what bothered her the most was that she missed Alex. She loved having him around her, his presence had a soothing effect on her. Becky couldn't imagine how she would manage without him. Especially in court. For now, the investigation was ongoing, and no trial date had been announced, but when it was, the person Becky wanted to see by her side was Alex. After several hours of nervously waiting for the time to pass, her shift was finally over. Becky walked home with a heavy heart, expecting something bad to happen. When she entered the house, it was quiet inside. Neither Alex nor Arnie were there. She set about cooking something, just so she wouldn't be waiting in silence, wondering what to think about. An hour later, the two men finally came home. They walked in together and smelled of beer. Apparently, they had met somewhere else before. Becky looked at them worriedly. They greeted her, kissed her on the cheek and sat down with her at the table.

'Arnie will introduce us to his girlfriend,' said Alex and smiled.

'Yes. I'm going to invite her over for a family dinner tomorrow night.'

'What's her name?' Becky asked, glad the topic had nothing to do with her.

'Veronica. We've been dating a short while, so don't have high expectations, but it's still good for you to get to know her.'

Becky smiled. Did her cousin know that she had been about to meet her yesterday.

'How is your father?' Arnie asked.

'He is fine,' Alex said and looked questioningly at Becky. She said nothing, leaving it up to him to decide whether to tell Arnie about what had happened or to keep it quiet. He chose the latter. Alex talked about his nephews and the dogs. Then he diverted the subject to political news. They sat and talked for a while. Finally, everyone headed to their rooms. Whatever Alex had wanted them to talk about, the conversation never took place that night, nor any of the next few days. Days passed and their daily routine did not change for months. Arnie introduced Becky and Alex to his girlfriend, but their relationship was short-lived. Suddenly, Christmas came again, and this time Ben called Becky personally to invite her to Christmas dinner. The condition was that Arnie came with them. Ben's call surprised Becky. She didn't know whether to accept or not. She decided it was best to talk to Alex about it first.

'My father likes you, Becky,' Alex told her. 'We will all be glad if you attend.'

'I don't want anyone to feel uncomfortable with my presence,' she explained.

'No one will feel uncomfortable. Arnie is coming with us, and he can't wait to see my family again.'

'Did you tell him about the argument with your father?'

'No, and I don't think I'll tell him.'

'Okay. I'll think about the Christmas dinner and let you know.'

Becky had already made up her mind not to go to Yorkshire. She was going to make Christmas dinner for her and her cousin and take a few days off for the holidays. However, Alex's father changed her mind. A few days before Christmas, sensing that she was hesitating, he called her again and insisted that she and

Arnie visit them. 'Alex's sister is upset. Your presence will have a good effect on her and the children.'

'Okay,' Becky agreed, though she wasn't convinced that was the real reason. She and Alex had become estranged since their last visit there. They talked, but it wasn't the same. Paul and Catherine told her that he was sad, wanted to talk to them about something, but never did. Whatever was bothering him, he hadn't shared it with anyone. In the past few months, he had devoted himself to work, enrolled in an extra course and studied for exams. Becky tried to talk to him several times, but he wasn't sharing with her like he used to. He was not talking to her, and she had felt alone for months. It was partly why she didn't want to celebrate with his family. She was sure they would feel her emptiness and loneliness.

The day before Christmas, Becky, Arnie, and Alex hired a car again and drove to North Yorkshire. The weather was cold, it was snowing lightly outside, and the small streets were icy. It was as if all of London was leaving the city. The traffic on the motorway was heavy, and their journey proved endless and arduous. Finally, late at night, Arnie parked the car in front of Ben's house. The door opened and the cheerful laughter of children spread out into the street. The dogs barked too, and a smiling Ben and Alex's sister appeared at the front door. And Becky felt like she was entering in a magical world with the smell of cookies and warm tea again. A homely family environment that she had missed almost all year. The warm welcome reassured her. It was as if a millstone fell from her shoulders. She laughed happily, hugged the children, and petted the dogs. Ben looked at her kindly, pulled her close and gave her a paternal hug.

'I'm so glad you agreed to come,' he said.

'You didn't leave me a choice,' she answered and kissed him on the cheek as a greeting and, entering, looked at the beautiful Christmas tree. Becky had a sense of déjà vu, only the children had grown, and the number of dogs had grown by one. Alex's sister stayed until late to talk with her brother and the guests, but finally woke the children and left. Ben also went to bed early, and Arnie, tired from the long drive, had been asleep for some time on the sofa. Only Alex and Becky were left in the kitchen, both in good spirits, drinking tea and putting presents under the Christmas tree. The tension in their relationship had started here and seemed to end there.

'I like coming here,' shared Becky.

'I like to come back at home too. Sometimes I think I should do it more often, but I've been busy with so many things and it's a miracle I was able to free myself for a few days at Christmas.'

'Maybe you should reduce your work and accept fewer clients.'

'That's what I tell myself, but I end up with more work than I could do on my own.'

'Then get someone to help you,' she suggested.

'I hired a woman. She starts in early January. She will help me with the administrative stuff.'

'Great,' said Becky. 'I was thinking of starting a second job, but I'm worried that when the process gets closer, I won't be able to work in both places, so I'm waiting for now.'

'I spoke to Inspector Ramsey a few days ago. There is still no sign of the driver, so they will probably make a decision soon and the process will begin in early or mid-March.'

'Yes,' the topic unnerved Becky and brought her back to reality. 'I don't even want to imagine for a moment what lies ahead.'

Alex saw her worry. 'Nothing has changed, Becky. I will be by your side and help you get ready.'

'I wish I could find a time machine and go to the future and skip this part of my life.'

'And I want to go to the past and do everything possible so that what happened to you does not happen at all,' he said.

Then he bade her good night and Becky was left alone in the cosy family kitchen. She looked at the Christmas tree and wished that next Christmas she would be here again.

The holidays passed without notice and when the day of their return to London arrived no one felt like leaving. The kids and dogs had surrounded the car again, and Ben and his daughter were waving goodbye from the front door. This time Alex was driving, and Becky and Arnie were in the back seat. Arnie was texting all the way, probably to his new girlfriend, and Becky was back outside watching the scenery. Alex watched her from time to time in the rear-view mirror. He was worried about her. Throughout their stay over the Christmas holidays, Becky had remained silent. She laughed, had fun with everyone, but hardly spoke. Unlike Arnie, who didn't stop telling the children various fairy tales and scary stories. Before they left, Ben had called Becky into one of the rooms. Alex had no idea what the two of them had talked about, but from the sad look on Becky's face, he could tell that it had not been an easy conversation.

Becky wasn't sad about talking to Ben though. And he, like Alex, had picked up on her silent mood and tried to make things right. He apologized to her, tried to explain his behaviour during her last visit, but to his surprise she understood him, even supported him. She explained to him that she had decided to leave the house as soon as she came of age.

After his conversation with her, Ben realized that her mood was not related to him. Whatever sadness this girl harboured, she did not share it with him. Alex's sister also tried to find out what was bothering her, but Becky didn't share with her either. She remained so silent until the end.

When they got back to the house, Arnie took the gift he had prepared for his girlfriend and immediately went out. Left alone, Alex and Becky decided to have dinner together.

'It struck me that you've been very quiet lately,' Alex said while arranging the dishes on the table. 'What is bothering you?'

'Nothing. I was just calm and relaxed with your family.'

'My father was probably worried and that's why he talked to you.'

'You must be right. He wanted to apologize, although I don't think he has anything to apologize for.'

Alex stared at her trying to figure out what was wrong with her. 'He likes you, Becky.'

'I know. I like him too. He and I both want only the best for you.'

Alex frowned. 'What does that mean?' he asked.

'What does what mean?' she asked distracted, not understanding his question.

'You told me you both want the best for me.'

'Yes. You to be happy, to have fun, to create a family...'

'Hmm. Okay,' Alex said, but his voice didn't sound pleased.

'Don't you want that?'

'For now, I want to work and create a career. Fun and family are next on my list.'

'Okay,' she said thoughtfully.

'What's up, Becky? You used to share everything with me, but now you are like an ice maiden in front of me.'

She was startled by both his question and the tone in which he asked it. She put down the fork she was eating with and stared at him. 'What you mean?'

'Something is bothering you, but you don't tell me what it is. Have I said anything to hurt or offend you? Because this silence is not from the calm family environment. It's been a few months,' he asked.

She wondered what to answer him. Finally, she decided it was better to tell him the truth. 'It's not just your father who spoke to me. So did Paul and Catherine. According to them, since I've been here you don't go out with friends; you don't have fun. You don't go out at all.'

Alex looked at her in shock and didn't know what to say. 'Right? And they told you it had something to do with you?' he asked.

'According to them, yes.'

'And what do you think?'

'I didn't know you before I came to live with Arnie, so I can't say if you've changed or not.'

Alex stared at her and sat back in the chair. 'They made you feel guilty, and you shouldn't be,' he finally said. 'I will talk to them tomorrow.'

'Is what they say true?' she asked him.

'They are somewhat right. I'm worried about you, that's why I come home early. But also, shortly before you came, I decided to focus on my career. I signed up for an additional unpaid internship, and this led to more work and therefore a lack of free time. The two things just coincided.'

'And Arnie worries about me and works in two places but finds time to go out.'

'Your cousin has a lot of catching up to do. Let's say I'm coming back from where he's going now.'

'That is, you've had your dose of fun?'

'You could say so.'

Becky nodded. She didn't want to have this conversation, so she got up, tired of the chair.

'Don't leave,' he begged her. 'I want to tell you something else.'

She sat back down and put her hands on her head. 'I see that you are tired, and I won't keep you. I haven't told Arnie yet, but I made the landlord an offer and I'm buying this house.'

Becky gasped in surprise. 'Great. I'm happy for you.'

'I wanted to tell you that this will not change anything. You can stay here as long as you want.'

But Becky was worried. It was another worry for her. She didn't know how Arnie would react to the news, probably the same way. 'I will only stay until I come of age. I don't want to change address before then, so as not to give my mother a reason to send me back to the farm.'

'You can stay as long as you want, Becky. You don't have to leave.'

Becky looked at him and there was sadness in her eyes. 'I'm tired, Alex. Thank you for a wonderful Christmas and for your understanding.'

'Okay. Goodnight.' He watched her struggle up the stairs to the second floor. Her shoulders were tensed, her back arched as if something weighed on her. The conversation had not gone well and had not had the expected result. Alex had imagined that Becky would be happy at this news, he hadn't expected it to make her sad. Something inside her had snapped and knocked her over. Alex got up slowly as well, his lower back aching from driving, and headed for his room. As he passed Becky's room, he heard her crying. He knocked on her door and, without waiting for an answer from her, entered. She was sitting on the bed with her back against the wall and her arms around her knees. Her head was resting on her knees and Alex couldn't see her face. He approached her slowly so as not to startle her and sat on the bed. 'What's wrong with you, Becky?'

She didn't answer. She continued to cry. He reached down and stroked her hair. 'Whatever it is, you can tell me.'

'I'm just tired,' she finally sobbed.

'I know you are stressed and under pressure. Soon it will all be over, and you can rest. You probably won't even need to work,' he interjected.

'How so?'

'The compensation you will receive from the three for rape and attempted murder, if they are found guilty, could exceed two million pounds.'

Becky looked at Alex in shock. She had never thought about compensation, her only goal was to put her abusers in prison.

'Didn't you know that you will be given monetary compensation if you win the case?'

'No, and I don't want their money either,' Becky said.

'I don't know what will happen when your mother finds out about the compensation. If you receive it before you reach the age of majority, the money will go to your parents.'

Becky looked at him once more with surprise in her eyes. Then her shoulders slumped again and her back arched. Alex realized that the information he was giving her tonight, instead of cheering her up, was weighing her down. 'I guess it's better to stop talking and let you calm down and sleep,' he told her.

She didn't say anything, just stayed like that, curled up with her back to the wall. Alex stood up, left the room, and quietly closed the door. Becky stared at the closed door, then without undressing she got into bed and fell asleep almost instantly.

10.

In early March, Inspector Ramsey called Becky. 'We can't find the driver. My boss is pressuring me to give all the evidence to the prosecution and the defence and the trial will begin.'

Becky sighed heavily. She was expecting this news.

'When do you think the process will start?'

'It depends on many things. Alex can inform you in more detail. We'll keep looking for him, Becky. He'll show up one day,' Inspector Ramsey tried to reassure her.

'I know, Inspector. Thank you again for everything.'

'Thanks to Michael and Tanya. They did the hard work.'

'That's right,' Becky agreed and hung up. She had to pull herself together and prepare for the battle in court, which, according to everyone, despite the evidence the prosecution had, would be very tough. According to Alex and the other attorneys assisting the prosecution, Becky had to leave work during the trial so they could prepare her to attend the trial. The police would be providing her with protection. After Becky got home from work, she called Alex to see if he knew the news. He did not answer. Shortly after, Becky's phone rang, an unknown number appeared on the display. Becky picked up and to her surprise she heard her mother's voice. 'Tomorrow, you catch the first train and come home,' she said.

Becky didn't answer. She waited to hear what her mother had to say.

'You didn't think that I would let you testify, do you?'

'We had an agreement,' Becky reminded her.

'It no longer applies,' said her mother. 'You must be at home by noon tomorrow. You understand?'

'No. I'm not going back to the farm.'

'You have no choice.'

'I have. I'll call social services.'

'And I will file a case against your cousin and the lawyer.'

'OK. If you want, hire lawyers, and sue them,' Becky's voice trembled. She had calmed down in the last two months. She went to work, went out with Arnie and Alex. She went to Catherine's shows, her life had become normal. And in just two days, everything collapsed. Now she not only had to mentally prepare herself to see her attackers every day in court, but also, she had to find a way to keep her mother from returning her to the farm. She and Alex had talked about it, and he had told her that he had a plan, but he would only share it with her if he had to.

'We will offer her a deal,' he said after learning about the conversation.

'What deal?'

'Half of the compensation,' he said and waited for her to understand what he said.

'But you said that my parents can take all the compensation if the trial ends before I come of age.'

'The process will start at the beginning of April. Albert's lawyer asked that we schedule it for then. These procedures take at least three months and, as yours will cover the Easter holidays as well as a few bank holidays, we all think it will be finished after your birthday.' Alex smiled as if it was all over. 'I'm sure your mother will investigate. It is unlikely that anyone from the defence will offer her all this money.'

'She will certainly agree. But what will we do if at some point she reneges?'

'I'll make her sign an agreement.'

'I don't know, Alex, I don't trust her. But we can try.'

Becky called her mom and let Alex talk to her. They argued for a few minutes, and finally her mother agreed to the terms Alex set for her and promised to sign an agreement.

'I would not like to meet your mother in person,' said Alex after finishing the conversation.

'Yes, she would sell me to whoever gave her the best price.'

Alex agreed with Becky. He hoped he was right, and the trial would be over after Becky's birthday.

At the beginning of April, everyone gathered in court. Becky quit her job and promised to appear in court every day. Alex took charge, backed by two lawyers, both of them were his good colleagues and friends. One was named Stan and his other assistant was a woman named Sandra. Sandra apparently had feelings for Alex. She looked at him lovingly and fulfilled his every whim. Becky hadn't seen Alex in a work environment before, but she wasn't surprised by his professionalism and the respect his colleagues had for him. She had seen how hard he worked on the cases he took on, but her case was the biggest of his career. The fact that the two were close was no secret to anyone, and his colleagues had warned him that this could at some point strain him emotionally and lead to problems.

However, Alex did not believe that the defendants would surprise him in any way. The three of them had participated in this gruesome rape and inflicted severe wounds on Becky, which he had already seen when she was wearing a t-shirt and shorts. He did not believe that anything could shock or surprise him in the process.

Becky, on the other hand, was having a hard time. The mere presence of the three accused made her nervous and worried. To calm herself down, she took sedatives, but that didn't always help. She had the hardest time giving evidence. She had to repeat what happened down to the smallest detail. And when the defendants' lawyer suggested that the skirt, she was wearing was too short, Becky broke down in tears. It wasn't her who decided the school uniform, and it wasn't her who bought and shortened the skirt, her mother did it, but she couldn't say that in court. All the time she was in court, the three accused men glared at her. For Becky, this was all very humiliating. The only thing that comforted her was Alex's close presence, as well as Arnie's presence on the days he could be there.

The trial was briefly interrupted for Easter. However, the four days off were not enough for Becky. The tension in the courtroom had taken its toll on her, and, towards the end of April, at one of the defendants' hearings, she collapsed and was taken to hospital. It took her a week to recover. When she got home, there was a bag of greeting cards and a small package waiting for her. Her case and the development of the trial were followed by some of the media and Becky was surprised to find that many people supported her. The people who sent her the greeting cards wished her courage. When she opened the package, however, she found the same socks she had worn on the day of the attack. The socks were new. The package was not delivered by a courier, it was found by Arnie outside the door. The message of the socks was clear. They wanted Becky to keep quiet.

'The fact that you passed out in court gave them a sign that you are mentally weak,' said Alex. 'They are trying to scare you, but now for you it is very important not to pay attention to them. Don't give in to the threat and keep coming to the courtroom.'

Becky looked at the socks and said nothing. The shipment had reached its destination. Her hands trembled and her lower lip too.

'Becky, if you surrender now, you'll let them get away. I know you, you're stronger than any woman I've ever met.'

She looked at him. His words calmed her somewhat and yet the sight of the socks bothered her.

Alex could sense her fear. He closed the box and moved it as far away as possible.

'Let's go for a walk,' he told her and asked one of the policemen at the door to accompany them.

Alex headed towards the park where she had walked when she first arrived in London.

'Do you remember our first meeting?' he asked her.

'I won't forget it for the rest of my life,' answered Becky.

'These people had brought you to this state. You couldn't even go to the park without our help. I want you to remember this, the efforts that not only you, but all of us have made for your recovery.'

'That's right,' Becky said, and understood why he had brought her here. She had to make an effort and return to court. She had drawn not only Arnie into this, but also Alex, Paul, Catherine, Michael, Tanya, and, to some extent, Alex's family. It would be a shame to give up now. Becky and Alex walked in the park for about an hour, accompanied by a policeman. She mustered up more and more courage every minute, and at the end of the walk she came home, eager to continue the fight in court. Her birthday was less than three weeks away. Becky couldn't wait to get her hands on that freedom, too.

With new strength and incentive, she appeared in the courtroom and looked at the accused with determination. Her demeanour was clear, she would not surrender.

One week before her birthday, her mother broke the agreement and called her home urgently on the pretext that her father was seriously ill. The week that Becky would be away was very important to the prosecution. The last defendant was to be questioned and two of the most important experts were to be called. Alex and Becky tried their best to reconcile with her mother again, but their attempts were in vain.

One sunny day, Becky was taken by a policeman in Cornwall to her parents' farm. Her mother locked her in one of the rooms and left her there for seven days. She said it was for her protection. Nobody visited Becky at that time and her phone was taken. Becky's sister, Summer, came one afternoon and opened the door to the room. Becky was glad to see her, all grown up and beautiful. She wanted to hug her and to talk like they had before, but Summer came closer and, instead of greeting her sister, she loudly spat at her. Then she glared at Becky, left the room, and locked the door. Becky was shocked. She didn't know what had triggered Summer's behaviour. Her mother had probably manipulated her, but Becky forgave her sister. She promised herself that one day a way would be found, and she would reconcile with her.

Her sister's actions made Becky's stay at the farm even more difficult. The days passed slowly and monotonously. Becky watched the sea from the window, watched each sunrise and each sunset, and told herself that each sunset meant a day had passed. She could hear the cows mooing and the horses whistling. Sometimes her cat named Blue would come to the door and lay there for hours. Becky found that she missed the farm animals. She had started working on the farm since when was very young and became attached to each new animal. Every calf became her friend, every dog followed her, and cats loved to lie on her lap. The love of animals was boundless, it was not like that of humans. Becky remembered how when she was little, she made friends with a little goose. When the goose grew up it followed her everywhere and, if it felt someone was threatening Becky, would spread its wings and chase whoever it was to peck at them. Becky felt protected then, protected by the wings of that bird. Until her mother got tired of the goose pecking her and slaughtered it in front of Becky. One of Becky's worst days as a child. After that, she never showed her mother that she was attached to any animal. Carla was a cruel woman, and Becky's father was a weak man. Now her sister had turned against her as well. Everyone seemed to hate her, and Becky couldn't understand why. After everything she'd been through, her family should have supported her and her sister should have sympathized with her, but instead she behaved with only malice and hatred so strong it didn't even need to be spoken out loud. Becky watched the ocean every day, watched the clouds in the sky and dreamed of the day she would be free.

When the seven days were finally up, Alex and Arnie personally came to get her. Her mother wasn't at the farm, only her father was around. Alex approached him and ordered him to bring his daughter. Her father nodded, gave Arnie a guilty look, and led Becky out of the room. She ran to the two young men, gave them a quick hug, and headed for the car.

'Get me out of this place,' she begged and sat in the back seat without looking at her father and sister who were looming from the back of the farmhouse. Alex handed two pieces of paper to her father, explained something to him, then got into the back seat next to Becky and Arnie drove the car. It was Sunday, Becky's birthday. Her coming-of-age day and she laughed happily just thinking that her mother no longer owned her. She hugged Alex tightly, then leaned forward and kissed her cousin on the cheek.

'I'm glad you're okay,' laughed Alex, infected by her mood.

'What did aunty do to you?' Arnie asked her, also smiling.

'She locked me in one of the rooms on the second floor. She brought me food twice a day and scolded me that I didn't deserve that either.'

'You were a prisoner, right?' Alex asked her. His smile was gone.

'You could say so. They took my phone and clothes and locked me in the room.'

'What kind of parents do this?' Alex asked in amazement.

'Ours,' answered Arnie and Becky at the same time.

Alex knew very well that some parents raised their children this way, but he had never thought that he would ever meet them in person.

'What happened in court while I was gone?' Becky asked.

'Almost nothing. Albert fell ill and his testimony was postponed until this week.'

The road they travelled to London ran alongside the ocean. The three stopped talking, enthralled by the beautiful sight.

'It's beautiful,' said Alex.

'That's right. Now I miss the bus trip along the coast,' admitted Becky. Then she remembered the driver, David, and asked Alex to call Inspector Ramsey.

'We talked to the driver,' she said when Becky asked if they had questioned him. 'He didn't see anything. He was berating himself for not waiting longer at the bus stop.'

'I was far away and there was no way he could see what was happening to me. But he passes this road at least six times a day, he might have seen the car before. David has a photographic memory. He remembers every car and even every driver he passed during the day.'

'I'll look for him again. He may recognize the driver or have seen him somewhere else.'

'Yes, that's exactly why I called you. He knows almost everyone in the area. He doesn't read newspaper and doesn't watch the news. He kept saying that his passengers told him all the news and he didn't need to read newspapers and watch TV. He probably didn't see the description of my rapists but if he saw them somewhere he would remember them.'

'Okay, I'll look for him. I will now send a police car to escort you. Alex and Arnie probably didn't tell you, but a package arrived for you at the courthouse yesterday.' Inspector Ramsey was silent for a moment. 'In the package there was a specially made picture. It was ordered from one of those online shops that make personal gifts. The account from which the picture was ordered is fake.'

'What is the picture?' Becky asked under her breath.

'A photo of the place where you were raped. There is also an inscription:

'Dear Becky,
There should be balance in the life.
Eye for eye,
Tooth for tooth
A friend for a friend.'

After hearing the message, Becky's breath stopped. It was a threat.

'Becky?' Inspector Ramsey called. 'I assume the threat is to your friends. Therefore, while the case lasts, everyone will be under police protection. Ask Alex to send the names and addresses of anyone you think is under threat.'

Becky didn't answer. She was terrified of the possibility of someone getting hurt because of her.

'Becky?' Inspector Ramsey called her again.

'Yes, we will send you a list. Alex is with me, and we will send it to you as soon as possible. I still don't have a phone, my mom got mine. I will text you as soon as I buy a new one.'

'Okay. Be careful while driving. A police car will be waiting for you at Truro.'

'Great. We'll call you from London,' Becky said and hung up. Her desire to celebrate was gone.

'They probably won't hurt anyone,' Arnie said. 'They just want to scare you.'

'I don't think so,' Alex disagreed. 'These people act exactly like that, they hit, intimidate, and bribe. I advise you to take the threat seriously, Arnie. Don't go anywhere without police protection until the court case is over.'

Arnie looked at Becky in the rear-view mirror and nodded at her. He didn't want her to worry about him and he would do what he had to do. His schedule was the same every day anyway. He hadn't been out with friends since the trial had started. Like Alex he would go home and wait for news from the day before.

Becky looked out the window but saw nothing. Fears clouded her vision. She couldn't wait for this nightmare to be over and for everything to go back to normal. However, her intuition suggested trouble. She felt Alex's hand on her shoulder. He was trying to calm her down, smiled and softly sang *Happy birthday to you*. Arnie sang too, and the mood of the three in the car quickly improved. After they passed Truro, a black car approached them. It was the undercover police car. Becky calmed down, sat back in the back seat, and smiled. Her life would not be the same from today, she told herself.

When they arrived at the house, Paul, Catherine, Michael, and Tanya were waiting for them. They had ordered a big, beautiful cake with the number eighteen in the middle. There were flowers all over the house, as well as balloons and greeting cards from the entire trial team and the investigative team in Cornwall. When Becky saw this, her face lit up. She hadn't expected a party, only phone calls and congratulations, but the birthday party and all the decorations surprised her. There was even a beautiful satin ribbon hanging on the front door that said *Happy Birthday*.

Becky and her friends quickly forgot about the threat sent, poured champagne, and toasted the birthday girl. After the emotions died down, Becky ate a piece of cake and watched her friends. Alex and Michael were discussing something animatedly, and Paul, Catherine and Tanya were telling each other interesting stories. They were so engrossed in conversation, smiling, with a glass of beer or wine in hand. Two years ago, Becky never imagined that she would be celebrating with them. And watching them now, looking at the unopened gift packages and the holiday cake, she felt grateful to have met them. Without them, her world would be dark and narrow.

'What are you thinking about?' her cousin pushed her.

'I can't believe I have so many friends. And all this is thanks to you, for sheltering me and helping me. Thank you, Arnie!'

'You are very welcome,' he smiled and raised a toast.

The party went on until almost midnight. It was so good that Becky officially put it down as the best thing that had ever happened to her. When she finally went to bed, she fell asleep with a happy smile and a blush on her cheeks.

11.

Two days after her birthday, Becky was back in the courtroom. According to Alex, the process was coming to an end and wouldn't last much longer. Becky watched Albert's interrogation and her body trembled as he looked at her. Alex leaned over her from time to time and spoke soothingly to her. For the first time since the trial began, he failed to calm her down. Becky was sitting on her trembling hands so that those present could not see her worry, her mouth was also visibly trembling, and the defendant laughed heartily when he noticed this. After nearly two hours of testimony, the questions ended and he was asked to step aside. Before he did, however, he looked at Becky, leaned into the microphone and spoke.

'A friend for a friend.'

There was a commotion in the courtroom. Becky got up and walked towards him, intending to slap him, but Alex and a policeman managed to stop her. The fury in her eyes pierced the criminal, but he seemed to like it. Before leaving the room, he flashed a cheeky smile and glared at Becky and her lawyer. The threat was vague but felt by everyone in the hall. Alex also shuddered at this look and in turn went after the defendant, but the bailiff stopped him. Alex turned, grabbed Becky by the elbow and quickly led her out of the hall. The two entered one of the offices, and a policeman stood in front of the door to guard them.

'Did you hear it?' said Becky. 'He threatened me, he threatened my friends.'

'I heard it,' Alex confirmed and forced her to sit on the sofa. 'Now calm down. Nothing bad will happen to anyone. The police and inspectors also heard and saw it. They'll probably beef up security.'

Becky was crying and looking helpless. Alex sat down next to her and put his arm around her shoulders. She leaned against his chest and cried even harder. He himself was not feeling better. He wanted to go out and beat the bastard up. Instead, however, he stayed with her until Inspector Ramsey entered the room.

'Scoundrel.' She was also angry. 'How dare he make a threat like that in court.'

'He's impudent and unscrupulous,' Alex said and gestured for Ramsey to take care of Becky. He had to go out and call Arnie. Things had started to get out of control, and everyone had to be very careful.

The next few days were agonizing for everyone. The process was coming to an end. All the evidence was given, but on the last day one member of the jury didn't appear. A few hours later, he was found beaten near a bus stop. No one knew whether he was attacked because of the trial or for other reasons. The jury was scared, and no one was sure how this trial would end.

Alex thought he had prepared for everything, but the events happening with each passing day wore him down. On the day of the verdict, he was already at the end of his strength. And though he stood upright and steady in the sight of all, inwardly he trembled. Becky was watching him, and she couldn't help but notice the tension radiating from him. She looked at him once more, this time not from the position of a friend, but of a bystander. Alex was handsome, his dark, close-cropped hair slightly tousled, which was not typical of him. However, his suit was impeccable and highlighted his well-trained body. His hands were shaking ever so slightly, but he quickly pocketed them when he felt her gaze. Becky also couldn't help but notice the adoring glances his colleague was giving him, along with several of the women in the hall. However, he didn't notice these looks, but looked at the jury intently and tried to understand their demeanour. No one expected a quick decision from the jury, but they returned after only half an hour of deliberations.

Becky was shaking with tension, her life depended on these people. She was looking intently at them, but they were all looking down. This process wasn't easy for them either, Becky thought. Then she looked around. Everyone in the courtroom was silent, waiting for the defendants to be brought. The reporters had their pens poised, and the relatives of the accused looked forward with hope. A few minutes later the verdicts were announced. Three sentences of forty years in prison for each of the defendants and compensation in the amount of three and a half million pounds. Vincent Geer and George Bell had to pay a million each, and Albert Levy, who had stabbed Becky first, had to pay a one and a half million pounds. Becky gasped when she heard the verdict. She didn't expect such a good result. She expected someone on the jury to be bribed and for the sentences to be lower. Alex grabbed her and lifted her into the air, excited by what he had just heard. Reporters took advantage of his reaction, and just a few minutes later several stories appeared on the internet with sensational headlines about the trial victory. Alex and Becky's victory became the number one news story for several days. Everyone rejoiced in the success and forgot the public threat made by Albert in the courtroom.

Becky and Alex indulged in a well-deserved rest and, together with Arnie, went to a hotel near the sea for four days. Two policemen still accompanied them, but in time the three got used to their presence and didn't seem to notice them. Becky, Arnie, and Alex were staying at a spa hotel that offered discretion and good service to its guests. The music, water and other therapies had such a relaxing effect on them that they decided to extend their vacation by two more days. It was as if they had entered heaven. Arnie immediately found himself some female company for the evening, but Alex didn't take advantage of the opportunity and decided to stay with Becky. The two of them lay on the sunbeds for hours, reading books and discussing the future. Becky, surprised by the large amount of money she would receive, explored her educational and business options. For some reason, remembering the goose with which she was friend as a child, as well as all the farm animals with which she had become close, an idea formed in her head to start a small business with food for all kinds of animals, not only cats, dogs, and birds but for reptiles, fish, and anything that people with pets needed. Alex and Arnie encouraged her to put her money into something, not just keep it in the bank. Her cousin promised to help her with the financial operations and teach her how to work with her money online, and Alex promised to help her with the legal side of the business. Becky wanted to finish school and then go to college or take a small business management course. Her dreams grew bigger and bigger, and she forgot about everything else. She was just sitting on the lounger near the pool, lazing around and discussing the future with Arnie and Alex.

A call from Inspector Ramsey quickly brought her back to reality. The driver, David, had recognized her fourth assailant. The man's name was Russell Taylor, and he was the son of a wealthy businessman who owned a fishing company. The family had a house in Cornwall, but they rarely went there. They also had a house in the south of France, where Russell lived most of the time. David knew Russell's father, they both shared a hobby—golf—and since there were only two golf clubs in the area, the two often saw each other, especially on weekends. David's son also lived in France, so David knew Russell well.

The news about finding the driver pleased Becky, but at the same time made her realize that these few days at the spa hotel would be her last vacation for a long time. A manhunt for Russell began. According to immigration authorities, he had arrived in Britain a few days before the trial, but police were unable to find him at any of the addresses they knew he usually stayed at.

Alex was also happy with the news, but he, like Becky, thought he would have a chance to take some time off from the strain they had been under for the past few months. He had planned to visit his father's house for a few days, but after hearing the news he immediately cancelled. If the police were looking for Russell, his father, who was undoubtedly influential, would find out and try to cover it up. Also, Alex's intuition told him that the money had come from this family, and they had most likely forced Becky's mother to take her in for a week. They were dealing with rich and powerful people and the battle with them would be very tough. Alex had asked Michael to investigate Albert further. There was something cocky about the man's demeanour at the trial, as if he knew something Becky and Alex didn't, and was snickering in their faces. Albert himself was very shocked when he heard his sentence. He had obviously expected the events to develop differently and was looking at someone in the hall with an angry look. It was this someone who Alex wanted to identify. Michael had called him to say he smelled some clues, but he couldn't give him anything specific yet because the police were hot on his heels as well as Tanya's, Paul's, and Catherine's. It prevented him from doing his job, complained the detective. Whatever he found, Michael wouldn't tell Alex until they got back to London.

Inspector Ramsey sent a picture of Russell and Becky recognized him. With that, everyone's vacation was over. Becky, Arnie, and Alex left the hotel, loaded their luggage into a car and returned home. Becky hadn't yet discussed moving out from Alex's house. She continued to pay him rent and share the bills, but it wasn't the same for her. She felt like she was intruding on his privacy and had decided to rent or buy a house for herself and Arnie to move into. For now, however, the police told them that it would be safer for the three of them to stay together at this address. While the search for Russell continued, Becky focused on online business courses and training. Alex also stayed home, filling out paperwork online and talking to prospective clients. Only Arnie went back to work in the office of the company he worked for. He was accompanied by an undercover policeman who followed him at a distance and tried not to attract attention. Everything seemed to be back to normal. Becky even planned to start going out to the park more often and to go to one of Catherine's shows in central London. That never managed to happen. Five days after they got home from the spa hotel, Arnie disappeared. He had gone to work in the morning, talked to clients all day, and by six o'clock in the evening they had lost track of him. Alex and Becky waited for him for dinner until half past eight, then they started calling him every five minutes, then they called everyone he might have gone to, and at ten in the evening, they finally called the police. The policeman who was supposed to accompany him had also disappeared. They found him a few hours later drugged up outside a bar. But there was still no sign of Arnie.

Alex and Becky sat in the house and didn't know what to do. All night they went around the rooms and the garden, talking to Michael and Tanya in an attempt to find some information about where and when her cousin disappeared, but until the morning no one knew anything.

'It's all because of me, Alex. I had to stop him, ask him to leave.'

'It's not your fault. The cops should have kept him safe,' said Alex with anger.

The two waited and dark thoughts ran through their minds.

Finally, at eleven o'clock in the morning, Inspector Ramsey came to speak to them.

'Did you find him? Where is he?' Becky asked when she saw her at the door.

'We don't know, Becky. We have no idea where Arnie is,' said the woman and sat down tiredly on the sofa. There were dark circles under her eyes, clearly, she hadn't slept all night either.

'The policeman said Arnie left work half an hour early. He told him that he had a meeting and when they walked down the street someone attacked them.'

'Who attacked them?' Alex asked.

'We don't know. They drugged the policeman before he saw anyone.'

'On the street, in broad daylight?' Becky almost shouted.

'Yes, in one of the alleys near Arnie's office.'

'And no one saw anything?'

'No, unfortunately everything happened in a blind spot.'

'*A friend for a friend*,' Becky whispered desperately.

'Everyone's looking for Arnie, Becky. We're also looking for Russell.'

Becky went out into the garden. She was so worried about Arnie, she couldn't breathe. It was all her fault, she continued to reproach herself.

'If you don't find him, she won't be able to survive,' Alex said while watching Becky walking in the garden. 'Nor will I,' he added.

'It's hard for all of us, Alex. It's not like we didn't expect them to try to kidnap one of you. I spoke to the French authorities yesterday. Russell is very well known for his crimes there, but his father still manages to get him out. The problem is, he's also very smart and usually manages to frame someone else.'

Alex listened to her and continued to watch Becky.

'I hope you find both of them soon. If I hadn't been afraid to leave her alone, I would have gone in the car myself and looked for him.'

'And putt yourself in danger,' said Ramsey, got up and headed for the front door. 'I will keep you posted.'

Alex nodded but didn't send her away. Instead, he went out into the garden and sat on the bench, pulling Becky close to him. She had picked up her phone and kept calling her cousin. However, the call only went to voicemail. Tears of helplessness flowed from her eyes, there were tears in Alex's eyes as well. The two huddled together, oblivious to the cold wind that blew and the rain that fell. Alex was the one who pulled away from her, shook off the rainwater running down them, and pushed Becky into the warm house. He made her change, made a tea, and waited for news with her. In the late afternoon, Michael and Tanya joined them. The two looked just as exhausted as Alex and Becky.

'I called everyone I know, all the policemen with whom I have even a small relationship. They're looking for Arnie, Becky. But at the moment there is no information about who kidnapped him and where he is now.'

'My father is also looking for him with his colleagues,' said Alex. According to Ben, if they didn't find a lead in the first twenty-four hours, the chance of finding Arnie was slim to none.

Becky just listened, not saying a word. Somehow, she knew in her heart that Arnie wasn't coming back. She couldn't explain this feeling, it was as if he was no longer alive and telling her this. Therefore, when she listened to her friends talking, she didn't join in on the conversations and remained silent. It was all her fault. She should have left and stayed away after the first month and not interfered with anyone's destiny. But she didn't, and now her cousin was gone.

'They will find him, Becky,' Tanya tried to calm her down.

'Yes, they will find him,' she agreed 'but they will find him dead.'

Her friends looked at her, surprised by the firm tone in which she had said this. Tears no longer dripped from her eyes. They were the eyes of a suffering girl drowning in her grief.

Alex hugged her again and tried to calm her down, but he himself was already exhausted from the emotions that flooded him. So finally, he just whispered to Becky that she better go to bed and helped her up the stairs to her room. Then, worried that something bad might happen to her, he took a sleeping bag and laid down in her room floor next to her bed. Michael and Tanya remained asleep on the sofa, unable to leave their friends alone on a night like this. There were also policemen left in Paul and Catherine's house. Inspector Ramsey didn't want to risk another one disappearing without a trace.

Alex woke up first in the morning. At first, he didn't know where he was, but after seeing Becky sleeping on the bed, he remembered the night before and immediately looked for his phone. He hoped there was a message that they had found Arnie, but the display only showed a few work emails and bank messages. Becky woke up feeling someone's presence in the room and was just about to scream when she recognized him.

'I couldn't leave you alone,' he explained to her, and she nodded in understanding. He got up and changed in his room. She recovered quickly as well. She looked at her phone, but there was nothing on hers either. They hadn't found Arnie that night. Alex and Becky crept quietly past Michael and Tanya, who were sleeping in each other's arms in the living room and shut themselves in the kitchen. While Alex made coffee, Becky dialled Inspector Ramsey's phone. The conversation was transferred to voicemail, apparently the inspector had finally fallen asleep as well.

'They didn't find him, did they?' Becky asked, but already knew the answer. Alex looked at her sadly, handed her a cup of warm coffee and sat down next to her. He opened the laptop and looked for information about the search for her cousin, but there was none.

'No news is sometimes good news,' Alex said, trying to calm himself down.

'I feel like he is not alive, Alex. Whatever happened, my heart says he's gone.'

'Your intuition can lie to you,' he said and pulled her to him. He felt even closer to her in his grief. He didn't want her to be far away from him at this point. They both needed each other.

There was a commotion in the other room. Michael and Tanya had woken up and Alex set about making coffee for them too. Then he heard Michael talking on the phone and looked towards the door, hoping that he had good news. However, Michael came in followed by Tanya and said nothing. Obviously, the news wasn't good, Alex resigned himself and concentrated on pouring the coffee into cups.

The two private investigators stayed with Alex and Becky for most of the day. In the late afternoon they left accompanied by several policemen. There was still no news about Arnie. After the detectives left, Becky went into the garden again. This time the weather was nice, she sat down on the bench, called Alex over and stared at the flowers. A kind of peace came over her that she had never felt in her life. She couldn't explain this feeling. Alex was sitting next to her, putting a hand on her shoulder, and also watching the flowers, but, unlike her, his gaze was intense. It was the first time Becky had seen him with a full beard, his hair was also a mess. The man who didn't give up on her and defended her even in front of his father had turned into a wreck in just two days. Becky moved his hand away from her and made him lie in her lap. At first, he was surprised, then he listened, dropped his head, and closed his eyes. She massaged his forehead and head until he drifted off and finally fell asleep. Becky thought that if Arnie didn't come back Alex was all she had left and she had to start taking care of him the way he took care of her.

The nap was a relief to Alex. It was as if he had been asleep for hours, but in fact he had only drifted off for a few minutes. It was getting cold outside, so the two moved inside, each with their phone in hand, waiting for a call. Late in the evening, Becky spoke to Inspector Ramsey again, Alex also spoke to Michael and

Ben, but there was no news of Arnie. The two stood in the quiet house, occasionally glancing at one of Arnie's belongings and hoping he would return. Alex even imagined him standing at the door, but the young man didn't come home that night either. Shortly after midnight Becky retired to her room, minutes later Alex followed her with his sleeping bag. Becky could hear his restless breathing for a while, then fell asleep.

The next morning, she woke up first. It was light outside and, according to the clock on her phone, it was not yet six in the morning. She didn't want to wake Alex, so she stayed in bed. She watched him sleep and told herself that there was no better friend in the world than him. She wished she had met him under different circumstances. If only she had come to visit Arnie without the heavy burden she came with. Then her thoughts drifted back to her cousin. She felt his absence and his presence somehow at the same time. She looked at her phone again, hoping someone would call her and tell her everything was okay. However, her phone's display was clear, only the date and time showing. Alex turned and apparently the light woke him up. He looked around confused then met her gaze. She just shook her head as if there was no news. He sighed heavily and rested his head on the small pillow he had brought along with the sleeping bag. He looked even more tired than the day before. Becky stood up and stepped close to him.

'Don't get up,' she begged him. 'You look very tired. Get some more sleep if you can. I'll be in the kitchen making coffee.'

He tried to protest and get up, but everything hurt from sleeping on the ground and he really felt tired.

'Lie on my bed if you want,' she offered and after Becky came out, he moved there.

Her sheets were still warm and smelled of her. He stayed awake for a minute, then drifted off again and fell asleep.

Becky went into the kitchen and immediately dialled Inspector Ramsey's phone.

'I don't have any news yet,' said the inspector tiredly.

'How is it possible for two days no one has found anything?' Becky was surprised. There was no reproach in her question. She was convinced that the police were doing everything they could to find her cousin.

'We're looking for him, Becky. We're also looking for Russell. We are doing everything possible.'

'I know,' Becky sobbed. 'I just want to know. Dead or alive, I want to know where he is and who kidnapped him.'

'I understand,' Inspector Ramsey said sympathetically. 'I'll call you as soon as I have news. You try to calm down. Also take care of Alex, the policeman who was with you yesterday is very worried about him. He said Alex don't look well.'

'Yes, he is exhausted. I let him sleep and rest.'

'I guess he's still afraid to leave you and sleeps on the floor,' Ramsey asked.

'Yes, that's right. How do you know about it?'

'Tanya told me. She went into your room the other night to see if you were okay and saw him sleeping in a sleeping bag.'

'I made him move to the bed,' Becky said and realized that Inspector Ramsey was right, she had to take care of him. He was also devastated by Arnie's kidnapping.

'I have to go, Becky. I'll call you if there's any news.'

'Okay,' Becky said and hung up. Then she went up to the second floor to see how Alex was doing, but after hearing his light snoring, she decided not to enter the room and returned to the kitchen. She picked up her phone and did what he had done yesterday, searched for news about her cousin's disappearance. The media had somehow picked up on the news and were speculating. One of them had taken a picture of Alex and Becky in the garden. Both looked distressed in the photo. Becky couldn't recognize herself, she looked so exhausted, and so did Alex. She searched for more information but found nothing more. The tension was starting to get to her again, so she decided to turn her attention elsewhere and looked for information on Russell's father. Judging by the photo he had at the company he ran, Kurt Taylor was Alex's father's age. He had founded the company when he was twenty-eight years old, and it was now one of the largest fishing companies in the country with subsidiaries in France and Portugal. Russell looked a lot like his father. There was no information on the internet about his mother or the presence of other family members. By all appearances, the father was as dangerous as the son. Former workers mentioned threats and traumas they suffered while working for him. Becky tried to find more information, but if there was anything, she didn't have the skills to find it.

'Good morning,' Alex's voice startled her. 'Is there any news?'

'No, no sign of Arnie or Russell.'

Alex sighed. He had hoped they would find Arnie.

'What were you reading?'

'I looked up information about Russell's father. The son has taken the character of the father.'

'Yes, Michael told me that the father is unscrupulous.'

'Do you think he's involved too?'

'Most likely. Inspector Ramsey is working on that lead as well.'

Alex poured himself some coffee and sat back tiredly in the chair next to her. He looked over at Becky, she was staring at the laptop screen. There were dark circles under her eyes, her lips pursed but her gaze lively. She no longer had the despair he had seen in the past few days. Something had changed.

'How are you?' he asked her.

'I'm fine,' she said. Then she looked at him and the desperation clouded her face again. She was about to say something, but her phone rang, and they both jumped in surprise at the sound.

'We found Arnie,' Inspector Ramsey said. Her voice was dry, and she seemed to speak with difficulty.

'Where is he?' Becky asked with hope in her eyes.

'In Cornwall. They found him dead on the same place where you were raped.'

Becky and Alex stared at the phone as if they couldn't make sense of what they heard.

'How?' Alex asked with desperation in his voice.

'He was killed with a knife. There are many injuries, but according to the pathologist, he died from the first wound.'

Tears welled up in Becky's eyes. Inspector Ramsey heard her sobs and hung up the phone. She should have let Alex and Becky deal with their emotions on their own. Alex was numb, unable to move from his chair. The news of his dead friend had shocked him to such an extent that his mind couldn't accept it. Becky, on the other hand, was crying, her arms around her knees and her head bowed helplessly. Then, seeing Alex motionless, she approached him and took his hand.

He looked up, his eyes weren't teary, but they were very dark, and, looking into

them, Becky saw a deep, genuine sadness. It was as if a storm had entered his

gaze. Rage, weakness, and fatigue. All these things rolled into one. Becky

caressed his cheek, pulled him by one arm, and led them into the living room.

Then she called Paul and Michael to tell them the bad news. Finally, she called

Ben and asked him to come over. Becky understood that Alex's condition after

hearing the bad news was not normal. He seemed to shut down and didn't speak

for the next few hours. He just stared angrily ahead without even moving. Becky

tried to get him to look at her, made him tea, tried a massage, but her best friend

was consumed with rage. Becky was also in shock, grieving for her cousin and

worried about Alex. She didn't know what to do, so she called Paul for help.

'Something's wrong, Paul. Please come and talk to him. Ben will come, but

it will take time. I don't know what to do,' Becky cried on the phone.

A few minutes later, distraught over the death of his friend, Paul arrived at

the house. When he saw Alex, he knew why Becky was worried. The person

sitting on the couch was shocked. The tension had taken a toll on him. Then he

saw his look, obsessional and angry at the same time.

Paul called a colleague who examined Alex and recommended that they take

him to hospital and do a few more tests. For Becky, it was the worst day of her

life. Paul accompanied Alex and Becky stayed home. Left alone in the big house,

she curled up on the sofa and continued to cry. That's how Catherine found her.

As if she hasn't suffered enough already, the young woman thought. Becky

noticed her friend and sobbed even louder, unable to even speak. Catherine made

her some tea and stayed with Becky until she fell asleep. Her breathing was restless as she slept, and it was obvious to Catherine that Becky was having a nightmare. She was waving her hands and crying in her sleep. She even tried to get up. The shock of what was happening in her life had carried over into her sleep.

Becky woke up a few hours later. Her head ached and her temples throbbed. Alex was sitting next to her on a chair, and voices were also coming from the kitchen.

'Are you okay?' he asked her. His eyes were tired, but they were already his eyes, with his concerned look.

'I am fine. How are you?'

'Better. Are you hungry?'

'Yeah,' Becky said, realizing she hadn't eaten in days. Then she remembered Arnie. 'He's gone, Alex.'

'Yes, he's gone. Your hunch turned out to be right.'

'How so?'

'Arnie was killed the day he disappeared.'

Becky's eyes watered again. Alex sat down next to her too, his eyes wet with tears.

'It's better to cry, that's what the doctors said.'

Becky nodded. She slumped against his chest and moaned softly. He kissed her hair, his tears falling on her. They stayed like that until Tanya entered the room. She sat down in the chair in front of them and expressed her condolences. Then Michael appeared.

'They found Russell. He was speeding on a road in Devon and the police stopped him without knowing it was him. The car he was driving was stolen.'

Becky thought this news would make her feel better, but instead she closed her eyes tiredly. Alex, however, perked up. That's who he could direct his anger at.

'Where is he now?'

'They're bringing him here, to London,' Michael said. Then the door opened, and Ben walked in worriedly. Alex looked at him in surprise.

'Becky called me. She told me to come because you are not well.'

Alex nodded and motioned to one of the vacant chairs for his father to sit down.

'I was hospitalized for a few hours, but I'm fine now.'

'And how is she?' Ben pointed to Becky.

'Paul will give her something to come down and she'll be fine,' Tanya said.

'They found Russell,' Alex informed his father.

'I want an hour alone with him,' Ben said angrily, and Becky could see now the similarity in the two men's personalities.

'They are bringing him to London. They'll probably want Becky to go tomorrow and identify him,' Michael said.

'Why don't they wait? Look at her, she can barely stand on her feet,' Alex looked at Becky worriedly. But she stood up and shook her head.

'Nothing will stop me from going and looking at that wretch in the face,' she said firmly. Then she turned to Michael, 'Is he... you know?'

'It is possible, but there is no evidence for this yet. Forensics will inspect the car.'

Becky nodded and looked at Alex. His look was again dazed, and his reactions slowed.

'It's from the medicine,' Tanya said, following her gaze.

'You should take your pills too and both of you try to sleep.'

'I'll eat something first. I haven't eaten in a few days, and neither has Alex.'

Tanya ordered pizza for everyone, helped Ben settle into Alex's room, then she and Michael left.

'I'll sleep in your room,' Ben said to Alex. 'And where will you sleep?'

'In Becky's room, I have a sleeping bag there,' he mumbled tiredly, drugged. Then he went up to the second floor and immediately fell asleep. Becky and Ben followed. The shock of the past day had broken them, they needed to gather strength for the next day, which was also expected to be hard.

Ben walked into his son's room. The troubles he had been worried about were now a fact. He had tried to warn Alex, but his feelings for this woman were clearly strong and he wasn't going to leave her now for anything in the world. Of course, Alex denied having feelings for her, justifying himself with his desire to help her, with his regret for what happened to her, but Ben knew his son well. Even if he didn't admit it, Alex loved Becky very much. What she felt, however, was another matter. There was no doubt that she was strongly attached to him, but whether her feelings ran deeper was hard to tell. Ben stared at the picture in the corner – Becky, Arnie, Alex, and Paul all in the eye of the lens. One of them was gone, Ben thought, hoping Alex or someone else wouldn't follow him. The people they dealt with were dangerous and would stop at nothing, even kidnapping in broad daylight and murder. Ben felt a pain in his heart, the tension of the day had worn him out. He sat heavily on the bed, stared at the ceiling, and thought about what was going on in his son's life. Ben wished his wife was alive, but she wasn't, and on days like this he missed her more than ever.

12.

Becky woke up first the next day. She jumped over Alex's sleeping bag and left the room quietly. Then, for the first time in days, she felt like taking a bath. She needed to wash away all the external and internal filth from herself. She put more scented oils in the bath than usual and stayed in it for almost an hour. After coming out she felt refreshed. When she got back to her room Alex had woken up. He watched her without saying a word as she took things from her wardrobe. Then he stood up, approached her, and slowly kissed her. Becky was surprised at first, then relaxed into his embrace. She didn't know what had triggered Alex to kiss her, but she liked it. He stayed like that, staring at her. Then he backed away slowly and took a step back.

'Sorry,' he said. 'I don't know what's wrong with me.'

'It's fine,' she reassured him. He nodded and left the room with his head down.

Becky was riven with emotion at the time. She had always looked upon Alex as an older brother, but now she was surprised to find that he didn't look upon her as a younger sister. Not now, not after this morning. And she didn't know what to do and how to react. She liked the kiss, but how was this going to last, she wondered. The ringing of her phone interrupted her thoughts.

'Becky, are you okay?' Inspector Ramsey asked her. Becky hesitated before answering, finally saying,

'I am fine.'

'Russell is with us now. Do you think you will have the strength to come and recognize him? Are you ready to stand up to him?'

Ramsey's voice no longer sounded so tired. Apparently, the inspector had managed to get a good night's sleep.

'I will find the strength,' Becky confirmed and agreed to go with Alex to the police station at noon. 'Michael said forensics were looking at his car. Did you find out if he ...?'

Becky couldn't finish her question.

'We are still working on it. We'll talk when you get here,' answered Ramsey evasively.

'Okay. See you soon,' Becky said.

'See you soon.'

Becky got dressed, went down to the kitchen where Ben was already making breakfast. He was a good cook, she remembered. Alex's father looked worried.

Another person suffering and worrying because of me, she told herself. Then she sat down at the table and told him everything she knew.

'Alex doesn't look good,' Ben said.

'That's right,' she admitted. 'That's why I called you.'

Alex's father looked towards the second floor, listened to the running water in the bathroom and sat in the chair next to Becky.

'I have to admit that some time ago I asked him not to interfere in your affairs. I was worried that things would eventually get out of control, and I was right.'

'I know. I'm really sorry,' Becky said with sadness in her voice.

'He is very attached to you, Becky. Although he won't admit it. So, I have a request for you. If you're not on the same page, cut it all off now.'

Becky looked at Ben in amazement. She wondered what exactly he was talking about. Had he seen Alex kiss her this morning? Before she could say anything, however, Alex came out of his room and joined them. Becky told him about the arrangement with Inspector Ramsey and the conversation moved in that direction.

'I will call now two of my friends. They can probably tell us more about Russell's capture in Devon,' Ben said. He took his phone and went out into the garden to talk to his friends. Only Alex and Becky remained in the kitchen.

'How are you?' she asked him.

'Okay. The shower refreshed me.'

Then he watched her, but she said nothing more. Becky started cleaning up in the kitchen, trying not to think, to stay practical and not give in to her feelings. Alex looked away from her and stared at one of the paintings on the wall. It was given to him by Arnie for his last birthday. The picture reminded him of his friend's death and the emotions of his death came flooding back.

'Do you want to talk about him?' he asked her quietly.

Becky turned and shook her head sadly. Then her eyes watered. Grief overwhelmed her again. She imagined Arnie curled up, abandoned in that dark place, stabbed with a knife. The ground there had absorbed not only her blood but his as well. Unless he was killed somewhere else. She also looked at the picture that had always soothed her – bright blue sea, sea foam and sunny sky. And on top of a wave was a surfer. Arnie joked that he was the one who rode the wave, and his surfing was so good that it inspired the artist to paint the picture.

He had promised Alex that he would teach him to surf like this, and that was why he had given him this painting. A promise that would never come true. Becky looked away from the picture and went back to clearing.

'Most likely Russell moved Arnie's body to that place,' said Ben entering the kitchen. 'He certainly didn't kill him there.'

Becky and Alex looked at him questioningly, waiting for him to share more information.

'Arnie was killed on the day of his disappearance, so claims the pathologist.'

Becky cringed at the thought of the autopsy. She imagined Arnie's cut body, her blood ran, and her skin turned pale. Alex caught her just before she fell. This time she didn't lose consciousness. She stood up after about a minute, refreshed by the water that the two men splashed in her face. She thanked them for their help and went up to her room. Becky had to change her clothes and pull herself together to identify Russell to the police. She wasn't going to let him get away with it, not after what he had done to her cousin.

In the kitchen, there was another argument between father and son. 'Alex, you have to back off,' his father was saying, trying to speak quietly so that Becky wouldn't hear him.

'I can't leave her right now.'

'Why not? She is already rich, she has money, she can hire any lawyer she wants.'

'You don't understand,' replied Alex desperately.

'Actually, I understand. My only son is in danger. The next one these people will want revenge on is you. Quit while you can.'

'We will put everyone in prison, they won't be able to kill anyone from there.'

'You can't be sure. Russell's father is like a mobster. He has people everywhere.'

'Don't waste your breath. I will not give up. Not just because of Becky and Arnie, but because I think it's the right thing to do.'

'If your mother was alive ...'

'Don't bring my mother into this!' Alex was angry, looked furiously at his father and left the kitchen, closing the door with a bang.

Ben looked at his son as he left and sat back tiredly in the chair. He looked at the untouched breakfast and the undrunk coffee and told himself that he didn't belong in this house. The tension here was very high. Alex and Becky were suffering, something was obviously going on between them too, and Ben realized that the conversations he was having weren't helping, but rather hurting.

Two hours later, Ben packed up and left the house, and Alex and Becky headed to the Police Station. Alex stared at her trying to figure out what she was thinking. Becky was silent. Before he left, his father had admitted to him that he had tried to talk to Becky. What had he told her about, Alex wondered.

Becky walked into the police station and felt all eyes on her. Inspector Ramsey approached her along with her colleague, Becks, and directed her inside the building. The four entered a room. There were four chairs in the room and Becky and Alex sat on two of them. Ramsey and Becks stood straight, pacing around nervously. Becky was worried by their reaction. She thought she was just coming to recognize Russell, but at one point she looked around and felt like she was being interrogated. She looked questioningly at Alex, who was also very confused.

'What is going on here?' he asked.

'We need to talk,' Inspector Ramsey said and finally sat down in one of the chairs across from them.

'Okay,' Becky said and looked at the inspectors questioningly.

'Did you know who Arnie worked for?' she asked.

'No,' answered Becky. 'A few months ago, he was fired, and he said he found another job. The office he worked in is in central London.'

'I know the name of the company he works for, but I haven't researched who owns it. Why? What's happening? What does his work have to do with his death?' asked a surprised Alex.

'There's a lot in common. Arnie worked for a government organization, helping Fraud Police to investigate possible illegal financial transactions and deals.'

Becky and Alex looked at each other. Arnie never shared with them what he was working on unlike Alex.

'You guarded him, didn't you know what he was doing?' he asked.

'No. Like you, we thought he worked for some financial company. Now it turns out that's he worked for the government.'

'I don't understand,' said Becky, visibly confused by what Inspector Ramsey said. 'Arnie worked from nine to five. I've heard that these agencies have long working hours.'

'Yes, but his work was mostly online. I guess he worked late at home without you knowing.'

'It is possible,' confirmed Alex. 'Only a laptop is needed to check financial documents.'

'Okay. There is a possibility that his death was unrelated to Albert's threat and that his body was left there on purpose.'

'You don't know exactly what happened, do you?' Becky asked.

'There is an investigation going on. According to the pathologist, Arnie was not killed there. His body has been moved, and there is no trace of it in Russell's car.'

Becky and Alex looked at the inspectors in surprise and waited for them to say something else, but they remained silent.

'Do you have any other suspects?' Alex asked.

'Yes, but we're not conducting that part of the investigation. We will only investigate the Russell lead.'

'Who will give us information about the other investigation?' Alex wondered.

'Someone will contact you,' Becks said and got up from the chair, signalling to them that the conversation was over.

Alex and Ramsey also got up, but Becky stayed in the chair.

'Tell me about him. How was he found, what exactly happened to him?' she said and turned to face the inspectors. 'I want to see pictures.'

'Becky ...' Alex tried to dissuade her.

'I want to see the pictures from where they found him,' she raised her voice, and this startled everyone in the room.

The two inspectors exchanged glances, then Ramsey nodded, and Inspector Becks left the room. A minute later he returned with a tablet and handed the device to Becky. Alex sat down next to her and stared at the picture that appeared on the screen. Arnie was dressed in the suit he had worn to work. His body lay in a strange position, as if he had fallen down drunk. His legs were crooked. There were dark red, almost brown spots on the suit in many places. In the first photo, his face was turned the other way. The second photo showed his lifeless eyes and slightly open mouth. There were photographs of the stab wounds.

'Did they compare the wounds to those inflicted on Becky?' Alex asked. It was hard for him to speak, but he had questions.

'They're doing it right now.'

'Do you know when Arnie was transported to this place?'

'I think the same day he was found. The previous day had been warm and there were several couples there.'

Alex nodded. Then he looked at Becky questioningly, waiting for her to ask her questions.

'When will I be able to see him?' she asked.

'You can see him the moment the pathologist is finished with the body,' replied Inspector Becks, and immediately regretted it. Horror appeared in Becky and Alex's eyes as they realized what was happening to Arnie's body right now.

'I will call you when you can see him. I advise you to look into his will,' she said, trying to brush aside what her colleague had said. Alex and Becky continued to look ahead.

Inspector Ramsey wanted to shoot Becks right now. These people had been through a lot in the past two years and didn't deserve to hear something so tactless.

'We'll leave you to recover for a while,' she said sympathetically and pushed her colleague out.

Alex was the first to recover from the shock. What the inspectors said distracted him. He imagined Arnie's body in the morgue in pieces. The years in the courtroom had prepared him for such sights, but when it comes to your best friend, the way you look at such an autopsy is different. He looked over at Becky and saw her despair written on her face.

She, like him, was imagining what was happening right now with Arnie. After all the tears she'd shed over the past week, her eyes were already dry. But her heart ached, and her mind refused to accept what Ramsey and Becks had said. Becky felt Alex's hand grab hers and give her an encouraging squeeze. Her gaze drifted to him, and tears finally flowed from her eyes. She didn't want to lose Alex either. She leaned forward and rested her head on his chest. He pulled her to him and stroked her hair. It had a soothing effect not only on her but also on him. The two stood like that, then slowly got up and headed for the door. When they left the room, Inspector Ramsey and Becks were waiting for them in the hallway.

'I'm ready to see the suspect,' Becky said and followed the two inspectors. Alex stayed in the hallway to wait. Becky recognized Russell, this time she didn't pass out, on the contrary, she was now firmly on her feet. The man in front of her was watching, grinning evilly and she wanted to go and nail him to the wall. She was no longer afraid. She would do whatever it took for him to follow his friends. And she would do anything to get him twice the sentence.

After giving a statement, which was also attended by Alex, the two left the police station followed by two policemen. Ben had called to tell Alex that he had arrived in Yorkshire. The thought of the empty house made both of them feel sick, so they headed for the park. They went to their favourite lake and looked at the birds floating there.

'Did he make a will?' Becky wondered.

'Yes, he did, immediately after the first threat.'

'Really? He didn't tell me anything.'

'We all made wills. Me, Paul, and Catherine witnessed each other's.'

Becky looked at him in surprise. 'Why didn't you tell me?' she asked him reproachfully.

'We didn't want you to worry, and we hoped that no one will need it.'

'Do you know what's in his will?'

'Yes.'

'I think I know too,' she said. 'He leaves nothing to his family.'

'It depends on what you mean by family. Arnie didn't have much savings. At least when we were making his will, but he left everything he had to you. You were his family.'

'To me?' Becky was surprised.

'To you, of course.'

'But I have a lot of money.'

'You had no money then.'

They made the wills before the trial was over, she thought. 'Probably I should make a will too,' Becky said.

'Probably. You might have to think about it.'

Becky nodded and looked back at the birds. She missed Arnie. It was hard for her to imagine her life without him. She began to remember what they had talked about last as well as incidents from her childhood, and tears welled up in her eyes again. Alex's eyes watered as well. He got up, gave her a hand to get up too, put his arm around her shoulders, and, walking like a married couple, they headed home. They had both suffered a lot. When they got home, no one wanted to eat, so they sat down on the sofa, hugging each other, each lost in thought. Then, almost midnight, Becky retired to her room, and, half an hour later, Alex followed her with his sleeping bag. He lay back on the ground and listened to her breathing. Becky wasn't asleep, he was sure of it. He wondered if he should say anything, but decided against it, returning to his thoughts and memories of Arnie and finally fell asleep.

However, Becky didn't get to sleep until almost the morning. Every time she closed her eyes, she saw the sprawled, dead body of her cousin. Then she drifted off and saw him as a ghost trying to tell her something, but she couldn't understand his words. She tried to hear it, but she couldn't, and she woke up from the effort.

At five o'clock in the morning, she finally fell asleep. When she woke up it was almost noon, the t-shirt she was sleeping in was damp with cold sweat. Becky got up, she saw that Alex was gone and headed to the bathroom to take a shower. When she walked into the kitchen a few minutes later, she found Alex reading something on his laptop. He was so focused that he didn't notice when Becky walked in and was startled by her good morning greeting.

'What are you reading?' she asked. He didn't answer right away, clearly hesitating whether or not to tell her.

'The autopsy report,' he said.

Becky took a step back as if to escape the words he spoke, then gathered herself and headed for the coffee machine. 'What does it say?' she asked.

He looked at her again.

'Tell me, you know I want to know.'

'He was stabbed eight times with a knife. The knife is different from the one you were stabbed with. But there is one incision that matches that of one of your wounds. However, this is not proof that it was inflicted by the same person.'

'But is it likely that Russell did it?' Becky asked.

'If I were his lawyer, I would dispute this,' said Alex.

'What else does it say?'

'No signs of dragging or other injuries,' Alex started to say something else, but hesitantly stopped.

'Alex, whatever it is, just say it.'

'He died from the first blow, but, according to the pathologist, the person who stabbed him inserted the knife very slowly and ...'

Becky fainted and leaned against the kitchen counter. Alex quickly got up and caught her. However, she recovered quickly. He didn't let her go even though he saw she was fine. He hugged her and stayed with her like that for a while. Then he let her go without looking at her. He went back to the laptop and continued reading in silence. She sat next to him and watched his reactions. When Alex finished reading, he leaned back in his chair and remained silent for a while.

'What's wrong?' she asked him.

'I miss Arnie. I'm reading this and waiting for him to come into the room and me to discuss it with him. Sometimes I did. I was digging into some document, and he would ask me what was bothering me, then I would discuss it with him. You have no idea how many times he helped me make sense of things.'

'You can discuss everything with me if you want.'

'You've been through enough. I don't want to burden you with my stuff. You have to start to think about your future.'

'Yes, after the trial against Russell I will think about it.'

Alex looked at her as if he wanted to ask her something but hesitated.

'Ask,' she encouraged him.

'It's not exactly a question, it's more of a request. I know you have enough money to rent or buy a house, but I would like you to stay and live with me. I would not be able to bear the thought of returning to the empty house.'

'I didn't even think about leaving you here alone now. I wouldn't be able to do it.'

'Okay,' he said and sighed with relief.

'What are we going to do, Alex? Should I inform my aunt that Arnie was killed?'

'I think she already knows. His murder was reported in the news and linked to Albert Levy's threat in court.'

'His mother probably blames me for this.'

'From what Arnie's been telling me about her, she's probably blaming everyone and will contest his will. But he is adamant that nothing be given to his family there. He wrote it twice to make sure it was understood correctly.'

'She won't like it.'

'And Arnie didn't like her attitude towards him and you.'

Becky was about to say something to him, but the doorbell rang. She opened it and to her surprise she was handed a summons. She opened the envelope and saw her mother's name.

'It's a court summons,' said Alex, amazed.

'What will she be suing me for?' Becky was surprised.

'She wants compensation for inflicted emotional and moral damages,' muttered Alex.

'What?'

'That's what it says. We're going to the courthouse tomorrow and I'll check just to be sure.'

Becky sat down in the chair next to him, dejected.

'I can't do it anymore, Alex,' she told him desperately. 'I'm tired. I'm tired of fighting all these people.'

'You will do it. I'll help you fight this time again,' he said. But she stood before him, small and as if curled up into a ball.

Alex turned off the laptop, pushed aside the envelope with the summons, and reached across the table for her. She didn't react at first, then put her hand in his.

'We will fight, and we will win. We are a good team,' he told her encouragingly. Then he got up and motioned for her to follow him. They sat on the sofa, and he hugged her. He didn't know what else to do to calm her down. Becky was abandoned and attacked by her own family. Alex wondered what would have become of her if he had done as his father had asked him to, to let her fend for herself. To fight all those wolves who were trying to tear flesh from her. She rested her head on his chest, then raised it and looked at him.

'Everything will be fine,' he told her and kissed her neck. He couldn't help himself. He didn't know what was happening to him and to her, but it was as if their grief and passion had merged. He kissed her again, longer this time and she didn't pull away. She seemed to enjoy the feeling.

Becky loved this intimacy, this closeness between the two of them that had suddenly sprung up. She let him kiss her, his hand caressing her hair, then moved down to her back, causing her to arch against him. She kissed his neck, then stopped and stayed like that, nestled in his arms.

Alex sighed slightly. He wanted this to continue, but he understood her hesitation. Hesitating himself, he removed his hand from her back and moved it to her shoulders. They looked at the beautiful garden and stayed like that until it got dark.

When Alex's phone rang, they were both startled. Paul called him, drunk and crying for Arnie. Alex talked to him for the next hour. When he entered Becky's room, she was already asleep. Her sleep was peaceful this time, Alex thought, listening to her steady breathing. He lay down in the sleeping bag and this time he was the one who couldn't sleep all night. He wanted this woman, he wanted to be with her, next to her. He could see in her eyes that she was not indifferent to him either. If it was another woman, he knew what to do, he would take her out to dinner, probably buy her flowers. Then he would court her for a while and eventually he would have her. That's how it's worked so far, and that approach has been successful. But with Becky everything was complicated. He respected her and worried about hurting her. Especially now, after the loss of her cousin, her mother's attack, and the new trial. He wondered if Arnie would approve of what he wanted to do. He would probably approve. He had even told him several times that Becky trusted and loved him more than her own cousin. All this was said in jest, but Arnie's eyes weren't laughing then. On the contrary, they were serious. Alex wanted to know what Becky was thinking and feeling and promised to ask her in the morning. At least that way he would sleep peacefully, he reassured himself.

Becky was also confused. She woke up early in the morning and got lost in her thoughts. She, unlike Alex, had other concerns. In her mind, she didn't deserve him, and she thought he only paid attention to her because they were both grieving. The fact that his father thought he had a crush on her didn't reassure her at all. Who would want to be with a woman raped by four men, she thought. Who would take that shame and live with her and her complicated life? Alex probably hadn't thought about it and when he realized what a burden she was, he would have pulled himself together and finally listened to his father's advice and walked out of her life. She finally got up quietly so as not to wake Alex. She made herself some coffee and went out into the garden. Then she called Catherine. She needed advice and didn't know who else to turn to.

'How is Paul?' she asked.

'He got drunk last night and had a long drunken conversation with Alex. He's in bed now, sleeping. Then he'll probably spend the whole day in the garden, that's how he calms down. How are you, Becky?'

'To be honest, I'm tired and very confused. But that's not why I called you.' Becky was silent for a moment, she hesitated whether to share her worries with Catherine.

'Becky, tell me what worries you, it's obviously something very personal if you don't know how to start.'

'Yes, it's personal. It's about Alex. Recently, our relationship has become more intimate.'

'And why does that bother you?' Catherine was surprised.

'I don't know if it's right ...' Becky tried to explain.

'Becky, Alex has adored you for years. Only you don't see that. Have you read what the journalists write about both of you? They call you the Knight and the Princess.'

'Really?' Becky was surprised.

'All women are crazy about Alex and what he does for you. And men are crazy about you.'

'But who would want a raped woman?' Becky finally asked worriedly.

'Have you ever seen yourself in the mirror? Becky, you are one of the most beautiful women I know. Any normal man would want to be with you. Let me tell you something, I know Paul loves me and would do anything for me, but if you gave him even a glimmer of hope, he would leave me and follow you like a puppy. So, nothing to worry about. You know Alex well, and if you have feelings for him, I advise you to seize the moment and immerse yourself in them. Otherwise, you'll regret missing the moment. He is a good man, he would never hurt you, and, let me tell you a secret, he has an excellent reputation with women.'

Becky blushed at Catherine's last comment.

'How do you know?' she inquired.

'From Paul and his big mouth,' Catherine laughed lightly.

'What if it doesn't work out?'

'At least you'll know you tried. But knowing you both, I think everything will be more than fine. Forget everyone and everything else and enjoy the moment,

Becky. I know you are sad for Arnie, and maybe you think now is not the time, but if Arnie were alive, he would tell you the same thing. He would support you. So don't worry.'

'Okay,' she said.

'Becky, I wanted to tell you personally when we meet, but we're having this conversation anyway. Before Arnie disappeared, I was offered a lucrative contract in Los Angeles. Paul and I decided to accept the offer and move there.'

Becky felt sad, her two friends wouldn't be here soon.

'I will call you often, we will come to visit you and you can visit us,' Catherine tried to calm her down.

'I know, I'm happy for you. But now I'm starting to feel lonely. When are you moving?'

'In a month. We are now sorting out the visas and documents we will need to work there. Paul's family is not particularly happy about the change.'

'And Ben is not very happy for me to be around his son.'

'Ben is worried about both of you. He has a lot of respect for you, he just doesn't like the situation you're in right now.'

Becky heard Alex walk in and turned and smiled at him.

'Are you going to tell Alex about Los Angeles? Paul didn't want to mention it to him yesterday.'

'Yes, I will tell him,' answered Becky and, after exchanging some more information about their trip, she hung up the phone.

'What do you have to tell me?' Alex asked and sat next to her.

'Paul and Catherine are leaving for America in a month.'

'Really?' he said.

'Yes. Catherine has received a good offer and they both decide to accept it and leave as soon as possible.'

'That will be good for them. Here the tension will rise again soon, it's better if they are far away and we don't have to worry about them.'

Becky nodded. Still, she was sad. And she thought again that it was all her fault.

13.

Over the next few days, Alex set to work. He formed a team of people to work with on both cases. Becky's mother had sued and wanted £1.5 million in damages. The very thought of the greedy woman made him laugh. She takes a bribe, sends her newly raped and multiple-wounded daughter away, then collects benefits on her behalf without actually using the money for what she has claimed, and ... Alex couldn't list everything he had entered into his computer. He had asked Michael and Tanya to research the woman who gave birth to Becky and her family and find any information that would be helpful to the case. The two detectives were very busy, so, in addition to them, two more people joined their agency. Becky, on the other hand, was busy making arrangements for her cousin's funeral. His body was finally released. In his will he had wished to be buried, if possible, in a sunny and peaceful place in Cornwall near the sea. Even though he couldn't wait to get out of there when he was alive, Arnie had chosen this very spot for his grave, and that surprised Becky a lot. She and Alex spent a day there and quickly found a cemetery and a beautiful place to bury him. Money will open all doors, Catherine had told her, and now that Becky had a lot of money, she knew what Catherine meant.

The funeral was for close family only. A few people from Arnie's office also arrived. Becky forced herself not to think about the body inside the casket and turned her mind back to their childhood days when she and Arnie would sneak out of the house and swim in the sea.

Alex and Paul, for their part, watched the coffin's descent with teary eyes. Catherine was supporting her boyfriend. Becky was leaning on Alex's arm. Ben, Michael, Tanya, and Alex's sister stood slightly off to the side, some crying softly, others just teary eyed. After the funeral was over, they all returned to London and stayed at Alex and Becky's house until almost dawn, telling each other stories about the deceased. When the last of the guests left, Becky, exhausted by emotions, sobbed. She looked at her cousin's picture and blamed herself for his death. Alex, also tired from the long day and emotional from a memorial in honour of Arnie, sat down next to her, hugged her and they stayed like that for a long time.

'Everything will be fine,' he finally said. 'We will get over it in time.'

'You think so?'

'Yes. When my mother died, I felt similarly angry, angry at the healthcare system and at fate.'

'Arnie mentioned to me that's why you became a lawyer.'

'Yes, until then I didn't know what I wanted to do.'

'Did you manage to overcome it? I mean her absence,' Becky asked and stroked his chin with her hand.

'Sometimes I think I've succeeded, but then something like this happens and...'

'I understand.'

'Sometimes I miss her a lot,' said Alex, remembering the argument with his father. What would his mother say if she were alive? Alex looked at the tired Becky, gently lifted her chin and kissed her. He knew he was addicted to this woman, nothing and no one could make him leave her, not now. He pushed aside part of the t-shirt she was wearing and kissed her shoulder. Becky didn't say anything, just relaxed and let herself be caressed by him. His touch had a relaxing effect on both of them and they drifted off to sleep just like that, his lips on her neck, hers on his arm. They slept for an hour until they were woken up by a knock at the front door. Alex got up tiredly and went to open the door. Then he entered the living room accompanied by two of Arnie's colleagues, whom they had met at his funeral.

'Sorry to bother you. We can see you're tired, but we'll only take a few minutes.'

Becky got up from the sofa, her body aching from the awkward position she had fallen asleep in.

'I need coffee to wake up,' she said and invited her guests into the kitchen.

'Arnie used to work for me,' said the older man named Max. 'He was very good at his job.'

'Is work the reason he was killed?' Alex asked.

'According to our investigation, he was not killed by someone who he was investigating officially.'

'So, it was because of me?' Becky said as she poured coffee. Her hand was shaking slightly, but she still managed to pour the coffee without a single drop falling outside the cup.

'Most likely so, but you should ask the authorities about that.'

'They're keeping us posted,' Alex said, walking over to the counter to help Becky carry the cups to the table.

'Arnie was working on two projects that I knew about, but which were not ordered by the agency, and this is the reason why my colleague and I came here.'

The man accompanying Max took two folders out of a leather bag.

'The one search he did was related to Becky's mother. All her financial records he could gather for the past two years. Arnie was trying to find proof that someone had paid her to keep quiet and send Becky away. The notes Becky gave to police were withdrawn two days after she was raped, by Russell's father from an ATM in Cornwall. Arnie found all this out two hours after the driver, David, recognized Russell. This gave him hope that he was on the right track. All the documents he found are in this folder.'

'And what's in the other folder?' asked Alex.

'Everything he found about Russell's and his father's companies. We have now taken over the investigation related to him as there are many unexplained transactions and concealment of taxes and fees in the documents. However, the management of our agency has decided to provide you with what we have found so far, so that you can use it in court if necessary.'

Alex reached over and picked up the second folder. He read the few conclusions, handwritten by Arnie.

'There is one more thing. We have allocated a pension in Arnie's name, and we don't know which name to transfer it to. We will ask you to give us a copy of the will to move this matter forward as well.'

'We will donate it to a charitable organization,' Becky said.

'You can do whatever you want with the money. Arnie was a wonderful man. We all mourn him,' added Max, and headed for the front door. His colleague followed him.

After the two left, Alex read the papers. He admired the good work Arnie had done. Then he called Inspector Ramsey to tell her about the new turn of events and made copies and emailed them to her.

Becky stood beside him, watching him. Alex was so excited by the discoveries that he forgot to even eat. She also looked at the documents that Arnie's colleagues had brought, but the numbers and facts told her nothing. This reminded her to re-enrol in school and look for business courses in their area.

Alex's day was spent researching the documents and Becky's was spent surfing the internet. They both tried not to look at Arnie's notes again. They were a reminder to them that he was not coming back. Becky had already put some things away that, just to look at, made her sad. However, none of them wanted to enter Arnie's room. It had been closed since the day he had last left for work.

14.

Alex worked for two days on the papers that Arnie's boss had brought him. On the third day, he went to his office to discuss strategy for the two cases with his colleagues. Becky accompanied him, but she felt useless and redundant. She understood nothing of the conversations the legal team were having, and it made her feel stupid. The office secretary noticed her confusion and asked her to step outside for a while.

'I often feel the same way,' said the older woman. 'It's like I'm from another world.'

'I feel useless,' Becky said. 'Everyone around me is busy with something, and I just sit and do nothing. I have been working for as long as I can remember myself and now that I am idle...'

'Then listen to my advice, find a job quickly. Otherwise, you will get very depressed. My daughter went through this. She lost her child, gave in to grief and lost her direction. We were all busy with something and she stayed at home all the time. We thought we were giving her time and a chance to rest and recover, but in fact, all the while, she became more and more depressed. Luckily, one of her best friends noticed this. You have the same lost look, Becky. Get a job, otherwise the hole you can fall into while waiting for the court cases can become big.'

Becky sipped the tea the lady had bought her and wondered what to do. The school she had enrolled in was two months away, and business courses also started in October. What could she do until then, she wondered. Then her face lit up. She could start working in a charity shop as a volunteer. She had heard the older women talk about it.

'From your smile, I understand that you have found a solution.'

'Yes. I think I know what I'll be doing while I wait for school to start,' Becky said with a smile. 'Thanks for that!'

'I only gave you a direction,' the woman smiled and patted Becky's hand encouragingly. 'You've dealt with much harder things, you'll deal with this too.'

After they got home, Becky looked for a few charity shops nearby and applied for a job there. As she browsed the Internet, she remembered what Catherine had told her about the media. They called Alex a Knight and her a Princess. She decided to read some of the articles and looked at the pictures they had taken of them, especially the one where Alex had picked her up after they won the case. And there she saw his adoration for her. Then, pictures of the crime scene appeared on the laptop screen, some of them close-ups. Becky was surprised by these pictures. She knew that the police had taken pictures of her when they found her, but the pictures she was seeing now were not the ones she had seen in her file. It was as if someone else had taken them. But when, Becky wondered. Becky took a picture of what was shown on the screen and sent it to Inspector Ramsey. Then she called her.

'I have not seen these photos,' the inspector was surprised after looking at them.

'And so am I. But someone took them, someone else was there, don't you think?'

Alex, surprised by the conversation that was taking place next to him, got up and looked at the pictures.

'I haven't seen them either. They were taken at the crime scene. I've seen similar ones, but they're from the hospital.'

Inspector Ramsey sighed heavily.

'We missed something,' she said.

'Or someone,' Alex put in. Then Inspector Ramsey asked Becky to send everything she found to her and Michael.

Becky looked at the pictures and was back in that place again, but this time with different feelings. She tried to remember what happened after the four men left, but she couldn't. The feeling that she was missing something out plagued her throughout the day. When she finally falls asleep, she tosses and turn restlessly. She had nightmares, pictures of her body as if it wasn't hers and someone hovering over her. She woke up to her own cries. When she opened her eyes, she saw Alex sitting next to her, holding her hand. He reached up and pushed her sweat-drenched hair away from her face.

'Everything is fine. You're safe,' he told her as he continued to stroke her hair gently. Becky moved away and made room for him to lie down next to her. Then she hugged him and pulled him closer to her.

'I had a nightmare,' she told him.

'I know. I was trying to calm you down,' he whispered in her ear, then kissed her. The touch of his lips soothed her. He continued with the kisses, moving to her neck. She squirmed, signalling him to continue. He hesitated for a moment then lifted her t-shirt and kissed her stomach gently, moving up to her breasts and then stopped. He looked into her eyes, saw that there was no fear in them, on the contrary, her hands encouraged him to continue.

'Trust me,' he whispered. And she trusted him.

Paul was the first to notice the change in their relationship. The looks, the touches, all this betrayed their feelings for each other. Alex seemed calmer and Becky more sensual. The three of them had gathered to see the latest musical in which Catherine was starring, and, as her relatives, they occupied some of the best seats in the house. When the music started, Paul turned to his friend and said, 'You're finally together, huh?'

Alex gave him a surprised look, then followed Paul's gaze. Becky had taken his hand and entwined her fingers in his.

'Yes, we have been together for some time,' said Alex with a happy smile.

'It was time,' Paul playfully nudged his friend.

Alex just nodded and looked at a smiling Becky. He had never seen her so happy before. Her eyes were shining, and there was a pleasant blush on her cheeks. He and she had indulged in romance and dreams. Love had changed their view on life. The two couldn't wait for the two cases to pass and start a new life. Arnie's death had brought them even closer together, thought until then Paul didn't believe that the two of them could become any closer.

The new musical in which Catherine participated was in tune with the mood of the two lovers, a romantic comedy that kept the audience smiling and dreaming. Becky identified with the role of the heroine, in love and happy, as if she had wings and was about to fly and didn't want it to end. She looked at Alex and knew he felt the same way. For several days, Becky had tried not to think about Arnie or the court cases she had to attend. She focused on herself and the man next to her. The two were inseparable. They would go to his office together so that he could discuss something with his colleagues, then they would walk the streets or be alone at home. On one of these walks, the two had entered a jewellery store and, surprisingly for both of them, came out with wedding rings. They had decided to get married, and although the decision was not made in the traditional way, it was something they both felt was right. The reason they came to see Catherine's new musical was because they wanted to invite their two best friends to be their witnesses. Alex was smiling as he asked her friends if they agreed to attend their wedding. It was as if another person had been born within the last few weeks. His face looked youthful, wrinkle-free, and fresh, as if he was ten years younger. His typical suit was replaced with jeans and a t-shirt, and the briefcase that was always with him was missing. You'd have to be blind not to see the change, Paul thought, and he and Catherine agreed to be their witnesses, as long as the wedding took place before they left for America. Mike and Tanya were also not surprised by the wedding invitation, but for Alex's father and sister the news came as a shock.

'So, you decided to go off the deep end and marry her?' said his sister.

'Yes. I know our father won't be happy...'

'On the contrary, I think he will finally calm down.'

'You think so?' Alex was surprised. 'Did he tell you that he tried to break us up several times?'

'Yes, he told me. I made him reconsider his position.'

'How did you do that?' Alex was surprised.

'I reminded him that mom's parents didn't like him at all. Our father didn't have the best reputation in his younger years.'

'Where do you know this from?'

'From grandma and mom. Grandpa even threatened to kill him.'

Alex and his sister laughed just thinking about their grandfather. The old man was a character until the end of his days and called their father a youth until the end.

'I can imagine Grandpa challenging him.'

'Yes, but our father didn't give up and married our mother. But, Alex, he's worried about you. And Becky too. And although he hasn't told you, he really likes her. He did everything he could to help her find the perpetrators and this case her mother filed against her just ruined him. He can't believe that Becky comes from this family.'

'Yes, me neither. So, you think he will be happy that we are getting married?'

'I don't know, Alex. You better talk to him. Our biggest fear is that if you stay close to her, something bad will happen to you. The same thing that happened to Arnie. Becky, on the other hand, has only you and there will be us too, when you marry her, we will be her family. So why not? It'll be nice to have a sister, especially if it's Becky.'

Alex understood his family's fears. He would feel the same way if his sister were in his place. Without even thinking, he was putting his family in trouble, but there was nothing he could do. He wanted to be with Becky, and he was going to marry her, with or without his father's consent. But to his surprise, after initial grumbling, his father agreed and even congratulated him.

'Better to be married to her than to be away from her,' said Ben.

Becky, for her part, had no one to invite. The decision about the wedding surprised her, and, although she was happy, organizing the event made her sad.

She had always thought that, if she got married, her sister would attend her wedding and that she would be her maid of honour, but after her time at the farm, it became clear to Becky that the two would never be close again. Perhaps in time they would become friends again, but for now Becky was alone, without relatives. She and Alex decided to get married in Yorkshire, the county where his mother and father had married. As there were fewer weddings there, the ceremony hall was free, and the wedding could take place before Paul and Catherine left. Becky had bought herself a beautiful wedding dress, one specially made for the event. Becky thought that everything had happened so quickly and had somehow come together easily. From buying the wedding rings to the ceremony itself, there were no problems at all. Within just two weeks everything was organized. The ceremony was short, and so was the visit to York. At the end of the day, Alex and Becky went home to their house as husband and wife and it was one of the most beautiful days of their lives.

15.

Their post-marriage euphoria ended the moment they entered the courtroom and faced Becky's mother and her lawyers. Becky hadn't expected to have any feelings for this woman, but when her mother noticed her ring and when Becky was introduced with her new surname, the hatred of the woman who had given birth to her showed in her eyes. This woman hated her own daughter, the child she had thrown away.

Alex had gathered a lot of evidence to support Becky and was sure he would win the case until he ran into her mother. He had never seen her before. Wicked and envious, but also smart, he thought, and immediately understood where Becky's intelligence came from. Although she had worked on a farm all her life, Clara spoke very well, one could tell she had graduated from university. And she really had, he found out later from Becky. But no one had bothered to check, and Becky had never mentioned it. Alex saw Becky's father in the court, as well as her sister, who looked a lot like her mother, only a softer copy of her. Alex's father and sister had also come to the court to support them. The battle would be Becky's former family versus her new family, he thought.

Becky took her mother's betrayal hard. Clara testified and described her daughter as a bad person who deserved what happened to her. According to her mother, Becky's behaviour and clothing caused the four men to have sex with her. Sex?? Becky was surprised. She had been raped and beaten to death, and her mother called it sex and gratification.

'It's going to be a tough case,' muttered Alex's assistant.

'That's right,' he sighed. He thought that Becky's mother proved to be a strong opponent. They should gather their strength and send her where she belongs, behind bars.

'But I don't want them to put her in the prison,' Becky protested.

'We have no choice, Becky. If we show all these documents in court, all the victims will file lawsuits against her. I know she's your mother and your instincts are to protect her, but if we don't use what we have she'll judge you and that'll give Russell a chance to get away. Because the accusations she levelled at you during her testimony also affect the case against him.'

'You think they paid her to say all that.'

'I am convinced that this case is precisely because of this. There was nothing stopping her from calling you and asking for money so she wouldn't file the case, and she didn't. She doesn't even want an agreement.'

'Try to come to an agreement with her again,' Becky asked him.

'After what she said today, all chances for an agreement have disappeared.'

Alex's sister listened to the woman testify and couldn't believe Becky's mother's speech, her recriminations, her accusations. All of this described in such detail that almost everyone on the jury looked accusingly at Becky and she saw disgust in their eyes.

'They think I did something bad, Alex,' Becky cried after her mother's testimony was over. Becky had expected a lot from her mother, but not this. To top it off at the end before it ended Clara accused Becky of Arnie's murder. Becky stared at her mother in disbelief and wanted to die and disappear again. It was easier for her to fight the criminals than her own mother. After the first day's hearing, Becky was not herself. She couldn't stand still because of nerves. She was squeezing Alex's hand, not realizing that she was squeezing it so hard it was causing him pain. Becky thought she was going from nightmare to nightmare. And her feeling of being betrayed once again by her family intensified. Even more after the testimony the next day and the day after that. Her father's account was rather tepid, but what affected her the most was her sister's testimony. The beautiful little girl that Becky loved to spend her free time with had turned into a vicious young woman.

'Ever since my sister had sex in public place, all my friends and acquaintances make fun of me. Boys ask me if I'm like her,' Summer said.

'How did that affect you?' asked her lawyer.

'I stopped going out. Everywhere I went my sister's name was mentioned. There is even a Facebook group named after her. So, I stopped going to school.'

Becky watched her sister and truly sympathized with her for the things she had gone through because of her. She did feel guilty that what had happened to her had affected her sister's life in such a way.

'Do you have friends?' the lawyer asked her.

'No, I don't have friends. Who would want to be friends with a rape victim's sister?' Summer said and started sniffling, which led to worse looks from the jury. Becky wanted to shrink and get out of the courtroom as quickly as possible. Alex patted her encouragingly. Then he got up and stood in front of Summer.

'Miss, do you know how many friends your sister had when she was your age?' he asked her.

'No.'

'So, you don't know she had friends?'

'No, I do not know. She said she didn't have time...'

'Yes, she didn't have time because she went to work. Instead of going home and studying like her classmates did, she worked and was raped after work.'

'Hmm...,' said Summer. That was not what her mother had told her.

'Did you know your sister worked till late?'

'I think so,' the girl said uncertainly.

'She was coming home tired from work because your family needed money. She had no time for friends and was raped on the way home. Did you know all this before you came to testify?'

'No. But...'

'Who told you exactly what to say in this court, miss?'

'My mother,' answered the girl, confused.

'You don't go to school, you work, right?' Alex asked.

'Yes,' Summer fidgeted uneasily, looking worriedly at her mother.

'And what time do you get home back from work?'

'At nine o'clock in the evening.'

'So, you mean you can go to work, but you can't go to school, right? Instead of going home at five in the afternoon, when there is no danger of meeting young drunken men, you voluntarily chose to go to work and come home in the dark.'

'I had no other choice ...'

'Who told you that you have no other choice?' Alex asked her.

'My mum,' muttered the girl and looked at her mother guiltily.

The look Clara gave her little daughter was searing. Becky felt sorry for Summer. She knew what the consequences would be for her sister after she got home from the case and she wanted to help her, but she didn't know how.

Summer stubbornly refused to talk to her, but one day Becky thought maybe they would.

The next two days passed with less emotion. Evidence, expert opinions, and studies followed. Becky watched her relatives and had mixed feelings. If her mother hadn't filed this lawsuit, Becky would have been more willing to give them some money to help them live a better life. But what was said in court hurt her deeply. It wasn't the requests for money, but the words that were addressed to her, about her. It was as if she no longer existed for them. That was the thing, the feeling that hurt her, and as she thought it, Becky looked behind her, saw Alex's father and sister, and calmed down. She was no longer alone. She had a family around her.

Three days after her sister's testimony, Becky was also called to testify. Her mother's lawyers tried to attack her, but since it was all about the rape and her wounds, they finally gave up. Their questions, instead of showing her in a bad light, evoked the sympathy of the jury. After Becky's testimony, it was clear to everyone that Carla would lose the case, and, after the evidence presented by Alex, there were already two claims from the charities that had donated the money to her. Her lawyers requested a meeting with Alex and Becky, but they refused to see them. They left it up to the jury to decide what happened. And the jury did, acquitting Becky and releasing her from all obligations to her family. Becky looked at Clara and her father, smiled gently at her sister, and happily left the court. She would think about the consequences for them later, now all she wanted was to go home and celebrate with her new family. Together with Alex, his sister, and his father she went to a small Italian restaurant.

'Surely that was hard for you?' Ben asked her. 'It's not easy to stand up to your family.'

'I didn't stand against them, but they against me,' said Becky sadly. 'Do You know what, before they decided to sue me, I had decided to send them a hundred thousand pounds. To help them, to give them the opportunity for a better life.'

'So, they made a mistake by getting ahead of the events,' said Janey.

'Yes.'

'I think that someone told them to sue you. This person wanted to direct attention away from themselves.'

'Maybe you're right,' Becky said thoughtfully. 'But if he paid them, where is the money?'

'Very good question,' intervened Michael, who had arrived with Tanya to celebrate the victory.

'If they were paid in cash, they should be spending that money now, right?' Tanya said. 'So, if we take a few banknotes they've used, we can trace from which bank the money was withdrawn.'

'Probably yes,' confirmed Alex. 'But how are we going to get those banknotes.'

'From the hotel,' Ben interjected. 'They will probably pay the hotel where they are staying at.'

'Then tomorrow morning we will wait for them to pay.' Tanya laughed and was already mentally organizing her appearance at Clara's hotel.

'Becky, I thought I had a bad family, but yours... well, it's unbelievable what they said about you,' said Michael.

Becky patted his arm sympathetically, then took Alex's hand again and squeezed it tightly. What she wouldn't have given to have been born into a family like Alex's, she thought.

Becky and Alex took a few days off and went to the Caribbean. Kind of like a belated honeymoon. The sun and smiling people around them restored their good romantic mood. Sometimes they remembered Arnie and wished he was with them, but most days they enjoyed each other's company. They had both turned off their phones and were only accepting messages through Alex's email. Tanya had written to them that they had confiscated the notes with which Carla had paid for the hotel and now they were tracking where they were taken from. That was the last thing the lovers knew before their vacation was over. After they returned to London, much news awaited them. Everyone had decided to wait for the newlyweds to return and then share their investigations with them.

'Money leads to Taylor,' said Michael. 'He withdrew it a few days before Clara's claim.'

'So, he's been paying her from the start?'

'We still don't have his fingerprints and I can't confirm it, but I assume he gave them the money they sent Becky away with.'

'What else have you discovered?' Becky asked.

'I don't think Arnie's death has anything to do with Russell.'

'Are you sure?'

'Yes. Inspector Ramsey found out that he was at a music festival, and he was stoned and drunk most of the time. Kidnapping and drugging a policeman would have been beyond him.'

'Maybe his father organized all this?' Alex asked.

'We are working in that direction, but for the moment we have nothing. The man Albert was looking at when they pronounced the sentence is something I want to talk about. I don't know how, but it's as if Arnie's work and what happened to Becky got intertwined at some point. I don't know exactly how, I'm still looking for details, but this guy I think is important. This man is Arnie's former boss, the one who fired him.'

Alex and Becky looked at each other. This news was unexpected.

'What's his name?' Alex asked.

'His name is Andrew Monaghan. He runs several companies involved in various financial services. According to me and the police, Arnie ran into something at the company while he was working there and that was the reason he was fired. I wanted to ask Arnie's new bosses if they knew anything about it, but they refused to talk to me and they promised to talk to you.'

'Okay,' Becky said thoughtfully, surprised by the turn of events. 'I'll call them right now.'

She got up, took her phone with her, and headed towards the garden. Max picked up almost immediately.

'Becky, I was expecting your call,' he said cheerfully. 'I assume you have questions about Arnie and his former boss.'

'That's right,' she said and called Alex with a gesture. She wanted him to listen to the conversation too.

'Arnie had detected many fraudulent transactions. When he asked Andrew Monaghan about them, he dismissed him instantly. He was furious and threatened to kill Arnie if he mentioned it to anyone.'

'What?' Becky exclaimed in amazement.

'Yes. Arnie never took his threat seriously because such things happen in many financial firms. In his opinion, Andrew would quickly erase his tracks and not bother with Arnie anymore.'

'That's why he came to you, and you hired him,' said Alex.

'Exactly. We didn't expect that what Arnie had uncovered was of such a large scale. We hired him and he was working on another case. However, we continued to investigate Andrew.'

'You came to us and told us that you were sure that Arnie was not killed because of his investigations,' said Becky. 'Do you still think so?'

'No, we already think he was killed for both reasons. He was the perfect target. Andrew wanted him dead, and Albert and his friends wanted you hurt.'

'Can you prove your theory?' Alex asked, still trying to understand the logic of the crime.

'Yes, somewhat. Andrew visited Albert several times in prison. There is a connection between them. We're still investigating, but we believe they were both involved in Arnie's death.'

'Okay. Our private investigators can also help if you allow them to participate in this investigation.'

'Yes, I spoke with Michael, and I would be happy if he would assist us. Once again, I'm sorry for letting you down. I really thought Arnie's death had nothing to do with our agency.'

'Thanks, Max. However, I would appreciate it if you could share your information with Michael and Inspector Ramsey.'

'I'll do it right now. But please, don't let anyone else know about this trail. The best way to catch these criminals is to catch them off guard.'

'Okay,' Becky agreed and hung up. Then she hugged Alex and told him she would like them to go back to the Caribbean right away. Their life was good there.

'We can't leave now. We have to finish what we started,' he said and headed for the kitchen. After their guests left, Alex called the law office.

'Is there any news about the case?' he asked his colleagues.

'No. They're not done with the evidence and the expertise yet, and Inspector Ramsey said they had a new lead they're working on. They won't be scheduling Russell's case anytime soon. But I have news about Becky's mother. She is going to be charged with tax evasion. Her and her husband.'

'What does this mean?' Becky asked.

'It means she could go to prison for a few years,' explained Alex.

Becky was standing up, but when she heard this, she slumped into her chair. She didn't want her mother to go to prison.

'It's not your fault, Becky. They were on her trail before she filed a lawsuit against you,' said one of Alex's colleagues. 'One of the organizations from which she raised funds to help you reported her to the tax authorities and they investigated her.'

'What will happen to my sister if my mother goes to prison?' Becky asked.

'As far as we know, your father is not involved, but as her husband, he will also suffer some consequences. I think he won't go to prison though so your sister can stay with him.'

'Okay,' Becky calmed down. Her sister was young, she didn't have to go through all this. But Becky could do nothing, she had to stay away and watch the events from afar.

After Alex finished his conversation with his colleagues, Becky contacted Inspector Ramsey.

'I understand that they have a new lead on Arnie's kidnapping and murder,' Ramsey said. 'I'll talk to his boss to see how I can help. Now, though, let's get back to your case. We have the evidence and will schedule a trial soon. We're working on another lead, but it's more related to the person who took the crime scene photos. We think there was a teenager there. We are looking for him and when we find him, we will know more.'

'Isn't he in Cornwall?' Alex asked.

'No. Now he lives and studies in Portsmouth. He went to the USA for two weeks. We'll wait for him to come back and question him.'

'Okay. So, we have no choice but to wait, right?' Becky asked.

'Exactly. Enjoy family life until then.'

With that conversation done, Alex and Becky relaxed and tried to enjoy the next few peaceful days. Then Alex went back to work, and Becky focused on her studies and her idea to start a pet food business. A month later, Becky opened a company in her own name and called it "Arnie's Family". She rented a small space, she wanted to start somewhere where she wouldn't have to invest a lot of money. Her idea was to try something small and if things worked out to expand her business. Alex also took a new career path. He and two of his best colleagues left the law firm they were working for and opened their own one.

Alex thought about doing all this after the Russell Taylor trial was over, but the investigation dragged on, and he decided it was time for a change. He and Becky supported each other in every new endeavour. She would often listen to him and help him make decisions on the cases he was working on, and he would help her make business decisions about her new store and the staff that would be working for her. Becky had also taken up studying and online training to become a small business manager. When she felt ready, she bought the merchandise she had already arranged for, hired two women to help her, and opened her first shop. The event coincided with Alex's first case with the new law firm. The two were equally enthusiastic about the store and the case. Fortunately for Becky, the store took off. She had researched the area in advance, researched not only if there was a pet store nearby, but also what pets the people there had. She did discounts, promotions, loyalty cards and everything she had learned about in the courses and her diligence paid off. Her first store was a success. After only a few months, Becky was forced to look for more staff and began looking for a new, larger premises in the area. In parallel, Alex won his first case and began preparations for the case against Russell. The police had finally finished everything the prosecution needed, and the case was expected to begin in the next two weeks.

'I'm not ready for this,' Becky told him one evening. 'I don't even want it to start. Look how well we live. I have you and my new job, you have me and your law firm. I have a feeling this lawsuit is going to change all that.'

'Yes, I feel that way too. I can't wait for all this to be over, and we can get on with our lives.'

'Have you heard from Michael recently? Any news on Arnie's murder?'

'No, he hasn't called me, and I don't want to worry him unnecessarily.'

'So, there is nothing new?' Becky asked.

'Nothing about him, but I have news about Carla. She was sentenced to three years in prison.'

'Right? Is she in prison now?'

'Yes.'

'And what will happen to Summer?'

'She will be staying with your father. Do you want to go to the farm and talk to them?'

'No. I will call them to ask if I can help with anything.'

Alex nodded and looked at his beautiful wife. He still couldn't believe he was married to her. He loved her, he had been impressed by her since their first meeting. Now she surprised him again with her humanity. Becky wanted to help the people who had turned against her. Not everyone would understand why she did it, but he did. Becky saw her father and sister as victims, just like her. She would help them, but only if they let her. Alex walked over to her, hugged her, and led her to their room. At times like this, he wanted her only for himself.

Becky called her sister a few days later. Gathering courage for this conversation, she went over what she would like to say to Summer in her head several times, what her first words should be, what she should offer her. Finally, she just picked up the phone and waited for her sister to answer her call. But she didn't. Not that day, not in the next few days. In the end, Becky gave up. When she remembered a week later that it was her sister's birthday, she bought a card, wrote a cheque for a thousand pounds, and sent them off. After a few days, the cheque was cashed. This pleased and reassured Becky. Still, she had a way of helping her sister, even if only on one day of the year. Until Summer decided to talk to her, Becky would be there waiting and hoping.

16.

Russell Taylor's trial began on a dark and cold January day. The headlines were already in the press, *The Knight Will Defend the Princess Again*, and a smile came to Becky's face when she read it. Alex was indeed her *knight.* He was her husband now too and she was very proud of him. Becky went to the courtroom every day. This time she was calm. The looks Russell was giving her didn't bother and startle her. No matter what this man would do, he wasn't going to stop her from testifying against him. And she did, stood in front of the jury, answered all the questions on the defendant's attorneys, and did it in such a way that there was no doubt that this particular man was the first to rape her. She described each pain in great detail, giving the jurors an opportunity to understand not only the physical pain she had gone through, but the emotional, mental pain she continued to go through every time she had to talk about that night. The jury watched her with pity, but the look that affected Becky the most was Russell's father. He seemed to enjoy everything his son had done, as if he was proud of him. Only she and the judge saw that admiration in his eyes. All other eyes were directed in another direction.

'He excited him,' Becky whispered to Alex after they left the court.

'Who?'

'His father. While I was explaining what happened he was enjoying the story.'

'Maybe that's how it seemed to you,' said her husband.

'No, Alex, if you don't believe me, you can ask the judge. She was also shocked by his reaction. I think only the two of us saw that.'

'The apple doesn't fall far from the tree.'

'Exactly,' Becky said and pressed herself against Alex, as if wanting him to protect her from that look.

Becky was going to court, but she hadn't given up on her business and her studies. Now when she had a good footing, her efforts were directed to doing something useful. And the sale of food and toys for the animals was seen as a useful deed. She managed to find a larger premises and moved her shop there. She sourced new and different goods that she and the salesmen arranged on the shelves and customers bought them. The prices were affordable, and the products checked for quality. Every single product that was for sale in the store passed through Becky's hands first. The last thing she wanted was to hurt any animal.

In just two months, the new store gained momentum and was making a greater turnover than expected. Some attributed it to the fame of the owner, but the truth was that Becky worked a lot, looking for new products for this market, of good quality and good price. She liked to stay up late and arrange the items in the store herself. Sometimes Alex would come over with pizza or some other food and the two would talk while she worked. They talked about both her business and the lawsuit they were having against Russell Taylor. The case itself was coming to an end and it was clear to everyone that Becky would win again. This time there were no threats from the courtroom. Russell, sensing where things were going, wanted to meet with Becky and make a deal, but she refused. In herself, she was done with him and his friends. Whatever they had done to her,

Becky buried it deep in her mind again and tried not to think about it. She attended the courtroom, listened to all the evidence and experts, but this time it all sounded like it didn't apply to her. What she was concerned about right now was her husband, his business and hers, and his family and their friends. Everything else didn't seem to matter. She had given several years to crying and worrying, now it was time to enjoy life. And she did, to the surprise of everyone around her.

Alex had also taken this direction. Although he had to fight this tough court case, he somehow felt happy. Becky made him happy, even his father agreed. So, after the case, he planned to take her on another beautiful romantic vacation. He wanted to enjoy her company while he could, to be with her emotionally and physically. The only thing that bothered him and darkened his mood was the lack of information about who killed Arnie and why. They now knew for sure that it wasn't Russell and his father. Somehow, this discovery helped Becky come to her senses and reassure herself that she wasn't the reason someone killed her cousin. Still, the mystery surrounding his murder hung around them, though they didn't talk about it often.

Two months after Russell Taylor's trial began, the jury announced the verdict. Forty-five years in prison and a million and a half in damages. Alex and Becky cried happily at what they heard and once again their hug appeared in the media. But Russell cried. He had probably expected a lighter sentence, though in Alex's opinion even that wasn't enough, but tears of helplessness were flowing from Russell's eyes. Becky was unimpressed by his tears. This man had gotten what he deserved and for the first time since she was a child she felt truly liberated. It was as if someone had dispersed the clouds above her and left her with only the sun's rays.

Becky and Alex went on their dream vacation again. This time they rented a cabin in the Swiss Mountains. They spent more time in the hut than outside and enjoyed the silence around. Becky had appointed one of the saleswomen as store manager before she left, and Alex had taken on two new cases, but they weren't scheduled for another month. For the first time in their lives, the two indulged in laziness. In the end, however, both were eager to leave. Laziness was not for them. They were working people, from those who couldn't sit in one place for long. Becky tackled her store and planned to open another, and Alex tackled the cases his new law firm had taken on. They get up together every morning, had breakfast and talked before going to work, then they separated and did not see each other for the whole day. Sometimes they called each other, exchanged loving texts, but, at the end of the day, they were always together. Often, Becky attended his larger cases, giving him moral support, and he always attended the opening of each of her new stores. Christmas and Easter they spent with Ben and Alex's sister, as well as her five children.

Their lives continued in this way for years. Becky's chain of stores became very famous, and Alex's law company was one of the best. They were an amazing team. The only thing that continued to worry them was Arnie's murder. It took Becky almost two years to recover from his death. For the first few months, she saw him everywhere, sometimes even heard noises from his room, but when she opened the door and he wasn't there, reality hit her and her eyes watered. Other times she would think of something, some new idea or something from her childhood and unconsciously dial his phone to share it with him, but then she felt it and the sadness came over her again. Alex felt the same way, and even though they were both happy, Arnie's absence from their lives left a void that no one over the years could fill. After five years of painstaking searching, no evidence was ever found as to who had killed him and why. With each passing year, Michael thought the chances of catching the killer were getting slimmer and slimmer, and he had declared the case one of the most complicated he had ever worked on. At least two people had a motive to kill Arnie, but there was no evidence that either of them did.

'Maybe we should publicize his murder. When it happened, it was reported that he was killed by one of Becky's abusers. That's the only information out there in the media. Maybe we should talk to a journalist and put the case to them again. Let's look for witnesses,' suggested Michael one day.

'And how will that help?' Becky was surprised.

'If anyone knows or has seen something, they can call. You never know where a lead can come from,' said Tanya.

'I think Tanya is right,' agreed Alex. 'Only we know that the murder is unsolved. If someone has seen something, they may think that the criminal is already in prison and not feel the need to pass on any information.'

Becky reflected on what Alex and Tanya said. They were probably right, and they hadn't done their best to look for eyewitnesses until now.

'A journalist contacted me some time ago. She wants to write a book about my life. I promised to call her if Alex and I decide to do it, but I can call her and ask her to write something about Arnie's case.'

'I think it's a good idea,' said Michael. 'An eyewitness can be found. To tell you the truth, sometimes I can't sleep thinking about Arnie.'

'It's the same with me,' Becky admitted and looked at Alex, who sometimes blurted out the name of his best friend.

'In any case, we will all be more relaxed if we know who killed him and why. I will talk to the journalist tomorrow.'

After finding Arnie's body, several forensic scientists searched his room and found nothing to give them a new lead. Becky suggested that Michael go in there again, review his papers and belongings. Although they had the opportunity to buy a new, bigger house, Alex and Becky didn't do it. The reason was that they couldn't face going into her cousin's room. Inside, everything was left as he had left it. Neither Becky nor Alex had gone in there. They had opened the door sometimes but remained at the threshold. They never managed to get inside, as if something or someone was stopping them. For them it was his room, his sanctuary. Michael agreed to go through Arnie's belongings again, though he doubted he would find anything. Becky, in turn, called the journalist, who agreed to write something about the case only if Becky reconsidered her request about the book.

'I don't know if the book would be a good idea,' Becky told Alex when they had dinner.

'Why not?'

'It will bring back all the memories, we will have to go through everything again.'

'But then people will understand what kind of person Arnie was, they will understand that in this difficult moment he helped you. Write the book in his honour,' suggested Alex. 'Tell the story from your point of view. Your rapists already told theirs.'

'You're right,' Becky agreed. The four who had raped her had made a very good deal and told their version of what happened that night. According to the media, each of them had earned over five hundred thousand pounds from their book sales. Becky didn't care about the money, her business was doing well, and so was Alex's. They probably wouldn't have to worry about money for the rest of their lives. What she cared about was the truth, and if the book could show how good her cousin was. She would do it.

One month later she and Alex reconnected with the journalist named Victoria Mace and signed a contract with her. Six months later, the book *Becky: My Story* was on the shelves of bookstores, and two months after that it was declared a bestseller. Becky didn't care about the book's rating. All she wanted to know was if it would help them find the killer. Unfortunately, no one contacted them.

'This book was probably a mistake,' Becky said one evening. 'So many people are asking me for autographs now. I can barely get into my office.'

'All this will pass soon. They accost me too. They ask me if I really poured coffee on you.'

Becky smiled at the memory of their first meeting.

'What do you tell them?'

'To read the book again,' Alex smiled as well. 'I checked, it says that you spilled the coffee yourself, but people read what they want.'

'Yes. Some readers forget that Arnie is my cousin and ask me how I chose to marry you and not him.' Becky's smile was even wider this time.

'Paul will be devastated. Your choice was between him and me.'

'Actually, it was always just you. I just didn't realize it and needed some advice and guidance.'

Alex reached out and pulled her close and hugged her. 'You and I have been a good team since the beginning. Arnie knew it.'

'Yes. Who killed him and why?' Becky asked.

'We'll find out someday. Sometimes things just happen. I'm sure the person we wrote this book for will read it and call us to help.'

'Victoria mentioned that there is an inquiry from a film company about the copyright. They want to make a movie about my story.'

'And what do you think?'

'I don't know, Alex. It's like this is getting out of hand.'

'Maybe only you think so. Your life is amazing, I'm not surprised people are interested in it. And being a part of this life of yours makes me happy. Some people don't like to read, maybe after watching the movie they will find an answer to their questions.'

'Such as?'

'Like, for example, is there justice. I think there is. The fact that rapists are in prison and you and I are here hugging and happy.'

'Yes, that's right. I'll think about it,' she promised.

'The decision is yours. I would take advantage and include Arnie's death in the contract. People need to know who he is, and I hope someone will contact us and tell us why he died.'

Becky thought about it for a long time. It was one thing to have a book about her and the people around her, but a movie, that seemed more than necessary. Before making any decision, she decided to talk to each of her relatives and friends. Again, Michael and Tanya thought that the film would be beneficial in spreading the word about Arnie's death. Ben was against having a movie about his daughter-in-law and his son. The motive of finding a witness to Arnie's murder wasn't working for him. For him, it was the job of the police, not the media and the film companies. Janey, like Becky, was hesitant about the effect of filming the book. Paul and Catherine were for the film. So, the scales weighed and a few months later, Alex and Becky signed a new contract, this time with a major American film company. Becky had decided to expand her business and make it international, so she was delighted when she was invited to America for the casting of the actors. Paul and Catherine were also thrilled. They still lived in Los Angeles and having their friends there was a nice event. According to the contract, Becky was supposed to be available and give recommendations and advice about some of the events that happened in her life, Alex didn't have to be there. Therefore, the two decided to leave together, but for Alex to stay only for a week. Then he would return to London and continue working. Becky didn't want to be apart from him, but she finally relented. She would be without him for a whole two weeks. They hadn't been apart before, and she wasn't sure how she was going to handle it.

The first casting was scheduled for September First. Becky and Alex left three days before and stayed over at Paul and Catherine's house with their two children. Unlike Becky, who was not ready yet to become a mother, Catherine wanted at least five children, but she and Paul had reconsidered after the second. Catherine's career began to wane after the birth of their second child, and she struggled to revive it by going to every audition for a musical that came along.

Paul, for his part, also worked a lot. He had become the boss of a paediatric clinic. It was interesting for Becky and Alex to watch Paul and Catherine as parents. Two new personalities seemed to appear in front of them, which disappeared immediately after the children fell asleep. They were a beautiful, happy family, and Alex and Becky envied them. Becky thought there were still a lot of ghosts and death around her and that it wouldn't bode well for a child, so she and Alex had put off having a baby for a while until they felt they were ready for it. Not that he wasn't ready, but he had agreed with her. They had to clear their lives of the ghosts, and that wouldn't happen until they found Arnie's killer. Before that, none of them would have been able to start their lives afresh.

After the short stay with Paul and Catherine, Becky and Alex moved into one of the apartments that the casting company provided them. There were two days of casting for the role of Becky and two days for the role of Alex. It wasn't easy to find the right actress to play Becky, especially since Becky was there, not a fictional character, but they found the right woman on the first day. She didn't look much like Becky, but her temperament, her character, the way she spoke— all of it was reminiscent of her. Becky was happy with the choice. In the casting for the role of Alex, things were different. The actor everyone wanted was busy with another role at the time the movie was going to be shot. So, they had to spend extra two days looking for someone to replace him.

'Maybe you should talk to him,' said the director. 'If you meet him and personally ask him to get the role of your husband, he might agree.'

Becky was surprised at the request. She had never participated in a film production. She didn't understand why an actor's decision should depend on her.

'He is famous, he can choose his roles himself. Therefore, I think that if you tell him why you want this film and attract his interest, he will agree and participate,' advised Veronica, who was kind of an assistant to Becky.

Becky nodded and promised to meet the actor the next day after seeing off Alex, whose few days off were over. The thought of living apart from him bothered her. Moreover, the two would be not only in different cities, but also on different continents. The very thought of him being away from her took her breath away, but she had made a commitment and she had to keep it. Alex left late in the evening the next day. Only after the plane took off did Becky call the actor and ask for a meeting with him.

'I have already refused the role,' he answered her.

'Still, I would like to meet you if you have free time and tell you why I want this film.'

The man on the other end of the line was silent. 'Okay. Let me know where you're staying, I'll drop by tomorrow to talk, sometime in the afternoon, is that okay?'

'Yes. Wonderful,' she was delighted. Then she headed for the quiet and empty hotel room. Becky already missed Alex. She tried to sleep but tossed and turned all night. She imagined that Alex's plane had crashed or that someone had kidnapped him. Her concern for him grew with each passing minute. Sometimes she got up and followed his flight path online, and it made her feel better knowing he was there and probably thinking about her too. Finally at eight in the morning he called her that he was at home, and she calmed down and fell asleep. She woke up at noon and, forgetting that she had a meeting, continued to lie down. Then she went out for a walk on the hotel's small private beach, expecting Alex to call her again after he woke.

Becky sat on the beach and stared at the waves. They reminded her of Cornwall and yet they were different. They came and went. They were calm that day, and that calmness and homesickness showed on her face. As she sat like that a man approached her and sat down next to her. She was worried at first, then she recognized him. It was the actor she was supposed to be talking to.

'You were not at the hotel and from there they told me that they last saw you here.'

'Yes. I thought you would call when you arrived.'

'I would have, but I was on the phone on the way over. I'm already here anyway.'

'Thanks for agreeing to talk to me,' Becky said and looked at the man next to her. She understood why they wanted him for the role. Victor Sean looked a lot like Alex. Same build, same eyes, and nose. Only his mouth and chin were different.

'I have half an hour, so...' said Viktor, who was already intrigued, but didn't mention this to her.

'I don't know if you've read the book,' she began uncertainly.

'I read the script and I admit that your life amazed me.'

'Yes. Actually, I agreed to this movie not because of me and my life, but because of my cousin's life.'

Victor frowned, trying to remember the script and who exactly her cousin was.

'I don't expect you to remember everything,' Becky smiled. 'I know how busy you are, so I'll be brief. My cousin saved me after I was almost killed. Unfortunately, a few years later he himself was killed. At first, we thought one of my abusers killed him, but we have no evidence of that. There is another clue, but the investigation has stopped there as well. The purpose of this film is to make more people aware of Arnie's fate and if there is an eyewitness or witness to his abduction or murder to contact us.'

'Wow,' Victor exclaimed. This was not what he had expected when he had agreed to meet her. He had expected her to be advocating on her own behalf. But what she said out left him speechless. Her beauty, too. Becky was one of the most beautiful women he had ever seen, and he had seen many.

Becky's phone rang, she apologized and picked up.

There was no doubt in Victor's mind that she was talking to Alex. Her gestures, her smile, her look, everything suggested that she was talking to him. That part of the script he remembered. The man who did everything for her, everything possible to protect her. Victor watched Becky as she spoke and felt a desire to feel that kind of love, to meet a woman who would talk about him and to him like that. And his interest in the film immediately changed. He would do it. He would participate in it. Not for Arnie or anything else, but for her. She had caught his attention and he wasn't sure exactly with what, but she had won him over to her side. Becky ended the conversation and sat down next to him on the sand again. She was staring at the waves as if she saw something there.

'Sorry, I had to talk to Alex. We are separated for the first time.'

'You miss him,' Victor smiled.

'Yes,' she smiled too.

'You managed to talk me into it, Becky. Tell Veronica I'm going to be in the movie. Have them contact my agent.'

Becky looked at him in astonishment and, moved by his change of heart, hugged him.

'You won't regret it,' she told him, and her eyes sparkled with excitement.

'I know I won't regret it. Come, I'll get you a drink before I leave.'

Becky got up and texted Alex and Veronica a quick message. She then followed Victor to a nearby bar, satisfied that she had successfully completed her mission. The two sat at a table overlooking the ocean and talked about the things of life. While they were sipping their drinks, his fans came and took pictures of them or asked for his autograph.

'The paparazzi don't bother you,' he was surprised.

'No. During the three trials we went through, me and Alex were constantly photographed.'

'And what if Alex sees a picture of us drinking cocktails at the bar.'

'I already sent him one,' Becky smiled and showed him the photo.

'So, you both trust each other,' he looked at her in amazement.

'Yes. Alex and I are very close, until yesterday we hadn't even parted.'

'There's always a first time,' he said, winking at her.

'If that's a pickup line, forget it. I will never cheat on Alex, and I'm not interested in you as a man, but as an actor.'

Victor looked away. Without even realizing it, Becky had hurt his ego. Until now, there was no woman who would stand up to him. He looked at her, saw that she was writing to her husband again, and decided that this woman was different. He was going to spend his time with her and, even though he had told her they would only have a drink for five minutes, he stayed and talked with her late into the evening. Becky talked to her husband from time to time. She looked like she was in love and thinking about him, and that surprised Victor even more. In the world he lived in, marriages were a one-day affair. People in his circles married and divorced in the same year. Into this world he was born, in this world he grew up. Women like Becky didn't belong here, not in this bar, not on this beach. She was like a rare, beautiful diamond, and Victor's desire to have her grew stronger with each passing hour.

'I have to go,' she finally told him, surprised that he stayed with her for several hours. At least that made the day easier, she thought.

'Okay,' he raised his glass. 'See you soon. I'll see you on set, I guess.'

'Yes. They plan to start the film in a few months. See you soon,' she said, smiled and hurried to the hotel.

The meeting with Victor surprised her. She'd thought he was one of those cocky actors who only thought of themselves, but he turned out to be cool and decent. Becky dialled Alex's phone and told him more about her meeting with the actor.

'He really looks like you,' she told him. 'Especially in the eyes.'

'You're not going to replace me with a younger version, are you?' Alex joked.

'Of course not. And he's your age, he's not younger, he's just had more plastic surgery.'

Becky missed Alex. She couldn't wait for the castings to be over quickly and to get home to him in their little house in Stratford.

'Michael called,' said Alex. 'A witness to the kidnapping called. The man worked in one of the offices where Arnie worked. He read the newspaper article and, as we assumed, decided the police knew who the killer was and didn't call the police.'

'Alex, this could really work. Maybe someone saw the murder, or someone saw who moved Arnie's body to that place in Cornwall.'

'Let's hope that we will be able to find witnesses,' Alex said in a tired voice. The travel was hard on him. He had hardly slept and now he felt tired and even though it was early he said good night to Becky and went to sleep.

Becky was tired and fell asleep in no time. A few days later she went home to her husband, happy to be home and that all was well again. She was due back in Los Angeles in two months, but until then she was going to enjoy her life in London.

The man who had seen part of the abduction was sitting in their kitchen sipping freshly made tea. Michael wanted to talk to him, but he couldn't use his office, which was under renovation, so he had asked Becky to set up a meeting.

'I read your book,' said the witness. 'Now I regret not going to the police immediately. At first, I thought it was a prank between friends because it looked like the two knew each other.'

'What did they say?' Michael asked.

'I don't know. I was inside the building talking to a customer on the phone. I couldn't hear what they were talking about, I didn't even see the other's face because I could only see the back of his head. Arnie approached him, said something to him, the other answered and hit him. Just then the car came and picked them up.'

'You mean Arnie got into the car by himself?'

'Yes, he turned as if to see for someone or something and then got into the car.'

'He may have thought the policeman was following him and had seen what was happening,' Alex said.

'What policeman?' the man asked. 'There was no one else around.'

'An undercover police officer was attached to Arnie,' explained Becky.

'Okay. As I said there was no one else. Everything happened very quickly, and since the man got into the car by himself, I decided that he knew his attacker.'

'They probably knew each other. Arnie wouldn't just walk into a stranger's car.'

'Will you describe the car and the man in more detail, as well as the driver of the car?'

'The driver was a woman.'

'Right? What age?' Michael asked.

'About forty. I managed to get a good look at her. You know... I was impressed.' The witness described everything as he had seen it and left.

'That's good,' Michael rubbed his chin contentedly. 'I have a new clue. I just need to confirm it.'

'You think you know who kidnapped him?' Becky looked at the detective with hope.

'Yes, I think I know, but I have to check first.'

'Okay. Let's go then.'

Tanya pushed her husband out and they hurried to the car.

'I hope you find him,' Becky muttered and sat down in the chair next to Alex.

'The book had an effect. The man remembered what happened to Arnie, and the photo he had them put on the front page helped with that. I won't even mention the money in our bank account.'

'We won't be able to spend all this money, Alex. Maybe it's time to donate some of it.'

'Okay. We'll talk about that tomorrow.'

Becky nodded. There was time for that. First, they had to find the killer.

17.

Despite the hope that they had a new and good lead, that lead led nowhere. Michael was hoping to see the man or the car from the dashcam footage they had taken of Arnie's disappearance, but the witness didn't recognize either. The only new thing he could think of was a tattoo of a small bird with outstretched wings on the woman's left arm. The investigation stalled again. They were waiting for someone else to call. While they were waiting, Becky's two months passed and she had to, as much as she didn't want to, go to the set. This film gave her new hopes, that someone would remember and help. But the idea of being away from Alex for a long time didn't sit well with her. So, they made a plan. Every two weeks, one of them would travel. Becky would leave and Alex would visit her two weeks later. In another two weeks she would be back in London for a few days, until the Christmas holidays, when the film shoot was due to end. After making the plan, they both felt better.

Becky left as always with some luggage. Even if she had millions in the bank, she was still a poor girl at heart, and although she spent thousands of pounds on merchandise for her shops, she never got around to buying expensive clothes and jewellery. She bought what she liked, sometimes even from the pound shops. She couldn't, like other wealthier women, set aside a whole day for shopping. She didn't have time, and she didn't enjoy spending money on clothes.

When she arrived on the set, the first thing she was amazed by were the sets. It was as if she was in London, on her street, in front of her house.

'Amazing, isn't it?' Veronica told her. 'They photographed your house with a drone and recreated it down to the smallest detail in just a few days.'

'Yes,' Becky answered, still amazed. 'I feel like I'm at home.'

'I'll show you around,' said the young woman and showed Becky all the sets for the film. Becky walked around and couldn't believe how realistic everything looked.

'Only the weather is not the same,' she finally said. It was very warm outside, and she couldn't wait to get somewhere with air conditioning. Veronica took her to the caravan designated for her, told her about the breaks for breakfast, lunch and dinner and left her to rest.

Becky was thrilled by the setting. She went out a few times just to take photos of the sets and send them to Alex. The guard then explained to her that she was not contractually allowed to do that and asked her to delete the photos from her phone. This brought her back to reality. She didn't know anyone here; she didn't know where to go or what to do. So, she did the first thing that came to her mind, called Alex.

'I think I was wrong to agree to come here.'

'You'll be fine, Becky. Just a few more days and I will come to you.'

Becky wasn't sure. Looking at the people around, all busy, knowing who should do what and where to go, she felt out of place. She wanted to catch the first plane to London and go back to him, to her husband. What kind of woman abandons her husband like that, she wondered.

'I miss you too,' Alex told her. 'And I know it's hard for you. Call Veronica and ask her when they will need you. If they don't need you, go to Paul and Catherine. You could at least help them look after the kids for a few days. I'm sure they won't mind.'

'You're right. I'm dramatizing again. I will call Veronica and then Catherine.'

'And then let me know what's going on.'

'Okay,' Becky smiled. Veronica didn't pick up right away, so Becky called Catherine, who was ecstatic that her friend was coming to visit her again.

However, Veronica thwarted their plans. They needed Becky in the next few days. Becky got up at half past five like everyone else, had a quick breakfast and went to the set where the scenes were to be shot. She stayed there until late at night. She had no idea that acting was so complicated and exhausting. The actors went from take to take and repeated everything until it worked. At the end of the first week, Becky was already very tired. Not only from the work but also from the heat. Veronica advised her to take a day off and go see her friends. That very day, however, Paul and Catherine had to go somewhere, and Becky was left alone all day in the caravan. The only consolation was her conversations with Alex. Her days were long and exhausting, but finally the two weeks passed, and Alex came to her for a few days. She expected him to call her and for her to meet him at the airport, but to her surprise, at half past five in the morning, the first person she saw when she got out of the caravan was him. Becky had never felt more excited in her life, she stood in front of him and wrapped her arms around his waist, and Alex kissed her head.

Victor Sean, who had arrived for the morning shots, watched the couple in love. They were like one. They didn't talk, they didn't go on and on about how much they missed each other. Becky and Alex just sat in each other's arms outside her caravan and stayed like that for almost a minute. Victor had never seen such closeness in his life. He looked at them a little longer, then walked thoughtfully to the breakfast room. It would be difficult for him to play this role. First, because his character was not fictional, but a person of flesh and blood. And secondly, because what he saw, the closeness between these two people was foreign to him. He didn't know how to get under Alex's skin. He didn't have that experience. Victor had never met a woman who could arouse such feelings in him.

'They are a nice couple, aren't they?' Veronica said after Alex and Becky entered the room.

'That's right,' Victor followed the two lovers again. In the past two months, he had read Becky's book and looked at every article and picture of her and Alex he could find online. According to the facts, Becky, and Alex had been married for five years and first met seven years ago. However, looking at them right now, they looked like newlyweds, as if they were still enjoying their honeymoon.

Becky and Alex felt the eyes of everyone present and couldn't understand why there was such interest in them. They had already met most of the team. Becky knew almost everyone, and the reaction to their appearance with Alex surprised her.

'Are we doing something wrong?' she asked Veronica after they sat next to her.

'No. On the contrary, you behave naturally and here this is appreciated as something rare. They will get used to your presence.'

'So, I'm the reason,' Alex put in.

'No, it's not you. It's hard for me to explain, but I'm sure you'll understand in time. Relax, eat, and come to the set. Victor's role begins today. Alex, you came just in time to guide your doppelgänger.'

Alex laughed and looked over to where the actor had been sitting until recently, but he was gone.

When they saw Victor two hours later, they both gasped. He was like a carbon copy of Alex. The make-up artists had removed the differences between the two men as if with a magic wand. Veronica laughed at their reaction.

'I wonder if they stand next to each other Becky will be able to guess who the original is?' she suggested.

'I'm sure I would recognize Alex even among twenty copies of him, but I have to admit that the resemblance is striking.'

'That's why we wanted Victor from the very beginning. He and your husband are like twins.'

'That's right,' Alex agreed and looked at his copy. Then he smiled. 'I don't look bad, do I?'

'Not at all,' answered Becky and hugged him around the waist again. She was glad he was with her.

The shooting started again, and everyone's attention turned to it. Becky and Alex helped the actors as much as they could, trying to tell them the events and feelings they had at the time, but it was hard for both of them when they had to explain something about Arnie.

After almost three gruelling months, the shooting of the film was finally over. Becky happily returned to London but was surprised to find that she missed the people from the film crew. While there she befriended Veronica and Victor. Alex's copy followed her almost everywhere. He had become one of her best friends and when Alex came over the three of them would often go off set and have fun in the big city. Victor showed them the good and bad sides of Los Angeles, told them about his life, which hadn't changed much since he was born. His mother and father, still working actors, had gotten him into the guild when he was three years old. There was only room in his life for good roles and cinema, he often told Becky.

'What do you do when you're not filming?' she asked him once.

'Have fun. I go out with friends to bars, sometimes I go on holidays. I like to visit Europe and Asia. But I always go there alone.'

'I can't imagine going somewhere alone,' thought Becky.

'You have Alex. Not everyone is lucky like you both are. You have each other,' he replied and looked at her.

'Yes,' she said thoughtfully. 'Two years ago, we made a trip around the world. We took three weeks off and visited almost all the places we had planned. Our best vacation so far,' she smiled, and her eyes sparkled at the memory.

Victor felt jealous for the first time in his life. Before he met Becky, his life was simple and orderly. All he cared about was work. Everything else was secondary. However, Becky and Alex changed his life without even realizing it. This closeness between the two of them, this trust, he envied it. He wanted to have it, to feel the same feelings, and for some reason he thought that those feelings were not so much caused by Alex, but by Becky's character: sensual and vulnerable on the one hand, and strong and determined on the other. A woman without pretence and pampering. Victor defined her in one word—natural. She wasn't even bothered by the scars on her thighs and shoulders that she had. She wore them as if they were something natural.

'They are a part of me,' she had explained to him. 'I see no reason to correct them. I have nothing to hide.'

In Victor's circles, Becky made an impression, people turned their heads attracted by both her beautiful face and healed wounds. When she was with Alex, the two of them attracted even more attention. There was something between the two of them, an attraction so strong that it was visible to other people as well. Sometimes Victor felt uncomfortable when he was with them, like he was an intruder and didn't belong with them. But he stood and soaked up their energy, excused himself, as doing it for the role, but the truth was that he wanted to be there and feel even a small percentage of that mutual feeling. When the filming was over, and Becky and Alex left, the feeling of missing something in his life was very strong. It was as if someone close to him had died and he admitted to himself that he had become obsessed with Becky's presence. For several months he had breakfast with her, talked with her, absorbed her every word. And now he missed all of that. Victor started looking for a way to get to London or find a reason for Becky and Alex to visit his hometown again.

Becky also missed Victor, but after a few weeks of work and commitments, she almost forgot about him. Her life got back to normal. She worked in the shops and Alex in his law firm. They spent the Christmas holidays with Alex's family, then plunged back into their everyday lives until the movie hit cinemas. The two went to the premiere and already at the first screening they knew that the film would be a hit. It was strange watching their lives on screen. The film itself opened with a personal appeal from Becky for anyone who saw anything related to Arnie's abduction and murder to contact the police in the United Kingdom.

After that, the movie itself was amazing. The performance of all the actors was so believable that Becky and Alex couldn't catch their breath with excitement almost throughout the film.

Victor was sitting next to them, watching their reaction.

'Unbelievable,' Becky exclaimed after the movie ended. 'I didn't expect it to affect me like that.'

'Thank you,' the actor smiled, looked around and noticed the same excitement among the other spectators. It became clear to him that this film would be recorded as one of the best in his career, and the credit was not his alone. Credit went to the whole team and especially Becky and Alex. It was worth the effort, Victor thought, and looked back at the couple next to him.

'Don't look at her so intently,' Veronica nudged him. What she said startled him. He forced his gaze away from Becky and stared at the crowd in front of them. Everyone was watching them, the attention this time was not only on him and his colleague playing the role of Becky, but on the two people sitting next to him. Under normal circumstances Victor would have been irritated by this, he didn't like being overshadowed, but now he preferred not to be watched so closely.

Becky and Alex were used to receiving the attention of the media, but what followed was something they had never faced before. Crowds of fans made their way to them and gathered around them. At first, they thought they were after Victor, who accompanied them almost everywhere, but after the crowd pushed him away too, they realized that all this attention was because of them.

'Welcome to my world,' the actor told them and put them in the car that was waiting for them as quickly as he could.

'This is crazy,' Becky complained after someone had yanked on her bracelet and taken it with them.

'It's not madness, it's called fame,' said Victor and laughed heartily. Alex would get more trouble than Becky since he looked so much like the actor playing him.

'That was not the idea of this movie. Our idea is to help find Arnie's killer.' Becky's displeasure grew with each passing minute. She was eager to leave America and go home to London, but, according to Inspector Ramsey, things were no different there. The police had received hundreds of false calls, all convinced that they had seen something related to her cousin's murder.

'There are always people in front of your house. We have security posted, but my advice is to go somewhere for a while and not come back here for now.'

Inspector Ramsey had moved to work in London and called them often. She and her family had become some of the closest people to them, especially after Paul and Catherine left.

During their short stay in Los Angeles, Alex had met Paul in private, as his friend had requested. It turned out that he and Catherine had not been living together for a long time and Paul had moved into his new girlfriend's house. Catherine, frustrated by her husband's infidelities, had finally made him move out, but hadn't shared this with Becky.

'But why didn't she tell me?' she wondered. 'I could go and help her with something.'

'According to Paul, she was ashamed of the failure of their marriage. He says it's all his fault. You know him, women are his weakness, and this movie presents him in a different light. I guess that's the problem. Paul asked that we not tell anyone and that you call Catherine to find out what will be told to the press and what won't.'

Becky made several attempts to call Catherine, but her friend never returned her call. Alex knew the real reason for that. Becky had succeeded where Catherine had struggled for years and had become famous. Her friend was jealous and couldn't swallow this easily. After a while, Becky figured this out on her own. Even if she were to hear from Catherine there would be nothing to say, she didn't know what to do to calm her down and with each passing day she regretted agreeing to the film more and more.

She and Alex were wondering where to go where no one would recognize them. They decided to rent their own beach and bungalow in Zanzibar. Only a few people knew where they were. Alex was tired from all this attention, and he really needed this break. They had stocked up on books and prepared to lay on the beach for days. On the very first day, however, the beach they had rented was filled with natives. They were all singing and dancing in their language, apparently performing some sort of ritual, and Becky and Alex watched them from the bungalow with bated breath. Then Becky went out and approached the dancing people. A woman pulled her up and invited her to dance with them. Becky refused but sat down by one of the fires that had been lit and gazed at the wonderful dance. Alex also joined her. With these people they spent the next two weeks. They learned to fish, to ride in something like a canoe, and to sing and dance in their own way. It was as if they had gone back in time, where there was no civilization, no internet, and no car noise. Here on this beach everything was primordial, people smiling and children free.

'I know It's unbelievable, but I love being here with them,' Alex shared.

'Me too,' Becky smiled as she prepared to swim in the sea. 'I have never felt freer.'

After a fortnight they both said goodbye to their new friends and returned to London, where the commotion was still the same. There were several people outside their door waiting for their autograph. Once they had signed all the pictures and posters there was finally just one woman left, apparently waiting to talk to them, but she wasn't a fan of the movie. Becky and Alex recognized the tattoo on her hand. It was in the shape of a bird between her index finger and thumb. The bird's wings folded when the fingers folded and spread apart when the index finger moved sideways. Becky invited the woman into the house, and Alex stayed outside for a while to call Michael and Inspector Ramsey and tell them about her visit.

'You didn't ask me who I am, but you invited me inside?' she was surprised.

'We heard about your tattoo,' Becky explained.

'Someone must have seen me.'

'That's right. What's your name?' Alex asked.

'Irene. My name is Irene.'

'We called Inspector Ramsey and the private detective we're working with. I hope you don't mind,' Becky explained.

'No, I don't mind. It's time to give you some answers.'

'Five years have passed. Why did you come now?' Becky asked her with reproach in her voice.

'I thought you caught Arnie's killer. I didn't think... I didn't think you needed my information until I saw the movie trailer and your plea for help.'

'So, you don't know who killed him?' Alex asked.

'No, but I can guess who it might be,' she whispered. 'I guess it was my ex-husband.'

'Was he in the car that day?'

'Yes. But I was driving. We took Arnie to a restaurant where he promised my ex-husband, he would never see me again.'

'You were his girlfriend, the one he was texting?'

'Yes, me and Arnie had a relationship. I had just broken up with my husband. I was in a coffee shop close to my office and Arnie was working in the building next door. I was talking to my ex-husband. I was very upset, and Arnie came over and handed me a tissue to wipe away my tears. That's how we met.'

'But why didn't you come and tell us after he was killed? Why didn't you come to his funeral?' Becky asked in a sharp tone. Alex pulled her back and stopped her.

'This woman was a victim of domestic violence. Isn't that right, Irene?' he asked gently.

The woman folded her hands and placed them in her lap. Her concern was palpable. She didn't need to answer.

'I'm sorry,' Becky said quietly. She approached Irene and gently hugged her by the shoulders. 'Sorry, but you were our only clue and to see you now in front of me, five years later, is shocking.'

The doorbell rang. Michael joined them in the kitchen, he sensed something was wrong and instead of asking questions he retreated to a corner and remained silent.

'I can tell you that my husband hated Arnie. The day he disappeared, I found out by chance that he was going to talk to him. Knowing his severe temper,

I became concerned and went to warn Arnie, only to find them arguing in the street. My ex-husband got mad when he saw me and made Arnie get in the car.'

'So that's why he voluntarily went inside,' Michael said thoughtfully. 'Sorry, I didn't mean to interrupt you. I'm Michael. What happened after you left?'

'My husband insisted that we go to one of his restaurants and talk there. His restaurant is on Palmers Green, so I took us all there. We went in, Arnie and I agreed not to see each other again, and immediately after that Arnie left. He said he was in a hurry and had an important meeting.'

'What happened to your husband after Arnie left?'

'He and I stayed to dine there.'

'Did Arnie say who he was meeting or where?'

'No.'

'Do you remember which direction he went?'

'No, I only remember his back when he was going to the door. Then he turned and looked at me with that look, you know, the one that says everything will be fine, and left. I was so upset that in order for my husband not to see that I was crying, I immediately went to the toilet.'

'Where was your husband at that time?'

'He headed to the kitchen. He said they needed him for some errand for an order.'

'Okay, but from what you say, you are his alibi. Why do you think he killed him?' Becky was surprised.

'He said he was going to take care of an order,' explained Michael, who immediately understood the situation.

Becky stared at the woman across from her. What she wouldn't have given if she had come earlier and explained what had happened. Arnie obviously loved her and cared for her.

'Where is your ex-husband now?' Alex asked her.

'I don't know. I haven't seen him in five years. I left him as soon as I found out about Arnie. I even though he killed him, but on TV they said someone else did.'

Michael sighed, reproaching himself that he hadn't thought to seek information sooner. The doorbell rang again, this time it was Inspector Ramsey. She listened quickly to Irene's story and asked her to go with her and testify. The woman agreed, then looked at one of the pictures in the kitchen and cried.

'He's dead because of me,' she sobbed.

'We don't know yet, Irene. I've been through this before. I thought my actions and what happened to me killed him. The truth is, until we know the truth, we won't know exactly what happened. But there is something that I don't think adds up. Arnie was escorted by a policeman. Did you see him anywhere nearby?'

'Yes, Arnie called him to tell him where we were going, and he followed us. Now if you ask me, he went after him after Arnie left the restaurant.'

'Then why didn't he mention it?' wondered Ramsey. Michael also asked himself this question. They needed to find Irene's ex-husband as quickly as possible. After everyone had left, Alex and Becky sat wearily in the living room, each lost in thought. Arnie's life was more complicated than either of them had imagined. And for the first time since he'd left the house, Becky felt like going up to his room and going through his things again. Alex followed her but stayed in the doorway. He didn't know what Becky was looking for, so he let her do it herself.

A memory haunted her, something she often dreamed about. That dream where Arnie was trying to tell her something, but she didn't understand, in that dream, the same one she'd had for years. Becky looked around his desk, then his closet, picked up a few shirts from the shelf, shuffled a few books, and then she saw what she was looking for. A small picture of a bird, the same as Irene's tattoo. On the frame was written *To feel the freedom.* Becky remembered the day she saw Arnie carrying that little painting and thought he'd bought it because of her, but now that she looked and saw the artist's name, she knew it was by Irene. Becky took the picture from the shelf and, when she turned it over, she saw a small memory stick attached to it. She and Alex went through its contents, but neither of them understood anything from the documents and photos that Arnie had stored there, so they forwarded all the information to Inspector Ramsey, Michael, and Arnie's former boss, Max. They hoped one of them would understand something.

'What a day, huh?' Alex muttered looking at his phone. It was almost midnight.

'Yes,' Becky agreed and leaned against his chest. She was thinking of Irene. Before he was killed, Arnie often talked to his new girlfriend on the phone, but, unlike his other girlfriends, he kept it a secret. Becky had decided that she was the reason, but now she understood that this woman's life had also been complicated and Arnie wanted to protect her. How little she knew about her cousin. Arnie had hidden parts of his life from her. He had hidden his job and his girlfriend, the most important things for a man like him. Becky was wondering why he had done it and Alex was asking herself the same questions.

'He probably didn't want to bother us,' he said aloud, assuming as always that they were thinking the same thing.

'We could have taken her with us to that spa hotel,' Becky suggested.

'She might have been there. He told me he had found a woman for the night, and I wonder if he was with her then. I knew he was a charmer, but I was amazed that he found a woman in just a few hours of staying at the hotel.'

'Of course, she was there. He suggested we stay two more days so he could spend more time with her.'

'Have we been so deluded?' Alex looked at Becky in surprise.

'No, we were absorbed in each other and didn't notice what was happening to him. We didn't even ask him how he was,' she remembered with sadness.

'I couldn't take my eyes off you, and he knew it. He leaved us both to rest. Irene's complicated life would certainly have been a new stress for us.'

'I miss him, Alex. But why did he withhold everything from us?'

'Maybe he was waiting for the right moment to tell us.'

'Maybe,' Becky leaned back against his chest. She felt best there, calm, and safe. She felt sorry for this woman, to part with her beloved like that. It must have been hard for her.

'We'll find out what happened to him,' whispered Alex quietly. 'That's the most important thing.'

I just hope there aren't any skeletons still to come out of the closet, Becky thought. Nothing would surprise her anymore. She had stopped blaming herself for Arnie's death. The possibility that he had been killed for his own way of life grew more and more every day.

Becky and Alex couldn't sleep all night. Before Becky's eyes was Irene, tormented, alone and miserable. Alex, for his part, was thinking about Arnie and the chances he had given him to get together with Becky. He had left him alone with her for most of their stay at the spa hotel and had told him that his cousin didn't realize how much she loved him, and that Alex needed to give her time.

Becky and Alex got up at four in the morning. They had both tossed and turned in bed, unable to drift off. Becky turned on the laptop and began to look again at the photos and documents from the memory stick they had found. She went through everything slowly, in order not to miss anything important. Alex was sitting next to her, also studying the files left behind. As they looked at one of the pictures, they both gasped and shifted in their chairs.

'That's him, isn't it?' Becky asked.

'I'm sure it's him. The person Albert was looking at in the courtroom.'

Underneath the photo was the caption, "Two days before."

'Who are the people with him?' Becky asked and looked at them but didn't recognize anyone.

'What did Arnie get his hands on?' Alex whispered and immediately dialled Michael's phone. To his surprise, the detective was also awake and looking at the information on the memory stick.

'He should have told me,' he was angry. 'Why didn't he tell me what he found?'

'Look at the date, maybe he was thinking of telling you. It is from the date of his abduction.'

'You're right. He must have been surfing the internet at night. As an employee of the agency, he worked for, he had far more access to classified documents than I did.'

'But who did Arnie meet?' Becky asked herself. 'Irene said that he mentioned twice that he was in a hurry and had an important meeting with someone.'

'I don't know. I will look again at his calls and the messages he sent.'

'And his work laptop? Where is it?' Alex asked.

'They never gave it to me. And his work phone. They said they took it to the police, and they told Inspector Ramsey they gave it to me.'

'Where are they then?' everyone was surprised.

'They may not have intended to give it to us at all. In all the commotion of his kidnapping and murder, we've missed that they didn't give us the phone and laptop. And didn't they say that they were sure he wasn't killed because of research he did there?' said Michael as if to himself.

'Maybe that was the goal, to direct attention elsewhere,' suggested Alex.

'You know what, Alex, I think you're right. I'll check something and call you if I have news.'

'How did we not notice?' Becky wondered.

'They played us well. They knew who it was, and they were covering it up. But I could be wrong. Although that would explain why we haven't found any messages from Irene. Arnie probably used his work phone for his relationship with her,' Alex continued to muse aloud.

'I'll call Inspector Ramsey,' she said and moved into the other room to have the conversation with her.

Alex and Becky spent the whole day checking the memory stick information, but they couldn't find anything that caught their attention. Michael and Inspector Ramsey wrote to them that they were working on a lead, so finally the two, exhausted from the past couple of days, retired to their bedroom, and fell fast asleep.

Alex and Becky didn't wake up until the next day at noon. They only had business messages and so they set to work. Becky had a meeting with new suppliers and Alex had a new client and headed to his office. However, neither of them managed to work. They had forgotten about the movie and everywhere they went they were chased by fans. So, they temporarily moved their offices into their house. Although they expected Michael and Inspector Ramsey to call them every day, they only received texts saying that they had no news yet. Until one beautiful sunny May morning they both stood at their front door.

'It's strange to see you two together,' Becky said after inviting them inside.

'We have good news. We caught Arnie's killer,' said Inspector Ramsey.

'Let me guess, the killer is Max,' suggested Alex.

Michael and Inspector Ramsey were surprised but confirmed. 'How did you guess?'

'He made a lot of effort to direct us to another track. I'm a lawyer, I've often heard of such things.'

Michael looked very tired. He sat heavily on the sofa and let his head rest. He let Inspector Ramsey to tell them what they find.

'Arnie's former boss is a very close friend of Max's. They had covered their tracks well, but the documents that Arnie found at his former company were the ones that signed his death warrant. It is very complicated to explain, but the two have assisted certain criminal circles. Albert had been paid to make the threat in court to divert any possible investigation. They took advantage of him, promised him a lesser sentence and some of the restitution he was supposed to pay Becky, but in the end, they didn't give him any of that. They threatened him that if he didn't keep quiet, he would meet the same fate as Arnie. They studied Becky's stab wounds and tried to imitate them. The meeting Arnie had was with Max's boss, but he never got there unfortunately. The documents and photos you found proved all of this, so Max confessed. We are looking for his friend, I guess by the end of the day the police will find him.'

'The evidence has been here all along,' thought Becky. If she had seen Irene five years ago, they would have known who this picture was by and found the memory stick sooner. But that's not how life works. Sometimes things happen later and sometimes never. Better late than never, she thought, and hugged her husband and friends.

'And while we are being emotional, I want to tell you some good news,' said Michael and his eyes suddenly shone. 'We will have a baby. Tanya and I decided four months ago to have a child, and surprisingly for us, everything happened very quickly.'

'That's why you're so tired,' said Becky. 'You're happy.'

'Yes, I'm so happy,' he smiled. 'Now I'm going to rest.'

Michael and Inspector Ramsey went out, and Becky and Arnie poured themselves a glass of wine and went out into the garden. It had lost its beauty after Paul left, but there were still some flowers here and there.

'It's over.' Becky sighed with relief.

'That's right,' Alex reached out and pulled her to him. Then the two sipped the wine and thought about the future. They were used to thinking about Arnie, wondering what had happened and when, but now satisfied with the revelations, they found themselves with more free time and less to think about.

'Still, the movie helped,' Becky said thoughtfully. 'I just hope the fans will forget us soon so we can enjoy our walks on the street again.'

'It won't end soon. It has a lot of good reviews.'

'I didn't want this, but it's a good chance for the actors,' Becky said and thought about Victor. He must be happy with that box office success.

18.

Five months later, the film *Becky: My Life* was named one of the best films of the year by several media outlets. The production company had invited everyone involved, including Alex and Becky, to celebrate. The couple had decided to combine their trip with a vacation and rented a house near the beach. Arnie's killers had been convicted and Becky hoped that this time they could rest both physically and mentally. Paul stayed one night with them, reminiscing about his good years in London. Catherine also stopped by with the children. Her career was on the rise again and her mood had improved. Becky and Alex were happy to see their friends, even though they were separated.

'I hope this doesn't happen to us either,' Becky muttered one afternoon.

'That we divorce? I don't think so,' he said and smiled at her. 'People have spoken to me about us many times, but I never really took what they were saying that seriously.'

'What did they tell you?' she asked him.

'People told me that they felt that there is something special between us. They could feel it if they were in the same room with us. Now I understand what they mean.'

'Victor and Veronika told me the same thing. No, you're right, nothing to worry about. No one can separate us.' Becky looked at him in awe. She didn't understand why people got married when they didn't love each other, but Victor had explained to her that it was part of the fake life that many people lived. They're trying to be what they want to be. 'What do they want to be?' she had asked him.

'Loved,' he answered briefly.

The days in the US passed quickly, Becky and Alex went home and started working again. The film was pulled from cinemas and their lives finally began to calm down and return to normal. Becky was happy, her work was going well, she and Alex and his family got along. The only thing that continued to bother her was her family. She had made several more attempts to contact her sister, but Summer never wanted to meet her. Her mother had finally been released from prison, but shortly thereafter her father had died. Becky had conflicted feelings about her father. She loved him, but at the same time she hated him because of his weakness. Before he died, her grandfather had told her the story of her mother and father. Clara had graduated from university, and she was the pride of the family, and was supposed to have a good career. However, her career quickly ended after she was twice fired from the schools where she worked for being rude to children. Left without a job and unable to find a new one, she decided to start a family. She entered the first pub she saw and married the first drunk who didn't mind her abrasive nature.

After Becky's birth, her father had tried to stop drinking, but was never successful. He could not find strength and will. Her grandfather told her not to be angry with her father—any man would drink if he lived with such a woman, he told her. And she wasn't mad at him, but she couldn't forgive him either. She could still feel that drunken kiss in the hospital on her forehead and his smell of beer and whiskey. There in that exact moment was his chance to stand up to his wife and do what was right, and he didn't dare. He probably regretted it later, at least that's what he had said, but that didn't do much to calm Becky's pent-up anger. She could forgive Summer though; she hadn't done anything wrong. But her sister didn't want to talk to her. Becky continued to send her a birthday card and cheque for her birthday, always leaving her phone number and email where she could be reached if needed. Summer never called. She found out from Michael that he still lived with her mother on the farm and that she hardly went out.

Becky had long planned to make her business international. During her stay in America, she had learned about the documents she needed to start a business there. That was what she had set her sights on, and that was what she was working on all Friday while she waited for Alex to get home from work.

Alex, for his part, had decided to take on less court cases and spend more time with her. He only worked four days a week. The other three days he and Becky spent time together at home or somewhere in the country. Their life was peaceful, and they both felt happy and lucky that they have each other.

However, the cases he accepted were always very complicated and sometimes required him to work more than he wanted to. One particular case was taxing him, and, instead of four working days, he had worked almost without a day off for the last month. When he got home from work on Friday night, he looked tired and asked Becky to have dinner later. He laid down on the sofa in the living room and never got up. Becky tried to wake him up, but when she touched him, his body was already cold. She panicked, then called an ambulance and started giving him CPR, but it didn't help. Alex had probably died the moment he went to sleep. Becky wanted her heart to stop with his, to go where he was right now. But her heart continued to beat, only her tears flowed and dripped from grief.

Becky couldn't get over his death, she became depressed, and Ben and Janey put her in hospital temporarily to keep an eye on her. She never attended her husband's funeral. She couldn't get out of bed the day he was to be buried. It was as if, if she had been present, she would have admitted to herself that he was no longer there, and that he would never return home. And she wanted him to be there for her, to open the door, to go to her, hug her and kiss her and tell her, like he always did, that everything was going to be okay. For weeks, Becky refused to accept his death and that from now on she had to go on alone, without him.

Alex had written in his will that he wanted to be buried next to her, no matter where, but for it to be sunny and peaceful, so even though they wanted him to be close to his family, Ben and Janey decided to bury him next to Arnie. Although she didn't want to think about it, Becky nodded and approved of their choice. She would go and visit them both. To be with them as before, she thought of them, and the tears continued to flow from her eyes.

Every day she prayed to die and go to them. Becky stayed in hospital for almost a month, everyone around her worried about her desire to kill herself and go where she thought she belonged. Finally, she realized that she would have to somehow continue her life on her own. She rented another house and settled in it temporarily. She couldn't go to the old one, she wasn't ready to go in there yet. Becky started working again and visited Ben and Janey almost every month, as well as the graves of those closest to her. She spent a lot of time traveling to Cornwall and back. The first time was the hardest for her to leave their graves.

Then she started taking the plane and went every chance she got. It took her six months to get used to the thought of Alex's death. Only then did she find courage, unlock the front door, and enter the house. His things reminded her of him, his favourite tea still sitting there from when she thought of making it for him and warming him up. Becky walked around the house slowly, went up to their room, opened the cardboard and sat down among his clothes hanging on the hanger. They still smelled of Alex and she felt safe here. She felt like he would come and hug her at any moment. Her eyes fell on a bracelet that one of the children on the beach in Zanzibar had tied to him. Becky took the bracelet and left the room relieved. She turned on the laptop and reserved the same bungalow in the same location for a week. She had to go there and tell them he was gone. Then, reassured that she had a plan, she slowly began to clean up. She wasn't going to stay away here anymore. This remained her house with her memories, and she would keep it.

19.

Two weeks later, Becky went to Zanzibar, stayed on the same beach, in the same bungalow, but the natives were no longer there. The tourist company owning the beach had kicked them out. Only one family was left and, after seeing her, they approached her. They came often, lit a fire, and prayed for the dead. For some reason, their ritual calmed her, as if she could feel Alex's presence around her, and for the first time in months, she was able to sleep.

Victor had heard from the media about Alex's sudden death. The first feeling he felt was shocked. He couldn't believe it had happened. The second thing he felt was sympathy for Becky. He didn't need to look at the pictures the press had taken of her to know she was devastated by Alex's death. Victor wanted to go to her right away, to comfort her, to help her get over the shock, but she wasn't taking any calls and, according to Victoria, she didn't want anyone to know where she was. A paparazzo had taken a picture of her in some hospital. Becky looked small, weak, and helpless. Then Victor found out again from the media that she had moved to another house. He sent her condolence cards and flowers several times. He sent her several messages and asked her to call him, to talk. But she didn't call back. Finally, he couldn't stand it and left for London. The film he was working on ended, and he refused to participate in the next one. He needed rest and time. Time to find her and do his best to calm her down and bring her back to life. So, he left and rented a house close to hers. He hoped that one day she would return there, and he would be able to talk her into it. Victor visited her friends hoping to learn more about her, but they, like him, had not seen her since Alex's death.

'Michael and I visited her twice in the hospital, but she refused to talk to us and asked the doctor to send us away. The only people Becky has contact with right now are his father, his sister, and their nephews. As far as I know she hasn't even met anyone officially, she only works with messages and emails,' Tanya explained.

However, Michael made him go outside to talk. 'We would do anything for her. I don't know what your goal is, but if you want to replace Alex, I'm telling you now that it won't happen.'

'I don't want to replace him. I'm just worried about her,' Victor was sincere.

'I know where she is now. I don't know if going to her will help her or if your resemblance to Alex won't confuse her even more. You can go or not, the decision will be yours, but be careful. She still hasn't gotten over his death and probably never will.'

'Where is she?' was all Victor wanted to know.

Michael wrote down the place in Zanzibar where she was staying and hoped that in giving the actor that information, he had done something wrong.

'You did the right thing,' Tanya called when she saw him enter the room. 'Becky needs someone to spend time with her.'

'I hope we are right, Tanya. I hope we are right...' Michael said and looked at his wife and son. He knew that he wouldn't be able to handle it easily if something happened to them. Like Becky, he wouldn't be able to survive it.

20.

Becky felt better on the beach, so she extended her stay by another week. She walked around the beach all day, played with the family's children, fished with them, and, for the first time in a long time, she felt alive. She had cut herself off from the outside world, wouldn't take calls, had given full authority to one of her managers to run the company while she was gone, with Alex's law firm handling the legal stuff. She hadn't told anyone where she was going or how long she would be gone, so she was very surprised when she saw Victor walking towards her. His resemblance to Alex was great and seeing him unprepared brought tears to Becky's eyes. One of the daughters of the native family approached her, spoke in her language, and began to carefully wipe them.

'Thank you,' Becky told her gently and moved her hand away. Then she pointed to the man walking towards them and explained with a gesture that she was going to him. Becky didn't know how to react or what to say to him. She didn't want anyone around her, especially someone who looked like her husband, but at the same time she was glad to see him. He clearly didn't know what to say to her either, he was speechless, and looked at her worriedly.

'I'm fine,' she told him. 'I just need time and to be alone.'

'I was worried about you. And not only me,' he finally said. He wanted to hug her, but her body language told him to stay away.

'I know. Sorry, I just have to get used to the thought of him being gone.'

'You have found new friends,' he pointed to the natives.

'Actually, they are not new. They were here before when Alex and I used to come. Only one family remains, the others have moved away.'

'Will you introduce me to them?' he asked.

'I hope I don't sound rude, but I really want to be alone,' she tried to send him away. She didn't want another in her memories.

'Okay. I understand. If you want to speak, I'm staying at the Palma hotel nearby.'

'How many days will you stay?' she asked him. He reminded her so much of Alex that she felt like she was talking to him.

'I do not know, we'll see.'

'I don't have internet or phone,' she explained.

'You don't need to call ahead. If you want to talk about him or something else, come. I'll be waiting for you there whenever you decide to come. If you decide to leave without talking to me, just call the reception so I know not to wait for you.'

'Okay,' she said.

'See you soon.' He slowly started walking away. Becky followed him with her gaze for a while, then returned to the beach with the others.

She didn't call him. She didn't go talk to him. She left for London and wrote to him that she was home the moment she landed the plane. Victor couldn't stand it, and, after a few hours, he called her. This time she answered the call.

'Sorry, I'm not ready to talk to people yet,' she said.

'I understand. Are you okay?' he asked her.

'I'm better. I'll make it up to you, I promise. The moment I can talk to you I will call you.'

'Okay. If you need anything, you know, you can count on me.'

'I know,' she said and hung up. All she needed was Alex, but Victor couldn't give him back to her.

Becky went to Yorkshire for a week to be with Ben and Janey. They were the only ones she could talk to. Janey's children were grown, but they still managed to distract her with their games and questions. She and Janey often just sat and drank tea outside but were rarely alone. Someone was always hovering around them.

'How did you survive it?' Becky asked her once.

'What?'

'Your husband's suicide.'

'It was hard. It was very hard for me, especially since I didn't know why he did it at the time.'

'Now you know?'

'Yes. And Alex knew, in fact he and Michael researched and found out why. I thought they told you.'

'They didn't. They probably didn't want to discuss something so personal about you with me and thought you would tell me.'

'Patrick had another family. At the edge of town. My children have a half-brother. You know him, his mother sometimes leaves him here to play.'

Becky looked at Janey in astonishment.

'But why?'

'I don't know, Becky. I ask myself this question too. I probably wasn't enough for him.'

'I don't understand. Catherine said the same about Paul.'

'Yes, Alex mentioned to me that they had problems. But Patrick having a child by another woman ruined him. He couldn't make a choice about which woman to stay with. It went around for months in a vicious circle, and, in the end, you know what happened.'

'I'm sorry,' Becky muttered.

'It was a long time ago.'

'You must be wondering if you couldn't have done something.'

'Yes, to this day I wonder how I didn't notice. But with four kids and a fifth on the way, I don't think I've had time to see the symptoms.'

'Was there anything I could do, Janey? Maybe stop him from working or not burden him with my work?'

'You couldn't do anything. What you can do now is start seeing other people. Your friends are worried about you, you haven't spoken to any of them since Alex died.'

'Yes, Victor told me.'

'Victor?'

'Yes, he came to the beach in Zanzibar. He wanted to talk, but I sent him away.'

'He came here to ask how you are.'

'Really? He travelled three continents to find me.'

'What are you going to do? Will you call him?'

'I don't think so. He reminds me a lot of Alex. Even if I look at him from afar, it's like I see him and tears flow.'

'And the others?'

'I'll call them when I get back to London.'

Janey nodded and stared off into the distance. She wished someone cared about her like that and visited three countries just to find out if she was okay. Becky was lucky to find not one but two decent men.

Becky stayed a few more days with Alex's family, then went back to work. She visited her shops again and worked up the courage to meet everyone else. She first visited Michael and Tanya. She managed to stay with them for only half an hour. Becky tried to talk to them about other topics and not think about Alex, but the moment they saw each other all three of them got upset and started talking about him. With Inspector Ramsey's family it was easier for her. She stayed there for almost an hour at one of their parties. Then she called Paul and finally Catherine.

'Are you okay?' her friend asked her.

'No. It's hard to be constantly asked if I'm okay. I want to say I'm fine, but I can't. It's hard for me without him. I see him everywhere, I look for him, I call him on the phone to ask him what he wants for dinner...'

'Calm down, Becky. This is normal. I called my mother to tell her about something I had bought five years after her death.'

'Do you think this is normal?' Becky asked.

'I think you've been through a lot and losing Alex makes your life even harder.'

'I thought we were going to have children, you know? That after we found out who Arnie's killer was, we were going to move... We had so many plans, Catherine.'

'Of course, you had plans. Believe it or not, I felt the same way after Paul dumped me. He is truly alive, but at the same time he seems to be dead for me.'

Becky realized that she had never talked to her friend about this. Not in this way. 'I'm sorry. I should have been there for you then.'

'No, I needed to be alone and clear things up. You need that, too, and everyone understands it.'

'Yes. Maybe I need more time.'

'If you need company, you can come visit me. I will be free for the next three months. Paul's mom will be babysitting this summer, so you can come over then, just the two of us.'

'I'll think about it,' Becky said. The idea of going to her friend's place for a while seemed good to her, but she decided not to promise Catherine that she would go. She talked to her some more and finally they ended the conversation. Becky thought about not calling anyone else but then she remembered that Veronica had left her many messages and decided to call her.

'I know you're not well, so I won't ask you how you are,' said the agent.

Becky mentally thanked her for her tact.

'I'm very sorry for the worry and for the many messages I sent you, but we need to talk about the income from the film. Alex and I agreed to send the money to you annually...'

As usual the mention of Alex's name upset Becky and she regretted calling Veronica.

'Sorry, I don't want to upset you, but we have to resolve this matter. I don't want all that money sitting in my bank account because I'll have to pay taxes later.'

'I understand,' answered Becky. 'I will give you a bank account details to transfer it to me.'

'Thanks, Becky. For everything. And I'm sorry for your loss,' Veronica said sympathetically. 'I guess you know that Victor is looking for you.'

'Yes. He found me. I'll call him when I can.'

'Do it as early as possible.'

'Why?'

'He is no longer accepting offers for films. He hasn't given up acting, but he says he wants to talk to you first and then take on new roles.'

Becky didn't answer.

'He likes you, Becky.'

'I know, but I'm not ready to talk to him.'

'Call him just to tell him how you feel.'

Becky fell silent again. She didn't know how to have this conversation.

'I will send you the bank details right now,' she changed the subject.

'Okay. See you soon.'

'See you soon.'

Becky stared at the phone. The last thing she wanted was for anyone to worry about her enough to stop working. Then she remembered Janey's comment, Victor had travelled three continents to find her and make sure she was okay. They weren't just ivy like she'd thought at first. He was really worried about her. So, she finally decided and called him.

'Hello,' she said.

'Hello. Do you feel better?'

'Yes. I'm calling everyone to apologize for my silence.'

'No problem, you needed to be alone.'

'That's right. Veronica told me you stopped accepting offers for roles.'

'That's right.'

'She said it is because of me. Because you worry about me.'

'And that's true.'

'Don't worry about me, Victor. I am fine. If you want to get some rest, it's good, but don't do it because of me.'

'It's not just because of you. I'm rethinking my life,' he said.

'Okay.'

'I've been working all my life. Have I told you that I've been in commercials and movies since I was four years old.'

'Yes, I think you mentioned it to me.'

'I need a break from all this. And I need something real in my life.'

Becky was silent. She wasn't sure she understood what he meant. Finally, she said, 'If you know what you're looking for, you'll find it.'

'I hope you're right. What are you looking for, Becky?' he asked.

'Time stopped for me,' she said, surprised that she was admitting to him exactly how she felt.

'And what will you do?'

'I will survive as long as I can. I will work, visit friends, and think about him.'

'So, you already have a plan?' he asked.

'Yes.'

'Great.'

'And what will you do?' she asked him in turn.

'I will wait.'

'What are you waiting for?'

'Something to change.'

She somehow sensed that she was involved in this waiting, but he didn't elaborate, and she didn't ask.

'I'll see you then.'

'Yes, we will hear from each other,' he said, and he wished the conversation had gone in a different direction.

Becky did what she told him. She worked and visited her friends and Alex's family. Two months later, she accepted Catherine's invitation and left for Los Angeles. The two spent two weeks together, walking, going to bars in the evening and trying to have fun. In one of these bars, they happened to meet Victor. Becky saw him before he noticed her. At first, she thought it was Alex. Their resemblance was striking, then she looked closer and thus caught his attention.

'Becky,' he was surprised. 'I didn't know you were here.'

'Catherine had days off and I came to her.'

'How are you?' he asked her, but there was no point in her answering him. She had lost weight and her eyes still had that deep sadness he had seen on the beach in Zanzibar.

'Okay. I'm trying to...' she stammered, 'get over it. You know...'

'I know. I have some work to do here, but I'll be free in ten minutes. Do you and Catherine want to wait for me and go have dinner somewhere together?'

'Okay.' answered Becky evasively, but Catherine nodded and pushed her towards one of the tables.

'I don't want to go to dinner, Catherine.'

'But I want to. Please do me a favour. Victor is famous, he has many contacts in our circles. It can help me with my career.'

'Okay,' Becky agreed and was surprised to see that he had finished his meeting in less than a minute and was coming towards them.

'But we will leave quickly.'

'Okay.' agreed Catherine.

But they didn't leave quickly. Catherine and Victor talked all the time about their mutual acquaintances, and Becky was silent. She felt so alone. Catherine had taken her from bar to bar, as if seeing other people would make up for missing Alex. For Becky, it was even worse. She had never gone out alone, she wasn't that kind of person. She was always with him, with her husband, and now it made her feel even more alone. And discussing topics she couldn't talk about made her even sadder. Victor could see Becky's mood dropping with each passing minute, her eyes beginning to water. He tried to shake off her friend's questions, but she wouldn't let him. She continued to press him for information. She was one of those women who had no tact when it came to their careers. Under other circumstances, Victor would have sent her away, but, if she left, Becky would also leave, and he didn't know what to do. Finally, he leaned down and whispered in her ear to shut up. This so surprised Catherine that she stepped back. Becky never saw the change, she was staring straight ahead and seemed to see ghosts.

'Are you hungry, Becky?' he asked her and gently grabbed her elbow. She looked away, looked at him and nodded. She didn't really know if she was hungry, but she knew what she was going to do the next morning. She would catch the first plane home and sit in the closet with Alex's clothes to calm down and rest. Catherine's constant chattering gave her a headache, and Victor's excessive concern bothered her. She didn't know how to communicate with him. He got up and led them to a small Italian restaurant.

'Here they make the best pizza and the best spaghetti.'

'Do you come here often?' Catherine asked.

'I grew up here. My parents and I lived in the house next door.'

Becky looked around at the houses and tried to guess which one he lived in. He pointed at a small, peeling building.

'You said that your mother and father are actors,' she said.

'That's right, they also worked as waiters and couriers. Not every actor gets paid well.'

'That's right,' Catherine confirmed.

The owner of the pizzeria seated them at a table away from the door so that no one would disturb them, but Victor was well known in the neighbourhood and a small line of fans formed inside the pizzeria. Everyone waited patiently, some recognized Becky or Catherine and asked for their autographs as well. Becky was amazed that people knew her. In Britain she knew the media were interested in her, but here, in this town? Some even took pictures of the three. Tomorrow everyone would know where she was and who she was with, Becky thought worriedly. She thought about calling Alex and warning him, but just before she pressed dial, she remembered that he was gone. Her eyes watered again, all this talk and noise and people making her nervous. She tried to focus on the menu, but her hands were shaking. Victor and the pizzeria owner both saw their trembling.

'Takeaway pizza, please,' said Victor to the owner, then turned to Becky. 'Calm down, we won't stay here. You will come to for dinner in my house.'

Becky looked questioningly at Catherine, who nodded.

'Okay, but we'll only stay for dinner.'

Victor wanted to kick her friend out, he was so irritated by her tactlessness. She obviously didn't see the state Becky was in. The owner of the pizzeria was worried that the woman was very pale and about to pass out and expressed his concern in Italian.

'Go on. I'll send my little son to bring them to you,' he finally said and helped Becky to her feet. She thanked him with a small smile.

'She recently lost her husband,' Victor explained to him. 'She's still in shock.'

The owner nodded in understanding and ushered the fans outside. Becky needed some fresh air, he thought, and possibly a new girlfriend. And he, like the actor, had noticed her friend's carelessness. Victor took the two women outside, hailed a taxi and took them home. He had read about Catherine in Becky's book, he didn't expect her to be so callous, but then he remembered what Becky had told him about her. Catherine had a good career in London and at one point accepted a contract in Los Angeles, where it did not work out. Apparently, it didn't work out for her with a husband either, because she mentioned several times that she was a single mother. Failures change people, make them negative, selfish, and bitter. Or at least most of them. Victor couldn't wait to take Becky to his house. It wasn't the done thing to admit it, but he was proud of it. He hoped she wouldn't give up on dinner halfway through. Catherine continued to chatter, and he could see Becky getting more and more nervous. Finally, Victor could not stand it, turned to the talkative woman, and told her in a loud voice to shut up. Becky looked at him gratefully, as if he had saved her from great harm. There's no way he was letting her go with Catherine. He had to keep her or get her a hotel for tonight. If Becky stayed with this woman, she wouldn't feel suicidal. Even he wished he kill himself when he was around her.

After the taxi stopped, Becky stood up and looked towards the house. In front of her was a beautiful patio with a small fountain in the middle. The stone fence and the house itself were painted white. She had seen such houses in magazines but had never been inside one. Victor saw her reaction and was glad, he had impressed her. Her friend too. Catherine had opened her mouth and was speechless for the first time.

'It's beautiful,' said Becky.

'That's right. Come, I'll show you around until they bring the pizza.'

He led the women in to look around, the only place he didn't let them in was his bedroom. He didn't want Catherine to go in there.

'You have a beautiful house,' Becky finally said.

'It is magnificent,' added Catherine.

Victor wanted to say something, but the pizza delivery arrived, and he invited the women into the kitchen. He poured them drinks and the three of them sat down to dinner.

'Do you feel better?' he asked Becky.

'Much better. Thanks for the dinner.'

'You're welcome,' he said and continued to wonder how to get her friend off and be alone with Becky.

'How long will you stay?'

'I don't feel well, and I've decided to leave tomorrow,' answered Becky and heard Catherine's protests.

'No, no. You promised to visit me for two weeks. Three days left.'

'I'm tired, Catherine. I want to go home and rest.'

'Alex has been gone for nine months. You haven't stopped resting since then.'

'Everyone grieves differently,' Viktor called. 'Some need only a few days, others need years.' He had read about it on the internet but didn't add that information.

'The more she stays at home, the more she will sleep,' Catherine did not give up.

Becky just shrugged and didn't get involved in the argument. She had already made up her mind anyway, she was going to sleep and catch the first available flight to London. Victor watched her worriedly. He didn't want her to leave. He wanted to stay and talk to her. So, he did the first thing that came to his mind. He called one of the producers he knew and recommended Catherine. He had never done this before, but he had to get rid of this woman. He handed the phone to Catherine and let her speak to the producer. At that time, Victor and Becky moved quietly into the garden.

'Has your girlfriend always been so talkative and sassy?' he asked Becky.

'No. She wasn't like that when we met. I think moving here really took a toll on her. Paul didn't stop cheating on her after the birth of their first child also didn't help.'

'Yes, I have often seen such people.'

'How are you?' she asked him and looked at him. He was emaciated and had dark circles under his eyes.

'I am fine. I was worried about you. At the pizzeria I felt like you were going to pass out.'

'I'm known for my seizures. The doctors explained to me that it was a consequence of the experience... you know.'

'Yeah, and Alex's sudden death doesn't help.'

'No, it doesn't help. That's why I prefer to stay at home and be sad,' she admitted to him. 'Anyway, it turned out that I wasn't good enough company.'

Becky looked towards the kitchen where Catherine was talking passionately about her career as a dancer and singer in Britain and America.

'She's unhappy just like me, she just doesn't show it.'

'That's right,' he said, although the subject of her friend did not excite him so much.

'You can stay here if you don't like her. You will be my guest for a few days.'

'I'd rather go back home, but thanks for the invitation,' she said. Then she got up and walked into the garden.

'We used to have a nice garden too. Paul took care of it. But it has been neglected for years. Maybe it's time to freshen it up, they say gardening is soothing.'

'Probably so. This one is taken care of by a childhood friend of mine.'

'He does a good job.'

'I will let him know.'

'Becky...' Catherine shouted from the kitchen. 'We have to go. Richard wants to see us tonight, we have a meeting in two hours, and we have to get ready.'

Becky sighed, 'I won't come with you to the meeting.'

'I won't leave you alone. You'll come with me, it'll be fun, you'll see.'

'I won't come, Catherine. I'm tired.'

'Okay, I'll go alone. You are coming?'

Victor let Becky make up her own mind.

'No, Victor invited me to stay here for a few days. I will only come to collect my luggage and return. Isn't that right, Victor?'

'That's right.' He smiled. 'I will call the cleaning lady to prepare one of the rooms for you.'

Becky got up slowly, barely able to stand on her feet from the strain.

'You know what' he suggested, 'tomorrow at noon we will come to pick up Becky's luggage. My mom and sister left some clothes here, I'm sure they won't mind Becky using them.'

Becky breathed a sigh of relief. She didn't know how right her decision was, but just the thought of spending almost an hour in a cab with Catherine made her sweat.

'Yes, that's better.'

'Good,' her friend agreed and this time she noticed Becky's tired look. 'Victor, will you order me a taxi, please?'

'Of course,' he said, pleased that she was leaving. He would even pay for her taxi. He knew that the producer he called would keep her for a long time in the evening and he didn't expect her to come back to his house. He couldn't wait to be alone with Becky. After sending her friend away, he returned with glasses of cold water and sat across from her.

'Are you tired?'

'Yes, but I want to stay here for a while. This garden has a calming effect on me.'

He nodded and made himself more comfortable in the chair.

'Did we interrupt your meeting today?'

'No, we were almost done. They gave me a new script to read, which I liked, and we were working out the details with the producer.'

'Don't you pay an agent for that?'

'I pay, but mine is out of town and that's why I went. They will specify the details later. How many days have you been here?'

'Almost ten,' answered Becky with a tired sigh. 'Catherine managed to wear me out. I have never been to so many restaurants and bars in my life.'

'So, you like to stay at home?' he asked in surprise.

'I own a chain of stores and I have to talk to customers and suppliers all day, so at the end of the day I prefer to cook something at home or order takeaway and have a quiet evening. Alex preferred it that way too.'

'I understand. I mostly eat out, but I would eat at home if I had a wife to cook for me.'

Becky smiled. She started to feel better. The casual conversation with him calmed her down.

'I want to clarify something,' she said.

'Okay.'

'I'm not insensitive. I know you like me, but I have to tell you that I'm not ready for this.'

'For what?'

'For a relationship or whatever you expect it to be.'

'Okay. But we can be friends, right?' he asked.

'We are friends,' she answered and smiled at him. 'I just want us to be aware of where we are. Have you lost someone yet, Victor? Someone you loved dearly.'

He stared at her. 'No. I've lost friends, I've been betrayed, I've been disappointed by some people, but I haven't lost anyone yet. Not in this way.'

'I lost Arnie, now Alex. It will probably take me years to come to terms with this.'

'I can wait...'

'You do not understand.'

'Probably not.'

'Let me try to explain to you,' she looked at him sadly. 'It's like having a very favourite cup. Very beautiful and special, made as if especially for you. Imagine seeing that glass fall from a height and break into thousands of tiny pieces. No matter how hard you try to put the pieces together, no matter how much glue you use to stick it together, there will always be something missing. And even if someone offers you a new glass that closely resembles the old one...'

'It won't be the same,' Viktor added and turned his head. He understood her feelings. She was trying to stop him from hanging around her.

'I know I'll never replace him, Becky.'

'That's right,' she whispered quietly and looked ahead in rapture. He did too. Still, he was grateful that she was here with him now. They sat in silence for a while, then he heard the cleaning lady coming and went to give her directions to Becky's room. When he returned, Becky had moved onto the lounger and was asleep. She might not need the room for tonight. He went into the house, found a blanket, and wrapped her up. Then he poured himself a glass of wine and stared at her as she slept. Sometime around midnight she awoke and met his gaze.

'I fell asleep,' she said apologetically and tried to straighten her hair.

'I know,' he smiled. 'Do you want me to show you the room?'

'Yes. Thanks.'

He took her to the room that was ready for her and bade her good night. Then after he heard the running water from the shower, poured himself another glass of wine and sat alone on the couch staring into nothingness.

When Becky woke up in the morning, he was waiting for her in the garden. There were still dark circles under his eyes.

'You didn't sleep last night,' she stated.

'Yes, I've been suffering from insomnia lately,' he admitted. Then he looked at her. 'You're not leaving today, are you?'

'No, I'll stay for another day or two, as long as I don't bother you. I still feel very tired.'

He nodded and smiled. He had dreamed of this moment. What he hadn't anticipated was that Alex was with them anyway. She was thinking about him, reaching for the phone as if to call him, then she saw the name written and her eyes watered. Becky was sad, suffering for her loved one, and Victor already knew that he couldn't fight it. It would take years for her to forget him.

'I asked a friend to go to Catherine and get your luggage. If you want, call her, and ask her what time Tom should go.'

Becky nodded, drank her first coffee of the day, and reluctantly called her friend. It went to voicemail.

'I'll have to go. My passport and personal belongings are there.'

'Okay. I'll give you a ride this afternoon. Do you want to go out or you prefer to stay here?'

'Let's stay here. You need a break too.'

Victor agreed with her. They spent most of the day in the garden, lounging on the deckchairs. He even managed to sleep for two hours. Catherine did not call until evening. She began to passionately explain to Becky about the producer, but the only thing Becky wanted was her belongings. So, she and Victor left immediately before Catherine went out on a new bar tour.

'I admit that if I had to lead such a life I would be exhausted,' said Becky.

'I used to live like this until recently.'

'What changed you?'

'You and Alex. The way you lived…'

Becky didn't know what to say. She began to wonder if the idea of staying with him for a few more days was a good one. She wasn't little, she wasn't a teenager anymore, she could tell when a man had feelings for her and even though he had made it clear, standing close to him and having him look at her like that was hard for her. There was no way to explain to him that even though he looked like Alex he wasn't him, and nothing in their relationship would change.

However, she did not regret the days she spent with him. The two went out twice for lunch and dinner, and the rest of the time they rested outside. When it was time for her flight, he decided to accompany her.

'But what are you going to do in London?' she asked.

'I will check into a hotel for two or three days and come back for the start of my new film.'

'Okay.'

Victor didn't want to part with her. It was as if he thought that if they were separated, even for a few minutes, he would never see her again. He packed his luggage, ordered a taxi to take them, and listened to her footsteps. A few hours later they were on the plane, and he was telling her funny showbiz stories. She listened and smiled. At some of the stories she even had a real, hearty laugh, then she would lightly touch his elbow and he regained hope. The plane ride was fun, at least for the two of them. An hour before they landed, Becky said she was tired and was going to get some sleep. She turned to the other side, looked through the portholes at the clouds, and smiled dreamily. Victor decided that this smile was for him, he calmed down and fell asleep too. An hour later he woke up to a noise around him and realized that something was wrong. He looked around in confusion to see Becky slumped to the floor. It took him more than a minute to realize she was dead. Becky, like Alex, had died in her sleep. One of the passengers who was a doctor was trying to do something for her but finally shook his head.

'After we land, we will find out what happened,' he tried to calm Victor down, but Victor already knew. Becky had died of a broken heart, Alex had taken her home, took her to him.

At the farm in Cornwall, Summer stared at the television screen, shocked by the news of her sister's sudden death. Journalists had surrounded the plane that had just landed and were broadcasting live. Everyone commented that Becky had not been able to get over her husband's death and that was the likely cause of her death. Summer watched the crying man who had accompanied her on the flight and her grief merged with his. Victor was sitting close to Becky's body and curled up, with his head in his hands. He looked desperate and helpless. Summer thought her sister must have been an amazing person, but she allowed herself to get to know Becky. Tears welled up in her eyes and memories flooded her. She remembered her childhood years with her, her attempts to make amends, Becky's willingness to help her despite the reproaches and insults her family threw at her. Too bad she hadn't realised that in time, Summer thought. She got up, walked over to the bookcase, and picked up the card she had gotten for her last birthday from her sister. Inside, Becky had written just one phrase, *Carpe Diem*. This wish had confused her before, but now she understood its meaning. Summer looked once more at the grieving man and, like him, curled up and gave in to her grief. It was time to admit to herself that she had always loved her sister, she just kept thinking that she still had time and that she would call her someday. But her time was up. A hard way to understand that sometimes in life there are no second chances.

'Rest in peace, sister,' Summer mumbled softly and let her tears roll down her cheeks and fall freely down.

Facebook: @Hristina Bloomfield Author

Instagram: @HristinaBloomfield

Email: hrisisart@gmail.com

hristinabloomfield@gmail.com

Also by Hristina Bloomfield

DEEPLY IN THE SOUL

Xena is forced to run away when she finds out her boyfriend sold her. After years of running, her past finally catches up with her...

The story follows Xena who finds herself in the situation of a victim but manages to escape. After her boyfriend is unable to return a loan, she is sold to the moneylender who wants her to work for him as a prostitute. She flees her hometown and tries to start a new life, but her past keeps catching up with her. Xena struggles to find her way as each time she gets to a good place, she has to run again. After months of solitude, Xena finally trusts Agent Dobrevski who helps Xena to face her trauma in order to finally live a normal life. The story begins in a small mountain town in Eastern Europe and ends in Cornwall, UK.

Deeply in the Soul is crime fiction; however, it also includes themes such as trauma, grief, romance, action and friendship. Xena's story is not only tragic but inspirational too. She is a survivor.

The Story of a Thief

Tony was born into a family of thieves. His life seems predestined, until his girlfriend Eva disappears suddenly. For several years he put all his skills into finding her, even working in the police, but there is no sign of his girlfriend. In several of the investigations he leads, Tony works with a psychic who uses Tarot cards. He is so impressed by her gift so he decides to tell her his story with the hope that she will help him to find Eva. However, it turns out that Isabella's life is no less complicated than his. The two have a lot in common and this creates tension and romance in their relationship. In the course of their investigation, Tony and Isabella discover that nothing is as it seems.

Printed in Great Britain
by Amazon

41244350R00166